Dear Friend,

At least I hope you will be my friend, since I'll need some support throughout the trials and tribulations of having to pretend to be married to a difficult man like John Slater. How ironic, when he is the troublemaker who complained about the marriage project I assigned to my high school sociology class and when it was his call that brought about the special P.T.A. meeting in the first place. I don't mind running a special class for parents, so they can see what the project is like, but I don't appreciate being forced to participate myself...partnered with John.

Not that John can't learn something, I suppose, since he went through a painful divorce. He was awarded full custody of two adolescent daughters, though, so he must be responsible. It's just that he's carrying too much baggage for a single woman to think about getting involved with him.

Involved! Where did that come from?

Oh, I just wish he wouldn't look at me like that. It makes tingles run up and down my spine. I simply can't let him get to me. I'm going to prove my teaching methods while not getting personally involved. Let me know if I start straying from that course, won't you?

Sincerely,

Gillian

Please address questions and book requests to: Harlequin Reader Service
U.S.: 3010 Walden Ave., P.O. Box 1325, Buffalo, NY 14269
Canadian: P.O. Box 609, Fort Erie, Ont. L2A 5X3

Make-Believe Matrimony

LYNN
PATRICK
THE MARRIAGE PROJECT

Harlequin Books

TORONTO • NEW YORK • LONDON
AMSTERDAM • PARIS • SYDNEY • HAMBURG
STOCKHOLM • ATHENS • TOKYO • MILAN
MADRID • WARSAW • BUDAPEST • AUCKLAND

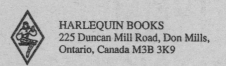

HARLEQUIN BOOKS
225 Duncan Mill Road, Don Mills,
Ontario, Canada M3B 3K9

ISBN 0-373-30125-1

THE MARRIAGE PROJECT

Copyright © 1990 by Patricia Pinianski and Linda Sweeney

Celebrity Wedding Certificates published by permission of
Donald Ray Pounders from *Celebrity Wedding Ceremonies*.

Printed in U.S.A.

A Letter from the Author

Dear Reader,

The idea for *The Marriage Project* came from some real-life experiments straight out of the news. High school students in social studies classes were participating in "pretend" marriages incorporating the nitty-gritty details that could make or break a relationship—division of labor, budgets, compromise, planning a family, etc. The goal was to make them aware that more than love went into a successful marriage.

But why not turn things around and make two unmarried adults work on the practical details, which would lead to their falling in love with each other? What could be more fun than playing Cupid with an innovative teacher and a conservative parent who is rightfully upset after overhearing his daughter's spicy telephone conversation with a classmate?

I hope you'll get more than a few laughs from their ensuing plight. Enjoy.

Thanks, Bev

PROLOGUE

"HEY, BOSS, phone call for you in the office."

John Slater acknowledged the workman's message with a wave, then carefully picked his way around the section of the restored wooden banister his men were reassembling. He suspected the job was taking so long because pieces were missing. Another detail to check. He crossed the mansion's marble floors and entered a small room off the empty front parlor. Blueprints lined one wall; a large bulletin board filled with business cards and memos, another. Looking for the card of the Glass Art Studio so he could phone later to check on the restored windows that were a week overdue, he picked up the receiver from the scarred wooden desk.

"Slater here."

A slight pause was followed by a familiar woman's voice that made the print in front of his eyes blur. "John . . . it's Kate. I'm back in town."

In shocked silence, he waited for the other shoe to drop, praying it wouldn't do so with a bang. He'd feared this moment for five years. All the feelings he'd stored away came back to him in an unpleasant surge.

"Actually I'm in Indianapolis," Kate went on when he didn't answer. "Permanently. I've already found an apartment and a sales position in a department store." She paused, then finished with a rush. "I want to see the girls." When he still made no reply, she laughed nervously. "Say something, will you?"

Say something? How often had he heard that during their final years of marriage? But now, if he said what was on his mind, Kate wouldn't like it, because his first instinct was to say no. And why shouldn't he? Kate had given up her rights, had thrown them away with both hands. But he had to think of what would be best for his daughters.

"I'll see what the girls have to say about it."

"Of course they'll want to see me."

"Don't be too sure about that."

"I'm their mother, for God's sake!"

"Isn't it grand that you finally took the time to remember?"

John could feel her hurt vibrate through the short silence, yet he steeled himself against pitying Kate. Forget her quarrel with him—she'd been unfair to their daughters. He remembered the tears he'd had to dry, the explanations he'd been powerless to make, and most of all, he remembered the nightmares. Kim had grown out of them, but Tracy still had occasional disturbing dreams.

"John, I know I hurt you badly, but please don't—"

"I said I'd talk to them, and I will." He couldn't help his clipped tone. "Where can I reach you?"

He wrote down the number, mouthed a polite if distant goodbye and hung up. Anger seethed through him. Not for himself—the love he'd once had for Kate was long gone, the wound to his heart long healed—but for his daughters. After five years of hastily scrawled notes or cards from various cities, five years of occasional phone calls that had become less and less frequent, Kate thought she could walk back into her kids' lives as if she hadn't abandoned them.

"Damn it all!"

John went back to the job but was so distracted that he couldn't concentrate. He kept worrying about Kate and her motives for this surprise return. Anger made him give abrupt orders, and his workers gave him a wide berth and strange looks for the rest of the afternoon. He hadn't felt so out of sorts, so short-fused, in years. All he needed was one more thing to go wrong and he'd explode like a keg of dynamite.

Mulling over the Kate problem as he entered his home later that evening, John couldn't quite figure out how to announce their mother's unexpected return to his daughters.

"Daddy!" Her carrot-colored hair tousled, Tracy ran straight into his arms. John held her close until she squirmed away. "You're early. Dinner's not ready yet. You'll never guess what I'm making," she said in rapid-fire style.

"Hamburgers or spaghetti."

Tracy wrinkled her freckled face in disgust. "You know I leave the easy stuff to Kim."

Smiling at the twelve-year-old's irritation over the insult to her culinary skills, John sniffed the air appreciatively. "Barbecued chicken?"

"With Tamari sauce."

"Something new. I'll bet it'll be wonderful. But before we eat, I want to talk to you and your sister. Where is she?"

"Where do you think?" Tracy heaved a sigh. "On the telephone, discussing boys." A mischievous twinkle lit her brown eyes. "Want me to tell her she has to get off the phone?"

"I'll do it myself. I want to wash up, anyway."

"Oh, all right," she said, already dancing away. "I'll finish setting the table, then."

"Tracy, honey."

"Yeah, Dad?"

"I love you."

She gave him a wary look. "I love you, too."

As John climbed the stairs to the second floor, Kim's voice drifted toward him. "Laura. You didn't." A giggle erupted from the sixteen-year-old before her tone lowered in pitch. "You'll never believe it, Laur. This is almost too gross to repeat."

Not really meaning to eavesdrop, John stopped outside of her doorway. Before he could announce his presence, his older daughter went on.

"Oh, all right, I'll tell. Scott actually wanted to negotiate how many times a week we're going to have sex."

Shocked, John tried to tell himself he'd misunderstood, but when Kim continued on the subject in a knowledgeable manner, her words lit the match to his fuse. He knocked but didn't wait for Kim's invitation to enter her bedroom.

"Hang up that phone, right now, young lady. You have some explaining to do."

Kim's green eyes widened as they turned to her father. "Uh, Laura, I think I'm in trouble. Later."

She hung up and, her expression embarrassed, faced her father as he slammed the door behind him.

CHAPTER ONE

FROM HER POSITION at the lectern, Gillian Flannery looked around at the members of the Greenville High PTA, most of whom sat forward in their seats expectantly. More than two dozen had turned out for the meeting. She tried to clear her throat. These people didn't seem as though they were ready to string her up. They looked like nice, ordinary suburban folks.

So where was he—the troublemaker who'd stirred up this commotion over one of the most valuable class projects her high school students would ever experience?

For a moment, Gillian felt ganged up on, like the times when she'd found herself at odds with the other members of her large, opinionated family. Thinking she'd be more in charge of the situation if she couldn't see any angry faces, she took off her glasses, set them on the lectern, then rested a sweaty palm along either side of the wooden base. There, now she had nice, fuzzy blobs to address. This technique had worked perfectly while doing her student teaching in inner-city Indianapolis. If she couldn't see her adversary, she wouldn't be nervous. Starting the meeting would help... and she knew exactly how to get everyone's attention. She cleared her throat again as she leaned toward the microphone.

"Sex," she said with deliberation, the single word quieting any remaining whispers, "is *not* a dirty word."

The drop-dead silence that followed lasted for about ten seconds before an unamplified masculine voice challenged her. "It all depends on the age of the mouth it comes from, Miss Flannery. In this instance, we're talking about a sixteen-year-old child."

"Young lady," Gillian automatically corrected him. Wanting to see her opponent more clearly, after all, she slipped her glasses back on. She was unready for the man standing in the open doorway at the back of the auditorium. He was dressed in a construction worker's uniform—tight jeans slung over narrow hips and a plaid shirt stretched across well-muscled shoulders. "You're Kim's father?"

Placing one work boot in front of the other, the man walked deliberately to the front of the hall. "I'm John Slater," he agreed, sitting in the otherwise-empty first row. Stretched out, his long legs ate up the space between his seat and the stage. Only then did he remove his hard hat, revealing auburn hair slashed with silver over his right brow. "So what's really going on in that class of yours, Miss Flannery? I want to know before things get out of hand."

Gillian wondered if what he really wanted was to put a stop to her class assignment. Why else had he called the principal?

"Mr. Slater," she said, staring at his mustache rather than at the whiskey-colored eyes that raked over her, "I get the feeling you don't understand the purpose of the marriage project I've introduced as part of my sociology class. I assure you, it has little to do with sex education. We merely discuss the responsibilities involved when two people have children."

"Then can you explain why Scott Ramsey asked my daughter how many times a week they were going to have sex?"

A growing murmur lit the auditorium, and the heat of embarrassment sizzled along Gillian's neck. Put that way, she could understand John Slater's concern. He waited for her answer expectantly, the generous mouth under the mustache straight and unsmiling.

Being put on the spot like this certainly wasn't a terrific way to start her first year at a new school. Few of these suburban parents knew her, and it was obvious that they were more concerned about what went on in the classroom than were the parents she'd dealt with in Indianapolis. Principal Martin Fowler sat to one side, watching her carefully. She swallowed hard and raised her voice so she could be heard above the continued undertone.

"I can assure you that wasn't part of our assignment, Mr. Slater. I'm sure Scott was merely teasing Kim, and I'll be happy to speak to him about his inappropriate behavior."

While the whispers subsided, giving her a feeling that the rest of the people in the room thought she'd proposed a reasonable solution to the problem, John Slater obviously had no intention of letting the topic rest.

"Speaking of appropriate . . . do you really think such a project is suitable for a high school sociology class?"

Gillian wondered why Slater couldn't accept her good intentions. He certainly couldn't think that she, a conscientious teacher, was trying to be a bad influence on her students. She looked away from him and toward the middle of the auditorium at a couple wearing almost identical navy pin-striped suits. Laura Talbot's parents. Both lawyers, they were leaders of the community. If she could win them over....

"Considering the frightening statistics on divorce in this country," Gillian said, aiming her appeal straight at the pin-striped couple, "I believe the project is important to the future of your children, to the stability of the families they will eventually start."

"So they have to know how to negotiate how often they're going to make love when they get married?" Mrs. Talbot asked, adjusting her tortoiseshell glasses as she stood.

"Arlene, come on," a blonde in a magenta jogging outfit objected. She shifted her ample figure so she could get a look at the other woman. "Miss Flannery already assured us they don't discuss that in her class. You don't have to worry about Andy getting out of line with Laura," she said, thereby identifying herself as Sarah Bigsby, Andrew Bigsby's mother. "Let's give Miss Flannery a chance to explain. That's why we came, to hear both sides. Right, dear?" She poked the rumpled-looking man beside her.

Seeming startled, he sat up straighter. "Right."

Arlene nodded her sleekly coiffed head and took her seat. "All right. Please go on, Ms. Flannery."

"As I said before," Gillian stated, relieved that the parents were willing to listen with an open mind, "this project isn't about sex, but about emotional responsibility and mature decision-making." She turned directly to Slater. "I'm talking about the more practical side of a marriage partnership. Everyday living. Setting budgets and finding ways to work through life's ups and downs. Learning to communicate, something missing in many marriages. And yes, that could mean assigning a certain number of children to each couple—*on paper*."

"I don't care what method you use." Slater leaned forward in his seat and stared at her as if they were the only two people in the room. "Don't you think you're pressuring these kids to grow up too fast?"

"On the contrary. I think I'm helping them to prepare for their future lives."

"And what makes you such an expert, Miss Flannery?" Slater asked evenly.

"I've never been married, as I suspect you well know, Mr. Slater. But I feel that I have properly prepared myself for marriage.

You've come alone tonight. How does your wife feel about my class project?"

"I'm divorced," he admitted. "Not that I'm happy about it. And not that it's a crime."

Uh-oh. She'd inadvertently hit a nerve. Realizing she'd embarrassed him, Gillian didn't know what to say. Slater's complexion reddened. And every muscle of his body seemed to define itself under his work clothes. Chagrined, she shifted her focus to the middle of the auditorium.

"Slater does have a point," Derek Talbot said. "How do we know that you—a single woman—have the necessary experience to guide our children properly?"

"My minor in college was psychology. I took several classes on family dynamics and one on marriage counseling—"

"College studies can't substitute for real-life experience," Slater said.

As the middle child in a family of seven, Gillian had had plenty of personal experience in dealing with life's problems: overcrowded living conditions, hand-me-down clothes, constant quarrels. The fighting had been the worst part—though her parents had always maintained they loved each other, even during a long separation when their father had moved out of the house, taking her brothers with him. Gillian believed her parents had married and had started a family when they were far too young to know what they were getting into. Two of her siblings had followed suit. Her older brother Donald was already divorced, and her younger sister had recently separated from her husband.

She hated the idea of their mistakes being duplicated time and again. Many people who were adults in other ways weren't ready for the numerous responsibilities that went hand in hand with a lifelong commitment. That's why she believed so implicitly in the marriage project as a valuable teaching tool.

Taking a deep breath, she said, "I assure you that I conducted similar experiments several times at my former high school in Indianapolis and—"

"A city school," said Arlene. "We moved to the suburbs purposely to remove our children from dangerous influences."

A quick look at the principal assured Gillian that Martin Fowler was openly frowning at her.

"The concept of marriage with all its problems is universal. We're not doing anything you'd object to," Gillian stated, knowing she could convince all of them—even John Slater, who sat in the front row, his expression enigmatic, his arms crossed over his chest. Her students' future well-being was too important for her to give up without a fight. "But, so that you can rest assured that this project is being conducted within your own principles, I invite you to participate." The idea had occurred to her soon after talking to Principal Fowler.

"Participate?" a woman in the back echoed. "How?"

"I propose to conduct a marriage project with this group, just as I am doing with your children." Gillian smiled at the startled looks passing between several of the PTA members. "I'm willing to volunteer my time *gratis* to prove that you have nothing to worry about and to convince you that your children are involved in a viable and valuable learning experience."

A low murmur set through the auditorium, making Gillian anxious. That's when John Slater rose to his impressive height. Though she stood a foot above him on the angled stage, they were almost eye to eye.

"And if we agree to participate in the project and decide it's not viable?" he asked.

A pulse beat in her throat as she registered the fact that this was going to be a tough battle to win. "Then I'll either change the way I teach it—or I'll drop the project, depending on the group's recommendation."

She could convince them, given the chance. Even Slater. She knew it.

"All right," he said reasonably. "I'll buy that. What do we have to do?"

Amazed that he'd agreed so easily, that he actually sounded as if he wanted to make a fair judgment, Gillian blinked at him and pushed at her glasses to cover her surprise. Perhaps he hadn't meant to stir up trouble. She appreciated a parent who was concerned enough to volunteer his time this way.

"Pair off, to begin with." She cleared her throat and stared over Slater's shoulder toward the Talbots. "Then each couple will be issued a computer printout listing the hypothetical circumstances of their relationship. New data will be issued each week, including where you'll live, on how much money, from what kind of job or jobs, in-law problems, how many children. The entire group will discuss each couple's progress once a week."

"Once a week?" a man echoed loudly. "Can't we do it in one night?"

"Well, you'll need at least six weeks to see how it really works," Gillian told him. "Otherwise, how can you share the problems and solutions you and your partner have come up with? Of course, you'll have to meet every week with your partner so that—"

"I don't have time to do this," a woman who'd been quiet until now objected.

"Well, I do," Sarah Bigsby countered, her wide, magenta-tinted mouth curving in an engaging smile. She nudged her husband, who by now had slid down into his seat. "We both do, don't we, Calvin?"

His watery blue eyes popped open. "Right. What?"

"We have time to get married for the experiment."

Looking distinctly confused, he smoothed his tousled brown hair as he attempted to sit straighter. "But, Sarah, we're already married."

Gillian bit back a smile. She had a feeling the Bigsbys would be interesting to work with.

"My wife would never agree to do this," said a man who sat alone. "And she would kill me if I had another woman . . . even if it's only on paper."

"Wait a minute," Slater objected, climbing to the stage and joining Gillian at the lectern. "These are our kids we're talking about here. I'm willing to give the project the benefit of the doubt and join in the experiment for their sakes. This way, we can make an informed decision on whether or not we think our kids should continue with the rest of the project."

"I agree." Arlene rose, obviously eager to get on the bandwagon now that she saw the current of interest racing through the crowd. "How difficult could it be for us if our children have been doing it? Count Derek and me in."

Suddenly everyone was talking at once.

"I can't see Jane's and my getting involved in something so childish," one man said, while the woman across the aisle from him countered with, "Well, Harry and I are game. And who said it's childish?"

The bickering continued between married couples and single parents alike for several minutes until Slater finally boomed, "Quiet!" His deep voice reverberated through the auditorium. "We have an issue to resolve here."

The proposed project was then discussed in a more organized manner, Slater giving Gillian the lead once more. With relief, she realized the tide had turned in her favor. While it was obvious that not everyone was willing to participate, the consensus that any amenable adults try the marriage project was positive. The parents were going to give it a chance.

Here she'd been worried about the imminent demise of her project when a half-dozen couples were looking forward to testing it for themselves. This was the kind of small-town enthusiasm Gillian had grown up with, the very thing that she'd found missing from her life during the years she'd spent living and working in inner-city Indianapolis.

Her energy and positive attitude renewed, she quickly passed around a notebook for signatures and phone numbers so she could keep up with the couples' progress between the "adult night classes" she planned to schedule for group discussion. Scanning the list quickly, she noted two of the twelve names were those of parents who were either divorced or who had lost a spouse.

"I'll need a partner," Slater said into the microphone. "Any volunteers?" The auditorium went silent for a few coughs. "Not even a divorcée or one of you women whose husbands don't want to participate?" No hands rose. "Well, then, who do you propose I do this project with?"

"How about Miss Flannery?" Martin Fowler suggested.

All heads turned to Gillian. Her eyes widened in alarm. Even though Slater might be a concerned parent, she didn't feel comfortable being his wife, pretend or not.

"I'll be busy offering guidance to the others, not to mention coordinating the meetings."

"These aren't high school students," the principal said, his expression meaningful. "They won't need as much guidance as their children. I think you should participate."

Put like that—what amounted to a direct order from her boss—there was no way she could refuse. Gillian turned to the man who suddenly seemed more intimidating than when he'd walked into the room. "I guess we're a team, Mr. Slater."

Lord, she didn't have to be so unenthusiastic about it, John thought, looking into her wary baby-blue eyes. Her small, tilted nose, half hidden by the frames of her glasses, was practically out of joint, and that smile seemed pasted on her mouth.

What was so wrong with him? After all, this experiment had been her idea; he was merely giving it a fair chance.

Realizing that everyone in the room was waiting for his reaction, he finally grumbled, "Yeah, I guess we're a team." Then he stepped down off the stage and retrieved his hard hat.

"Well, that's it," Martin Fowler said, rising. His round face beamed with delight all the way up into his receding hairline. "We can conclude this meeting. Miss Flannery will coordinate the activities of our wonderful volunteers. The rest of us will be anxious to hear your report at the regular PTA meeting in November."

"Couples should pick up their initial envelopes in the high school office tomorrow and meet on your own to get started. Be back here the same time this Thursday for the first group meeting," Gillian stated while everyone rose. "We'll decide on a regular meeting night then."

They headed for the doors, some escaping as quickly as possible, a few lingering in small groups, talking while inching up the aisle.

"'Night, John," his neighbor Sarah called, her husband ambling along behind her, looking half asleep.

Calvin probably *was* half asleep, John thought as he waved to the Bigsbys. Anyone who knew the couple could testify to Calvin's uncanny ability to fall sound asleep wherever and whenever he got the chance. Slow-moving Calvin claimed that years of working night shifts as a security guard had permanently damaged his body clock. He and bright-eyed, busy Sarah—who ran a day-care center and was also active in several community organizations—were a study in contrasts.

When John turned his attention back to Gillian Flannery, she seemed a little flustered. He couldn't help grinning at her. "What now?"

"We leave." She placed a bag over her shoulder, bounced off the stage and led the way. They exited the auditorium and crossed the short hallway to the outside doors. "We can meet tomorrow afternoon here at the school and get things rolling."

"Evening," he corrected, opening the outside door and waiting for her to go first. She stopped and frowned up at him instead.

"What?"

"Tomorrow evening," he repeated. "I can't make it in the afternoon. I'm behind on an important job."

Her baby blues narrowed behind the mask of her glasses as she left the room. "I thought construction workers started at sunrise and ended their day early."

"Not when you're the boss. And I'm in the renovation business, not construction. So we'll meet at seven-thirty, but not here."

"What's wrong with meeting here?" She didn't look at him as they continued walking across the parking lot. She scavenged through her large shoulder bag, undoubtedly searching for her car keys. "Or do you have something against the school, too?"

He didn't have anything against her, if that's what she was intimating. He was concerned about the project. That's what this was all about. He wouldn't be involved with Miss Gillian Flannery otherwise. Actually, to be fair to her, she did seem very earnest and obviously had her students' best interests at heart. When Martin had suggested this special meeting, he hadn't known what to expect from her, but Miss Flannery's enthusiasm and sincere belief in her project had almost won him over.

"I'd like to meet near a place where I can get something to eat, if you don't mind," John explained, trying to pacify her. "I'll be more receptive to giving this project of yours a fair try if I can get some food in my stomach before we meet."

Gillian looked up at him, her face framed by soft, light brown curls. A smile lit her eyes. She really was pretty. Although she was probably at least thirty, John imagined some of her male students probably had crushes on her.

"I hope you mean that about being fair, Mr. Slater. I wish you would have talked to me directly, given me a chance to tell you about the marriage project, before putting me under the gun."

Standing in the middle of the parking lot wasn't exactly conducive to playing true confessions, John thought. And yet, hadn't his ex-wife accused him of being too closemouthed, of not being able to communicate effectively? And Gillian Flannery made him want to be completely honest.

"Look, I'm a concerned father," he finally said, trying not to resent having to explain himself to a stranger. "When I heard my sixteen-year-old daughter talking to one of her friends on the phone, complaining about how many times she was supposed to have sex, I got a little worried."

As a matter of fact, that conversation had been enough to light his fuse so that he'd forgotten all about Kate for the moment. But his ex-wife's return was something he'd have to deal with, and soon.

"Maybe I should have called you first, but I've known Martin for years. I wanted an explanation and some assurances. I wasn't trying to get you in trouble. It's not easy being the only real parent to two girls who are growing up faster than I can keep up with," he went on. "It's damned scary. Sometimes I don't even know how to talk to them. But I try, Miss Flannery. I do my best, because I love them and I think they deserve at least one parent who looks out for them.''

John Slater's speech, obviously wrung from the depths of his heart, made Gillian sorry she'd doubted his good intentions. The man deserved her respect. He wasn't merely taking a potshot at her class project because it was new and different; he had his daughter's best interests at heart, as did she. That was the important thing to remember.

"Why don't you take the time to eat, Mr. Slater, then meet me at the public library at your convenience?'' Gillian smiled naturally this time. "It's the proper environment, isn't it?''

"All right. The public library, at seven-thirty.''

She held out her hand. He didn't hesitate, but engulfed it in his own immediately. His palm and fingertips were callused. He might be the boss, but he obviously wasn't afraid to pitch in and get involved—whether with his kids or his employees. She liked that about him, even if he had questioned the appropriateness of one of her class assignments.

Suddenly his lips turned up under his mustache. The genuine smile that reached his eyes and the tiny lines that crinkled around them sent a thrill through her. Gillian let go of his hand immediately.

"See you tomorrow,'' she said, backing off toward her old compact Ford parked a few dozen yards away.

He stood there staring after her while she whipped around and jogged to her car. She felt his eyes on her back the entire distance. And yet, when she got to the Ford and glanced back in his direction as she unlocked the door, Slater was climbing into a four-wheel truck rather than watching her.

Gillian coaxed the engine of her beat-up car to life. She had absolute faith in the marriage project and was sure the parents would appreciate her class when they delved into the work themselves.

She only wondered how she'd feel being "married'' to John Slater for the next six weeks.

CHAPTER TWO

"WOW, YOU'RE PLAYING HOUSE with some guy?" remarked Vicky, Gillian's younger sister. "And this is fully endorsed by the PTA? How liberal of them."

"That's not what I said and you know it." Gillian kept her voice hushed. "Don't talk so loud." She gazed around the Greenville restaurant where she and Vicky had met for dinner, relieved when she didn't recognize anyone. After the PTA meeting the night before—where the morality of her assignment had been questioned—she couldn't help feeling a bit uneasy. "John Slater and I are participating in the same type of marriage project that I usually assign to my junior sociology class. It involves nothing more than a few meetings and paperwork."

Vicky took another bite of her chicken salad sandwich and grinned. "Still sounds like fun to me. Is John good-looking?"

"He's attractive, but that's not important. This is a serious experiment."

"Ooh, real serious, huh?" Vicky laughed and tossed her blond hair, making her long bat-shaped earrings jingle. "The man is attractive, divorced and available, right? You should try to score a few points with him while you're filling out all those papers together."

"Trying to score points isn't a positive way to approach any kind of a human relationship."

"Oh, come on, you know what I mean."

Tiring of her sister's teasing interrogation, Gillian hastened to change the subject. "Have you seen the waitress? I'd like some more coffee."

"She's over there." Vicky waved. Then she turned back to Gillian. "Now that both of us are single, we can hang out together more often."

"How about a movie on Friday night?" Gillian's numerous siblings, most of whom lived in the Indianapolis area, provided her with a social life, even when she wasn't dating someone.

"A late movie," Vicky agreed, "say at nine or ten o'clock? And let's drive into Indianapolis. Afterward, we can drop by Rochesters."

"Isn't Rochesters that new pickup bar?"

"I've heard it's a great place to meet men."

"Mostly the kind of men who think that buying you drinks gives them the right to breathe down your blouse for the rest of the night."

"You're exaggerating . . . and there's nothing wrong with a little flirting."

Gillian didn't like the sound of that. "How long have you and Tim been separated now? A month?"

Vicky frowned and tugged at her oversized black sweater, the neck of which kept sliding down to reveal pretty shoulders and a black tank-top underneath. "Do we have to talk about Tim?"

"Don't you think you need some time to mull things over before you jump into the swinging singles life? I thought this was a trial separation."

Vicky's lower lip jutted out, making her look even younger than twenty-two. As the pretty baby of the Flannery family—Gillian's junior by eight years—Vicky had always been good at pouting.

"I've wasted enough time on Tim Harper. The month after we got married, everything started to go downhill."

"A month? Now who's exaggerating?"

"Well, maybe it took a year or so." Vicky sighed. "You were right about us getting married too young. I should have listened to you. I thought our love would last forever."

High school sweethearts, Tim and Vicky had married a year after Vicky's graduation while she was attending a local community college. They'd only been together for three years now and were already having problems.

"You don't love Tim anymore?" Gillian noted the sudden flash of emotion in her sister's blue eyes that was just as quickly shuttered.

"Not in the same way. We're better off apart, believe me. Marriage has to be more exciting than waiting on some guy, getting his meals together, cleaning house, doing laundry, picking up his dirty socks. Our social life consisted of watching television together. Big deal."

Gillian had discussed the matter with Vicky many times before it had come to the point of separation. "I thought you were going to try to negotiate household duties and arrange to have a romantic evening once a week."

Not that such an evening had to be elaborate. Lighting candles for dinner or even going for a long walk could be romantic. Personally Gillian had always dreamed of reading love poetry to someone special, though she knew most men would think that was silly.

"Tim is impossible and so was the marriage."

From Vicky's guilty expression, Gillian figured her sister hadn't tried to negotiate anything.

"I don't want to talk about Tim," said Vicky belligerently. "We're not part of your marriage project, all right?"

"All right."

Gillian obligingly backed off, though she intended to continue the conversation whenever she got the chance. Tim and Vicky had indeed married too young, but she didn't think they had really tried to work things out. She wondered how much her little sister's immaturity had added to the strife. Tim, on the other hand, had always seemed easygoing.

"I don't want to be in a bad mood, okay? Let's enjoy ourselves." Vicky nodded toward a booth in the far corner of the restaurant. "See those two men over there? They've seen staring at me since they came in. They must like my new look."

Gillian hadn't been impressed with Vicky's new black leather miniskirt or her over-bleached hair. "You've always been pretty," she said truthfully.

"But I look more funky now, you know. I had the hairdresser leave the lightener on longer yesterday."

"Yesterday? Your roots are showing." Not to mention that her sister's medium-length hair was ratted up until it was almost standing on end.

"The roots are supposed to show." Vicky picked out a strand of hair with plum-lacquered nails. "The contrast of the darker roots and lighter ends frame my face. See? Isn't it flattering?" Vicky glanced toward the men in the corner. "Blondes get more attention."

Gillian laughed. Vicky was so open and bubbly and charming that she could get away with almost anything.

Vicky turned her attention on her sister and scrutinized Gillian's hair. "You could turn blonde real easily, too."

"I like it just the way it is, light brown."

"Pooh, at least you should let me play up your makeup, especially since you wear glasses. On Friday, I'll come over early and do your eyes before we go out."

"I don't need special makeup for a movie."

"Oh, come on. And if you just loosen up and stop being so picky, you might find someone interesting at Rochesters."

Gillian sighed. "All right...I suppose I can stand it for an hour or so."

Hopefully Vicky would quickly tire of loud music and pushy men looking for one-night stands. Gillian didn't think that was what her kid sister was looking for any more than she was.

Indeed, Gillian was particular about the men she dated; long ago, she'd set certain standards for herself. She wanted someone who was mature and responsible...and deep. She longed for a man who wanted to communicate, ideally a man who was willing to share the secrets of his heart and soul. She'd never find him in a noisy singles' bar where even making small talk was difficult.

For years she'd met dates through mutual friends or siblings, and sometimes while participating in sports. So far, though, no relationship had blossomed into the kind of love she sought. She'd broken off with Edwin a couple of months ago, not because she didn't care about him, but because she didn't care enough. When the arguments had started, she called it off. Through the years, she'd heard enough shouting matches between her parents to last her a lifetime. Constant fighting would never help a couple grow closer.

Gillian glanced at her watch and rose. "I have to be going. I'm meeting John Slater at the library in half an hour."

Vicky followed Gillian to the cashier's desk. "You sound pretty eager. Sure you're not planning on having any fun?"

"I told you, it's just a project."

Though at the moment the prospect of working with John didn't look half bad. Gillian would far rather spend an evening with him than with the most eligible singles' bar Romeo.

GREENVILLE LIBRARY was a few blocks from Gillian's apartment, the second floor of a Victorian house. Since the September evening was mild, she left her car parked in front and walked.

Gillian loved her neighborhood with its cozy old homes and quiet streets. The larger, three-story Victorian standing on the corner reminded her of the elaborate dollhouse she'd constructed as a hobby while in college and to which she was still adding miniature furniture and authentic detailing.

As she strolled toward the library, she gazed up at the stars, which blazed so clearly that they seemed to hang in the branches of the tall oaks and maples lining the sidewalks. She was happy she'd chosen to live in the established section of town rather than the newer, barren-looking housing tracts at Greenville's eastern edge.

The small library was lit up brightly as Gillian entered. She greeted Mrs. Derekson, the librarian who was always there in the evening. Gillian had introduced herself the first week of school. As a local teacher, she liked to know everyone.

She spotted John Slater when she headed back toward the stacks. Wearing a becoming turquoise pullover sweater rather than a plaid work shirt tonight, he was sitting at a long table near the encyclopedias and watching her approach with interest. She smiled, her pulse beating in an irregular pattern. Annoyed, she told herself to settle down. Vicky's teasing had gotten to her. But as she'd told her sister, John's attractiveness had nothing to do with the situation.

John eyed the large manila envelope and the spiral notebook she was carrying. "Are those our marriage plans, Miss Flannery?"

"Please call me Gillian," she told him, pulling out a chair and sitting down across from him.

"All right, Gillian."

But he still sounded formal. She laid her materials on the table. "And, yes, this contains all the information we'll need to begin." She opened the envelope and pulled out a couple of multiple-page computer printouts, along with several letter-size envelopes. She handed one of the printouts to John. "This is your copy of the 'setup,' as I call the initial description of our hypothetical marriage. The smaller envelopes contain the random possibilities we'll draw at each meeting as the project progresses."

"Random possibilities?" He didn't look impressed.

"The only changes or problems I've included are those that are logical for this particular marriage," she explained. "I have twenty-six different types of marriages mapped out on the school's computer, along with two years' worth of various changes and problems I print out on slips to draw from as we go along. So even though the setup for a marriage is repeated in different classes, the problems are never exactly the same."

He tapped a long finger on the table and gazed at her measuringly. "*Types* of marriages? People are a little more individualistic than that—each marriage has its own laws and inherent problems."

"Maybe 'examples' would be a better word for what I've set up." Beginning to feel a bit defensive, Gillian hoped she wouldn't have to deal with his skepticism every time they met. "Some of the marriage examples for this project were drawn from real case studies. The rest were made up from a variety of sociological statistics—professions of young people today, familial backgrounds, popular hobbies and interests...."

"Okay," he interjected. "You don't have to give me a lecture." Then he grinned. "Of course, I asked for it. I'm sure you're trying to be as accurate as possible. I recognized your commitment and sincerity at the PTA meeting."

Relieved, she smiled also. "I do my best."

"We'll need to relax while we're working or this project is going to be quite a chore."

"Right, I hope we'll both feel at ease," Gillian agreed, though she wasn't sure she would ever be able to do so if John kept gazing at her the way he was now, his light-brown eyes as warm as heated brandy. She wished she could remove her glasses and reduce him to a nice, safe fuzzy blob. But then she wouldn't be able to read. "Um...want to take a look at the printout?"

He nodded. "Good idea." He unfolded the pages.

She examined her own printout at the same time, having no idea which "marriage" they'd gotten. She'd pulled one out of the pile she'd prepared that afternoon, placing the others in envelopes for the rest of the adult group. She hoped everyone had remembered to drop by the school to pick them up.

"We're Mr. and Mrs. X?" He sounded amused. "Like people who want to remain anonymous when they write to Ann Landers for advice."

"To make things simple," she explained. "I labeled each married couple with a letter from the alphabet."

"Couldn't get any sociological statistics on names?"

Surely he wasn't serious. "I didn't think spending time on that kind of research was necessary."

He grinned. "Loosen up, would you? That was a joke. How about if we call ourselves Mr. and Mrs. Xerxes or Xylophone or something? That would feel more personal."

She couldn't resist his sense of humor. "Mr. and Mrs. Xerxes it is."

He ran a finger across the page. "So Mr. Xerxes is working in the commercial art department of a university and Mrs. Xerxes has an MBA and is employed by a bank. A banker and an artist—what an odd combination. How did we ever get together?"

Gillian leaned over to point to another section of his printout. "It's right here. We met in undergraduate school."

"I see. And we were so opposite we were attracted, I guess." He smiled and kept reading. A few seconds later, however, the smile faded. "You're earning more money than I."

Uh-oh. He didn't look very happy. "That sometimes happens with today's couples."

"I guess so...though I've never been in that kind of situation." He tapped the page. "And we're living in an apartment in a city's downtown area. I don't like that. Why can't we buy a condo or a town house in the suburbs?"

"We can make that one of our goals." She opened her notebook and jotted it down. If that's what he wanted, she was willing to go along. "The assignments for this project include keeping weekly, monthly and long-term budgets, adjusting them when necessary. We'll also be making out a list of goals and keeping a daily diary of our accomplishments and responsibilities. You'll need your own notebook."

"I'll bring one next time." He gazed at the computer list and raised one auburn brow. "You know, this really isn't fair."

"What's not fair?"

"In marriage, two people contribute to the problems and solutions. You have to deal with the other person—that's what it's all about. In this case, you've set up this entire scenario. As your partner, I think I should have some say-so from the very beginning."

"You don't like this particular marriage?"

Gillian was sure the income discrepancy was bothering him. But then, even the most open-minded man was likely to balk at the idea of a woman making more money.

"I just want to include some input of my own."

"What kind of input?" she asked, certain he was about to suggest upgrading Mr. Xerxes' profession.

"I'll feel better about this if I can add a few small details here and there," he told her, avoiding being specific. "Can I have a piece of your notebook paper?"

Deciding he would think her unfair if she didn't give him a chance, she tore out a page and handed it to him. She warned, "Everything has to be logical given the basic situation, you know."

If they didn't stick to the rules, the purpose of the project would be ruined. A real married couple couldn't magically change their circumstances whenever they felt like it.

"I realize that." He took a pen from his sweater's front pocket and quickly made a list.

She leaned closer and tried to read his handwriting, a difficult task since it was upside down. "Do you want me to enter that data into the computer?"

"We don't have to be so mechanized." John tore the paper into sections. "We can draw a few slips right here and you can write them down on the printouts."

Oh, she could, could she? Gillian didn't object, though she liked everything the way it was now—well-organized and logical.

He folded the strips he'd torn off and made an untidy pile in the middle of the table. "Why don't you draw first?"

"How many do you want to use?"

"Three or four will satisfy me."

She only hoped his additions would be acceptable. Hesitantly she picked up a slip. "This says you're going to pick up some free-lance commercial artwork." Not too bad. That should make him happy. "Free-lancing will increase your income."

"Our income," he corrected her and drew a slip himself. "Let's see, we have a dog, a beagle. He's small enough for our apartment but we'll have to work pet food into the budget."

"And make sure someone walks the animal morning and evening." Feeling more enthusiastic, she drew another slip and unfolded it. Her eyes widened. "You can't do this. It won't work at all."

"Why not?" He reached for the paper she held. "Oh, this one— you're having a baby in a few more months." He explained, "You got pregnant the first week of our marriage."

"I can't be pregnant," she insisted, then realized her adamant tone had attracted the attention of an elderly man who was reading a newspaper nearby. She flushed and looked at John, lowering her voice to a whisper. "There are no children in the X marriage, at least not for a while."

"I thought one of the purposes of this project was to learn to cope with problems and change."

But why on earth would he want to add a baby at the very outset? "This is quite a change. I'll have to sit down at the computer and look over the X marriage's profile from the very beginning."

"Extra work for you, hmm?"

"It's just that the X... the Xerxes may have a difficult time dealing with an unplanned pregnancy."

"Most newlyweds would have a hard time." He tapped his pen on the table and smiled wryly. "Actually I added the pregnancy to the possibilities because of my own personal experience. My ex-wife and I found ourselves expecting our first child barely a month after we were married."

"I see." And the problem must have had serious impact or he wouldn't still be thinking about it. "Well, I suppose I really don't have to change every detail on the computer," she said grudgingly, not wanting him to think she wasn't being cooperative. It was just that she wasn't used to being on the experiential end of her own assignment.

"Don't change anything. When we draw our slips every week, we can discuss how these additional items will alter things. We can do the work together." He scooped up the rest of the slips and crumpled them into a ball. "That's enough input from me. I'll throw the rest of these things out."

She nodded. "All right." From the corner of her eye, she thought she saw the elderly man trying to turn up his hearing aid.

"I hope maternity costs are covered in one of our jobs' insurance plans."

"We'll have to make a guess about that."

"And how many weeks will you be taking for maternity leave? Or are you going to quit the bank and stay home?"

"Stay home?" She suddenly confronted the real issue that had probably prompted John's insistence on the pregnancy. "I can't quit my job. I'm the major breadwinner in the family."

He looked disapproving. "You're planning to hire a nanny, then?"

"That would be terribly expensive, especially if we want to save for a house." She paused for a second to consider. "You're the one who should stay home. You can free-lance while you take care of the baby," she stated, certain he wasn't going to go for the suggestion.

"Hmm...sure, why not?" he agreed, completely surprising her. He rubbed his mustache thoughtfully. "Might be fun taking care of a new baby. My daughters were half-grown when I had to take complete responsibility for raising them."

Gillian couldn't help wondering what had happened to his wife, but she didn't think he'd appreciate being asked to explain the situation to her. Always efficient, she spread out both the printouts, writing down the new information John had forced her to add. Then she made some notes in her spiral.

"Tracy's now twelve, Kim's sixteen," he went on softly. "Five years went by so fast, it makes my head spin."

His expression and the love apparent in the man's voice warmed Gillian inside. "I can tell you've enjoyed child-rearing."

"Most of the time." He leaned closer, resting his elbows on the table while he watched her scribble. "But children come with their own set of problems. Parents should be aware of that."

She nodded. "As the middle child of a family of seven, I've had some experience with child-rearing and problem-solving myself."

"Then you learned responsibility at an early age."

John was obviously a loving, responsible and protective parent. That's why Gillian had so quickly forgiven the ruckus he'd made over her class project. He took fatherhood seriously. What would it really be like to have a baby with him? she mused, imagining the situation. Would he want to have more children, when and if he got married again?

"Put diapers and formula, baby clothing and furniture on that budget list," said John, interrupting her thoughts.

"We don't have to have diapers and formula until later on."

"But you should add the cost of a crib now, maybe Lamaze classes . . . if you want to go through natural childbirth."

"Natural childbirth?" Considering, she knit her brows.

"And put vitamins on the grocery list. In fact, I suppose you should even plan out your diet. Plus you'll be needing maternity clothes. . . ."

She stared up from her notebook when she heard him chuckle. His eyes crinkling with mirth, he broke into full laughter.

"I know this project is for a serious purpose," he said, "but I feel kind of silly right now, planning for cribs and maternity clothes. Don't you?"

"It does sound silly," she had to agree, joining in when he laughed again. "We were really getting into it, even bickering like some married couples." Amazing that she hadn't gotten hyper about that. "I almost forgot we were working on a project."

"Now I can see how the kids got into talking about sex." He made an effort to be serious, though his eyes still danced. "Not that Scott wasn't pushing things too far."

"I already talked to him about his inappropriate behavior, and he apologized, both to me and to Kim. When...and *if* we go back to the class's marriage project, he'll behave himself."

They finished the task quickly after that, actually joking as they made up a basic list of items to think about, then discussed the following night. Teasing her about outrageous names they could give the baby—mixing them up with others for the dog—John borrowed a second sheet of paper and copied her notes.

The library was almost ready to close when they rose to leave, though the elderly, white-haired man at the next table was still perusing his newspaper.

"No, I don't think Attila is a good name for the baby," Gillian told John with a chortle. "And it doesn't fit the poor beagle either. He's not likely to be a vicious animal."

"But Attila H. Xerxes has such a nice ring to it."

The elderly man glanced up as the couple passed by. He waved an arthritic finger. "Don't worry, kids. Marriage will get easier as you go along. My wife and I have been together for fifty-one years and we've solved a lot of problems in that time."

Turning red, Gillian smiled, then traded self-conscious looks with John and hurried on. "I just knew he was listening."

"He didn't mean any harm," John told her, amused she was embarrassed. Noting the color of her cheeks, he decided pastel pink was as flattering to Gillian as pale gold, the color of the silky blouse she was wearing this evening.

They paused on the steps outside.

"I'll walk you to your car," he offered.

"That won't be necessary. I'm on foot." She gestured toward the west. "My apartment is only a couple of blocks away."

"Really? That's certainly convenient for both the library and the high school."

She backed away slowly. "See you tomorrow night."

"Wait." He followed. "I'll walk you to your door."

"You don't really need to. The neighborhood is safe."

"You could still use an escort—it's dark and you're a woman alone." Plus he was oddly reluctant to see the evening end so soon.

She made no other objection, and they set off, strolling through a mosaic of shadows and glowing pools created by the street-lights.

"I enjoyed your company," he told her. "I enjoyed the whole evening. I like the project."

"Good. We're agreeing about something. That's progress."

John recognized a special sort of tension hanging between them as they walked along. He noticed how the streetlights picked up the gold strands in her light brown hair. "I can see how high school kids could learn something about life from a project like this."

"I thought you would appreciate the idea once you tried it."

He gazed around at the houses as they passed. "I heard you just moved to Greenville. Like it?"

She smiled. "So far. It's a lot quieter than the city. I had to get used to that. The first week, I kept waking up in the middle of the night and couldn't figure out why. Then I realized the silence was causing the problem. I used to live near a freeway."

"Maybe you should get yourself a tape of traffic noise."

She grinned. "I thought about something like that. But actually, I'm acclimatized now."

"What made you move from the city?"

"I grew up in a small town, and I missed that kind of atmosphere. Indianapolis was fine during my wild youth—"

"You were wild?"

She laughed. "Don't let this demure demeanor fool you. I used to shop until I dropped, eat enough spicy foreign food to give heartburn to a basketball team, and stay up until all hours."

"Whew." He liked her sense of humor. "That is pretty wild."

"But now that I'm older, I've slowed down a bit. I appreciate knowing my neighbors and the clerks in the grocery store and even the parents of my students."

They crossed an intersection and walked half a block before she paused and turned onto the sidewalk leading to a white frame Victorian house. "This is where I live, on the second floor."

He examined the building's exterior with an experienced eye. "It's a beautiful place, must be at least ninety years old. The owners could stand to give the gingerbread trim another coat of paint, though."

"You'd notice little details like that, being in the renovation business."

John followed her up the steps leading to the wide porch. "I own an interesting house myself. You'll have to see it sometime."

She stopped beside the door and stared at him, her heart-shaped face tilted at an angle. The pose suddenly made him realize the source of the tension he'd been feeling. "I guess this is where there'd be a good-night kiss . . . if we were on a date."

"Which we're not," she added, almost sounding regretful. She reached into her purse for her keys. "Well, good night. See you tomorrow."

"I'll be looking forward to it."

He really was. On the way back to the library where he'd left his car, he hummed a little tune, thinking about the project they'd be working on. He wasn't going to mind doing homework at all, especially with such an amusing and attractive partner.

How interesting that Mr. Xerxes was an artist, something he'd planned to become before his parents talked him into pursuing a more practical career. In recent years, he'd gotten back on track, though, doing more what he liked to do. He and David, his architect brother and business partner, mixed creativity with practicality in their work. An intuitive feel for materials and an eye for the visual helped when one was renovating beautiful old buildings. John even took pleasure in the small things, like restoring authentic woodwork or creating some new details of his own.

Kate had never appreciated his talent and had been so concerned with his improving their life-style that she'd fought his quitting his job to go into business with his brother. He'd tried to convince her that doing so would save his sanity, since he hated his job, and would afford them the best possibility for their future. She hadn't seemed to care about what he'd wanted.

She'd been furious when, despite her objections, he'd invested the money he'd saved from his engineering salary in the business. She'd planned to use the money as a down payment on a larger house. And even though both girls were in school, Kate hadn't been willing to work outside the home herself to make that goal possible.

To this day, John wasn't sure exactly what had been the worst of their troubles—opposing goals and egos, unrealistic expectations, the pressures of having a family while he was still in college. But when Kate had left him less than a year after he'd involved himself in Slater and Slater, John had regretted the high-handed way he'd handled the situation. If he'd tried to make her see his point of view, perhaps Kate wouldn't have left him. Kim and Tracy didn't deserve to suffer because their parents couldn't see eye to eye.

Still brooding about his daughters—the subject foremost in his mind since Kate had called the day before—John paused when he reached his car. He unlocked the door, slid in and started the engine, then pulled out into the street and headed for home. Gillian Flannery had been nonplussed when he'd thrown in the pregnancy issue for their project, a problem that had naturally occurred to him because he'd dealt with it in real life. He only wished the complications facing him at the moment could be solved with computer printouts and pencil and paper.

"WHY DOESN'T HE CALL?"

For at least the tenth time that evening, Kate paced the perimeters of her small furnished apartment. She stared at the phone, willing it to ring. John had more than twenty-four hours—surely that was enough time to talk to Tracy and Kim about seeing her.

But the phone remained as silent at ten o'clock as it had at seven. "Ooh!"

She hated waiting. She flopped down in a living room chair, then picked up the receiver, determined to take the initiative. It wasn't as if she didn't have John's home number.

She paused before dialing, however, remembering how harsh and unfriendly her ex-husband had sounded the day before. He could really be cold when he wanted to be. Perhaps she'd better give him some time after all, though she didn't know why he was balking at uniting a mother with her children. Hadn't he complained about her lack of contact with them since the divorce? Well, now she was ready to make up for their separation.

Kate replaced the receiver and sighed. She loved Tracy and Kim with all her heart. When she'd left John and run away with Howard, she'd planned to take her babies along. Howard had talked her out of it, however, assuring her they would send for the children when they got settled in California. She'd been too stupid to realize her spontaneous action would cost her custody of the girls, probably forever. And she'd been naïve about Howard's intentions—he'd never really wanted her kids, anyway.

She'd made a big mistake running away with him. They'd hardly been married a year before she was seeking a quickie Las Vegas divorce. Depressed and mixed-up, she'd soon gotten involved with another man. Chuck had made her feel better with his compliments and personal attention, but she'd been reluctant to marry him. Instead, she'd lived with him and told herself that she'd see her daughters as soon as she got back on her feet.

When Chuck broke up with her, she'd been forced to learn to support herself. She'd saved a little money and had come back to

Indianapolis, assuming she could depend on her children for a permanent, ongoing relationship.

She really had tried to keep in touch with Kim and Tracy through the years. If she hadn't encountered so many problems, hadn't moved so many times, had been able to earn more money, she would have come to see them as well, Kate assured herself.

Picking up her purse, she riffled through her wallet for the treasured photos she always kept with her. When she found them, she spread them out on her lap—Tracy as a smiling baby, Kim as a grade-schooler dressed in a cowgirl suit, both girls opening their Christmas presents the year before she had walked out on her marriage.

Last but not least, Kate gazed at the Polaroid her widowed mother had managed to send her a few months ago. Both girls were so tall now! And Kim was a real beauty, a younger version of her mother except for the hair color. Kim's was auburn rather than dark brown. Kate knew she and Kim could have fun shopping together . . . if they ever got the chance.

Kate put the photographs back in her purse, determined anew to see her darling girls. She was being deprived of watching her own children grow up. When her eyes filled, she brushed away a tear and rose to pace the apartment again. This waiting game was going to be impossible for her. She couldn't rush home and stare at the phone every night.

Should she call John again tomorrow? He'd probably be angry, always having complained about her impatience. But he was going to have to make some arrangement within a reasonable time period . . . or she was going to contact a lawyer.

Every parent had some legal rights, at least a few days of visitation each week. If John didn't cooperate, she would be forced to take action.

CHAPTER THREE

WHEN KATE called him a second time at work, John knew he had to quit making excuses and talk to the girls about their mother. She undoubtedly could obtain visitation rights if she tried, no matter what he thought about the idea. Though he'd have to leave to attend Gillian's class later on, he decided he would have enough time to discuss the situation during dinner. He waited until they'd all settled down at the table.

"I have something important to discuss with you," he told Kim and Tracy.

Kim threw down the fork she'd been using to toy with her meat loaf and scalloped potatoes. "Oh, no, I just knew it!"

"Knew what?" John asked with a thrill of trepidation. Had Kate dared to contact the girls directly?

"You're dating Miss Flannery, aren't you?" Kim's voice was ripe with accusation.

"Dating?" Completely taken aback, John stared at his daughter. "Where did you hear that?"

"It's true, isn't it? Yuk!" Kim pressed her cheeks with her hands and rolled her eyes in horror. "How could you do this, Dad? It's s-o-o embarrassing . . . and creepy!"

"Dad's dating that new high school teacher?" Tracy chimed in from the other side of the table. She turned from Kim to their father. "Wow, good going. Miss Flannery's cute. I saw her at the library one time."

"Ever-r-ybody saw Miss Flannery at the library . . . with Dad," said Kim mournfully. "They were all talking about it today during class."

John was still stunned. "Who's talking about Gillian and me?" He hadn't noticed anyone paying attention to them the night before other than the librarian and the older man reading the newspaper.

"Andy drove by and saw you two leaving together," Kim stated breathlessly. "And Melissa dropped some books off and..."

"Saw us sitting at a table," finished John. "That's hardly dating, Kim. And it's certainly not romantic."

"But Melissa said your heads were close together."

"Sure, we were working on the project I told you about, the same one you were doing with Scott."

He'd given the teenager a complete rundown after the PTA meeting. She hadn't seemed upset then.

"But why were you walking down the street with Miss Flannery after the library closed?" Kim asked, sounding suspicious.

John could hardly believe the way his older daughter was carrying on. "She didn't bring her car, it was ten o'clock at night, and I saw her to her door as any gentleman would do. It was common courtesy."

Kim appeared slightly relieved. "Then you really aren't going out with her?"

"No."

"But why not, Dad?" Tracy, who'd been following the conversation avidly, jumped in to give her own two cents' worth. "She's single. You could go to a basketball game with Miss Flannery or a movie."

"Be quiet, motormouth," Kim snapped at her sister.

Tracy scowled. "Be quiet yourself, pimpleface—and there's a new one coming up on your nose."

Kim's hand flew up to cover that part of her face.

"That's enough." Disgusted, John gazed from daughter to daughter. "Stop the name-calling. You're acting like little girls instead of young ladies. And I don't know why you're both so interested in Gillian Flannery in the first place."

He'd dated a couple of women over the past five years, discreetly of course, and neither of the girls had gotten upset over it. Not that he wouldn't expect a mixed reaction if and when he became serious about someone.

"Oh, Dad." Kim sighed, then spoke slowly, as if he couldn't possibly understand. "There's got to be lots of single women around. You can't date teachers, okay? I mean, it's so gross, I would never live it down."

"Who says he can't date teachers?" Tracy came in again, obviously spoiling for a fight. She enjoyed annoying Kim. "Miss Flannery seems real nice. She even likes sports. She plays volleyball with the Taylor kids on Saturdays sometimes. I think she'd make a great wife for Dad."

"Wife!" shrieked Kim.

His ears rang. "Settle down," John admonished the older girl, drawing the line at hysterics. "I already told you there's nothing going on." Not so far, anyway. "If I were you, I'd quit speculating about Gillian Flannery's love life and concentrate on learning something from her class. I'm sure she's a very dedicated teacher."

"She's okay," Kim agreed.

An understatement, of course, but what had he expected? Kim's teenage hypersensitivity was responsible for her negative attitude. The biggest shock about the whole discussion was that there had been gossip about Gillian and himself in the first place. He remembered their discussion of the advantages of living in a small town. There were drawbacks as well. Everyone knew everyone else's business and liked to extrapolate to entertain themselves.

"Now that we have things resolved, let's finish our dinner, shall we?" His meat loaf had cooled but he was so hungry he didn't care. "Pass the potatoes, please," he asked Tracy.

"Want some more green beans, too?" The younger girl handed him the serving bowls and wrinkled her nose. "These are kinda blah, though. Mrs. Hoffman doesn't put lemon juice and fresh pepper on them the way I would."

"We'll try your version another night," John assured her.

Since Kate had left him with the kids, he'd paid his neighbor Reva Hoffman to be a part-time cook, housekeeper and babysitter. Although the girls were now old enough to take care of themselves when he was away, the aging widow still came over to clean and to prepare meals two or three times per week. She'd been a godsend for a single, working father.

Thinking about the status in which Kate had left him reminded John of the discussion he'd been sidetracked from having with his daughters. But Kim was finished with her meal. She got up and went to the sink to rinse off her plate and silverware before placing them in the dishwasher.

"Done already?" he asked, wanting her to stick around. "You hardly ate."

"I wasn't very hungry."

"She probably had French fries and ice cream after school," Tracy said.

John figured Tracy was correct. Kim liked to munch and hang out with her friends.

"I don't like meat loaf, okay?" the teenager said defensively.

"Besides, she's too worried over you and Miss Flannery to eat," jibed Tracy, earning a dirty look from her sister as the older girl flounced out of the room.

John frowned at the twelve-year-old. "That wasn't nice. You knew she'd get mad." Now he'd have to call Kim back to the table.

"She just doesn't want you to get married again, Dad. But it's all right with me," said Tracy seriously.

He had to smile at her earnestness. "I'm glad you're giving me your approval, but I don't need it yet." He started to rise, intending to go after Kim.

"When you do, let me know. Will you have an affair first?"

"A what?" The word seemed to reverberate through the room. Shocked, John fell back into his chair and stared at his daughter. "What do you know about affairs?"

"Uh, I hear about them on TV programs all the time." She spoke a little too casually, obviously aware that she'd said something wrong. She jumped up. "Want some dessert? Mrs. Hoffman left us a pan of peach cobbler."

"Sit down. Dessert can wait. What television programs are you talking about?"

He knew Tracy was aware of the general facts of life, but she'd never brought up anything like this before. And he felt distinctly uncomfortable, considering her mother had run off with another man.

Tracy slipped back onto her chair and squirmed. "Um, in TV movies or on *Dallas* and *Dynasty*, stuff like that, people are always falling in love and having affairs. They go out a lot and . . ."

"And?"

She giggled nervously. "And they kiss and stuff."

Stuff? John wasn't a man who was usually concerned by censorship, but he couldn't help wondering if he should curtail Tracy's television viewing. "You shouldn't be watching movies or programs made for adults."

Her expression become alarmed. "You're going to make me stop watching TV? D-a-a-d . . ."

He held up a hand. "I won't take away your television privileges." That kind of censorship was unrealistic. He didn't want his kids living in a prison camp. "Relax." His daughter was growing up fast.

Tracy let out her breath in relief. "Whew."

"Why don't you get that peach cobbler out of the refrigerator? We'll have some dessert together . . . and talk."

He rose to pour himself a cup of coffee, passing the antique stained glass windows that he'd hung from the ceiling to divide the cooking from the eating area. During the day, light poured in through the skylights and the greenhouse window he'd installed above the sink, making colors dance across the kitchen.

"Are you going to tell me about the birds and bees again? Give me some more books?"

He'd done so a couple of years ago, and he knew he hadn't done the best job. Luckily his sister-in-law Julia had rounded out the basics with details.

"You already know the facts, Tracy, but I'm not sure you have an idea of the emotional responsibility involved. I just want to stress that responsibility," he explained, hoping he'd find the right words.

"Okay."

She got the cobbler and brought a couple of plates and forks back to the table. Both of them helped themselves.

"People are attracted to each other, they date, sometimes they fall in love, they decide to get married," John began, "but they don't have 'affairs' lightly. Anything beyond a kiss on the cheek is something to think about first."

"Uh-huh," Tracy murmured while eating a big bite of cobbler.

"They overdramatize television programs just to get high ratings. Real life and real love are more serious than television portrays them."

"So you shouldn't kiss and do all that other stuff with someone unless you're in love and have been going out with them for a long time."

As in the past, he was amazed at Tracy's sophistication. "And maybe you shouldn't do anything at all, especially if you're young. . . ."

"Oh, now I get it," she broke in knowingly, making a face. "Don't worry, Dad. Geez, there isn't anybody in my class I'd even kiss. They're all dorks." Then she paused for a moment. "I socked Billie Taylor when he tried."

John laughed, his tension having ebbed away as he talked. "Billie might look better to you in a year or so." When Tracy would probably be as boy-crazy as Kim. He rose and leaned over to hug his daughter and ruffle her carroty hair. "I just want you to know that television isn't real life. I only wish problems were solved as easily as they are in hour-long programs.''

Speaking of problems, he realized he wasn't going to get around to the Kate discussion tonight. He glanced at the clock. Kim had retired to her room and was probably on the phone. Tracy had homework to do and he was supposed to be at the high school in less than twenty minutes. Well, his ex-wife would have to wait a little while longer.

But the problem with Kate was still very much on his mind as John entered the classroom where the first group marriage project meeting was being held. Gillian hadn't arrived yet. Several of the other PTA members had seated themselves around the room. John slid into a desk next to the Talbots. Intent on their printouts, the couple barely nodded, seemingly too busy to talk.

Which was fine with John, who wasn't feeling very outgoing. What were Kim and Tracy going to say when he told them about their mother? How would they feel about her being back in town? Kate hadn't even left them a note before taking off that night.

The rest of the project group drifted in gradually.

Gillian herself rushed in at seven o'clock carrying a handful of envelopes. "Good evening, everyone."

The couples smiled and murmured their greetings in return. She made eye contact with John. When she glanced away, he looked her over admiringly. Her long corduroy skirt and soft sweater expressed innate femininity. Maybe her students gossiped about her because she was so pretty. He wondered if she knew they had her linked up with him.

She gazed around. "I guess we should start. Most people are here."

Four out of six couples, anyway. A couple of seconds later, Elaine Parker, the widow, and her divorced partner Wes Meyer showed up, and after that, the Bigsbys.

"Sorry we're late," Sarah Bigsby apologized, her rumpled husband following her.

"Probably had to wake Calvin up," someone behind John whispered, then laughed softly.

The teasing but good-natured remark made John smile. Despite their idiosyncrasies, the Bigsbys were very well-liked in the community.

"I assume you've all read what I call 'the setup,'" announced Gillian, standing at the head of the classroom, near the teacher's desk. "The printout details the initial logistics of your marriage for this project. Does anyone have any questions or comments?"

A man spoke up, "Looks pretty good to me. Of course I'm sure my memory's going to be jogged a little." He laughed. "Our couple is so young."

Arlene Talbot nodded. "They have to be young so that high school kids can identify with them." She gazed up at Gillian. "I just want to say I think this is very well laid out."

Derek Talbot agreed. "This project is definitely going to be interesting to work with, if a little time-consuming."

Arlene smiled at her husband. "It won't take us that much time, darling." She told Gillian, "We've had quite a bit of experience over the years, participating in couples workshops on various subjects. Are you handing out special problems tonight? We're eager to get to the next step."

"These contain our first set of problems." Gillian walked around the room and passed out the envelopes.

Soon everyone was involved in discussion. John glanced over at the Talbots, who were muttering and jotting down reams of information in their matching leather-bound notebooks. Both lawyers, they were obviously "paper people."

Gillian joined John as soon as she was finished, scooting her desk close to his so they could work. "As the project coordinator, I might have some interruptions while we talk. I hope you won't mind."

"We can tie up any loose ends when we work together alone."

Something in his tone sounded possessive, Gillian thought, as if John preferred to get her off by himself. Or perhaps it was her own wishful thinking. She had to admit she found him even more attractive and actually charming after getting to know him better.

John drew a slip from their envelope, and they were reading it when she became aware of loud bickering at the back of the room. Gillian glanced up, concerned.

Sarah Bigsby, who'd been arguing with her husband, flushed. "Don't worry," she told Gillian with a laugh. "Calvin and I are just having our usual house-repair disagreement." She waved the slip they'd drawn. "According to this, our couple bought an old house that needs a lot of work. Good luck. I can't get Calvin to fix up the one we own in real life."

"I'm renovating the basement," he objected.

"Sure, you paneled half a wall . . . two years ago."

There were chuckles from other class members, though Gillian didn't think the situation funny. She could imagine the arguments the Bigsbys' house provoked. Suddenly realizing the married members of the adult class could run into more complications than the single ones who had no problematic history together, Gillian asked, "How about compromising, Sarah, at least on paper?"

Sarah smiled. "Compromise. Right, I guess it's easy to forget these are only assignments we're working on."

"I'm happy you find them so realistic. The assignments are meant to mirror actual situations," said Gillian, pleased but still concerned.

She hoped she hadn't stirred up an old battle between the Bigsbys. But, to her relief, the couple went back to work quietly and Gillian turned to her partner.

"So what's on the slip you drew?"

He quirked his brows. "Your mother is coming to stay with us for a week and she's always disliked me."

"Is that what it says?" Not remembering such a factor, Gillian reached for the piece of paper to read it for herself. "She doesn't dislike you. She just thinks you don't earn enough money."

Wonderful. Another reference to his lack of income. Of course, the money discrepancy had been worked into the entire fabric of the X marriage.

"She dislikes me."

If that's what he wanted to think, Gillian decided to go along with him. In-law problems were definitely realistic problems in many marriages. "We're going to have to get along with her some way. She'll be very hurt if she can't stay in our apartment. We have two bedrooms. What do you want to do?"

He frowned. "I'm not sure."

Since he was usually decisive, at least during the short time she'd known him, she was surprised.

As if he guessed what she was thinking, he explained, "At the moment I'm a little distracted. Do we have to make a decision right away?"

She wondered if something was wrong. "We can take more time if you want."

"Why don't we meet again...say, on Saturday afternoon. Is that good for you?"

She hesitated for a moment. If her sister or one of her friends wanted to do something later on, she'd still have time to meet them. "Fine. Is there anything in your notebook you want to discuss?"

"Notebook?" He looked a little embarrassed. "Oh, great, I didn't even buy one yet. It was on my list of things to do today, but I totally forgot about it."

Forgot? She thought this project was important to him. "We also need to figure out what kind of effect the coming baby will have on all this."

"Right, why don't we talk about that on Saturday, too?" He smiled. "I promise you I'll get a notebook and have it started by then . . . honest."

So what were they supposed to do tonight? Once again, she wondered why he was putting off making decisions.

"Miss Flannery?"

Gillian turned to Elaine Parker. "Yes?"

"I'm sorry to interrupt you, but I believe the problem we've drawn is a little too serious," the widow went on, her inquiry attracting the attention of other class members.

"What is it?"

"As the wife in this marriage, I'm supposed to deal with my younger brother when our parents are divorced. I didn't know we'd be concentrating on this kind of outside pressure. Aren't there enough problems within the marriage itself?"

"Outside pressures are real influences on a marriage," Gillian told her. "That's Marriage M, if I remember correctly, and the brother blames his mother for the divorce."

"And he wants to move in with us or else he's threatening to run away," said Elaine.

"You'll have to use your common sense to figure out a solution. That's all the project asks from you. Right off hand, what do you think?"

"My three kids never did that," complained Wes Meyer.

Arlene Talbot joined the discussion. "But I've heard of situations where kids did."

"How awful." Elaine shook her head sadly.

"Well, you can't let the brother move in," said John, leaning forward so he could see Elaine better. "That would be an imposition on the marriage."

"But you might want to try to understand the brother's pain," cautioned Gillian. "You could warn him of the dangers in running away and give him some space. It takes time for kids to recover from a divorce." She noticed John staring at her curiously.

"Hmm, I see. There's no one solution, I guess." Elaine exchanged looks with her partner. "Wes and I will have to discuss this."

"That's the right idea," Gillian told her. "Jot down your best conclusions as homework and share them with all of us next week."

"It's only paperwork, but people can't help taking it seriously, can they?" John mused softly when he had Gillian to himself again.

She chuckled, remembering their discussion at the library about babies and maternity leave.

He leaned closer, his warm arm brushing against hers. "And you give good advice. All those psychology courses helped."

"I've also had to deal with divorce in my family as well," Gillian hastened to say, not wanting him to think her knowledge ended with books. "My older brother is divorced, and, at the moment, my younger sister is separated. I hope Vicky and Tim will work things out, though. Our parents did when they went through a separation."

"I forgot about your large family. No wonder you're so together and down-to-earth."

"Large families don't guarantee a well-adjusted outlook."

He gazed at her with a wry grin. "Are you that uncomfortable with compliments? You keep throwing them back at me. I'm trying to tell you that you're great."

"Um, well, thanks." Her face grew warm and her pulse picked up. She knew he wouldn't compliment her unless he meant it.

"You are uncomfortable, aren't you? Guess I'll have to add modesty to your list of virtues."

She smiled and felt compelled to joke. "If you think this is going to get you an A in this class, you're on the right track."

His thick brows shot up. "Are you giving us grades?"

"Grades?" asked Derek Talbot from his seat in the next row.

"There aren't any grades for this project," Gillian told him quickly.

"I wouldn't mind if there were," Derek said, obviously confident he and his wife would do well.

If not as confident, the rest of the group seemed to be as content with their assignments so far. At eight o'clock, the end of the meeting, the parents decided to schedule the rest of the weekly group meetings on Wednesday nights. A few people left. Sarah Bigsby stopped to chat with Gillian for a few minutes, as did Elaine Parker.

John lingered behind, waiting for Gillian to turn out the lights. He accompanied her through the empty halls. "Are you sure Saturday afternoon will be okay? I wouldn't want you to have to alter any plans."

"I haven't made any plans yet." And she was pleased that he hadn't, either. She could almost imagine he was asking her for a date. "How about five?"

"Make that five-thirty. I have to feed the kids. Meanwhile, how about going out for coffee tonight?" He added, "Just for a while. I'd appreciate the chance to talk to an intelligent woman."

Flattered that he wanted to spend more time with her and certain he was interested in her personally, Gillian agreed. "Sure."

Perhaps John had felt distracted because he'd been pondering the difficulties of a parent-teacher relationship. She hadn't wanted to admit it, but she'd been hoping he'd ask her out. "I have some papers to grade, but it won't take me that long."

"I'll deposit you on your doorstep by ten. You walked, didn't you?"

She nodded, remembering his remark about good-night kisses the evening before. She felt a tingle of anticipation as she wondered if he counted this invitation as a date.

After everyone left the school, she and John made small talk on the way to the nearest coffee shop, joking about their visiting "mother-in-law."

"I think we should lock the woman in the basement of our apartment building," John teased. "Or, better yet, send her an announcement saying she won a ticket to a quiz show in Hollywood."

"She'd know better than that by the time she was ready to visit us," Gillian objected, chuckling.

"I'll do extra free-lance work to pay for the quiz show *and* a ticket to California."

"You're truly desperate."

Laughing, John parked the car and helped her out. He kept a solicitous arm around her shoulders as they entered the restaurant. Somehow, the simple gesture seemed romantic.

After they were seated in a booth, Gillian ordered tea and a piece of cantaloupe. John asked for coffee.

As soon as the waitress delivered their order, he turned to her, his expression serious. "You know the advice you were giving Elaine... I was wondering how much time it takes for kids to recover from a divorce. I thought you might have some kind of idea, since you're up on statistics."

Puzzled as to why he'd brought up the couples' problem rather than discussing something more personal, she searched for words. "I don't think there's a specific time boundary. It depends on the child and on the divorce."

He heaved a sigh. "You mean the *type* of divorce? That doesn't sound good. I had the worst kind."

Why did he want to talk about his divorce? Did he feel they'd grow closer if he got all the personal details out in the open? Gillian wasn't sure she felt comfortable with that. And now that she thought about it, she wasn't totally comfortable being attracted to a divorced man. She wasn't unrealistic enough to expect that every marriage would work out, but she couldn't help being wary of a man who'd already gone through a bad one. Divorces were rarely the fault of only one person.

"My wife ran off with another man five years ago," John suddenly told her, staring down at his coffee as he stirred it. "If you weren't new to Greenville, you would have heard the gossip."

"How awful."

"It was all over town. Kate left me and our two girls without so much as a note. She sent intermittent letters through the years, a few cards. She called once in a while, but Kim and Tracy were devastated. They had nightmares."

"I can imagine." While Gillian's heart went out to the girls, she had to wonder what kind of problems had forced such a drastic measure.

"And now Kate's back."

"In Greenville?"

"No, but close enough. She's working in Indianapolis and she's called me twice already about seeing the kids. I hate to be heartless, but I really wish I could keep her away from them. Unfortunately she can probably obtain visitation privileges. I just don't want to force them into anything."

"How difficult," she said, keeping her voice even. The conversation was definitely making her squirm.

He took a sip of coffee. "Very difficult. That's why I was so distracted tonight. I haven't told Kim or Tracy anything yet."

"But you're going to have to."

"And soon." He gazed at her candidly. "That's why I wanted to talk, to confide in you. I thought you might have some good ideas."

Disappointment washed through her. So he'd wanted professional advice rather than a chance to explore a possible attraction. "You'll have to be completely honest with them." She swallowed her expectations along with a bite of cantaloupe. "If Kim and Tracy are still angry at their mother, they may refuse to see her."

"What then?"

He leaned closer; she moved back. He was too close for comfort as it was. She was beginning to feel very foolish.

"That's up to you," Gillian said. "Surely you have the legal upper hand, considering how your wife left you. It would take her a while to obtain visitation rights, and even then you could limit the days and hours she got to see the girls. But that's only my opinion. I'm not an expert."

"You sound like an expert. Besides, it helps to just talk about the situation. You're the first person I've told."

She should feel complimented again, she knew, but she still felt only disappointment. Of course, she was usually disappointed when she trusted her heart rather than her mind. That's why she tried so hard to be logical about life and relationships.

She would get over it, Gillian assured herself. She would just have to focus on the marriage project and forget her silly notions. She was more likely to find a suitable date when she went to Rochesters with Vicky than she would by mooning over a man who saw her as a walking volume of statistics.

CHAPTER FOUR

GILLIAN HAD CAUSE to reconsider her thoughts about finding a suitable date at Rochesters upon entering the shiny new establishment. The copper-foil ceiling reflected the copper-trimmed Plexiglas dividers and lamps that glowed from every nook and cranny. Vicky led the way toward the curved Plexiglas bar which was lit from within. Large monitors showing rock videos were suspended around the raised dance floor where couples gyrated to loud music.

This wasn't Gillian's sort of place—too trendy. And the people matched their surroundings.

Whether dressed according to standards set by *Vogue, G.Q.* or *Taxi,* they all appeared too studied, too aware of the impression they were making on everyone else. They stood in tight little knots, talking, laughing, their voices adding to the cacophony of sound.

Vicky leaned back, her lips practically next to Gillian's ear, when she said, "Great, isn't it?"

While Gillian would have preferred going for a drink at a cozy bar, she didn't want to dampen her sister's enthusiasm. "Very glossy. Chic."

"Like the new me," Vicky said with a giggle as she slid toward the bar when a man left, two Coronas crowned with lime wedges in his hands.

"Can I get you ladies a drink?" asked the bartender.

Vicky leaned over and tossed her blond head flirtatiously. "Do you have flavored seltzers?"

"Raspberry, lemon-lime and cream."

"I'll take a raspberry."

Surprised by her sister's unusual request, Gillian raised her eyebrows. "I'll have a glass of white Zinfandel," she told the bartender. To Vicky, she added, "You don't like beer anymore?"

"Seltzer is healthier. Besides, it was Tim who was the beer nut."

Gillian remembered Vicky enjoying beer as well. But she was obviously doing everything she could to change herself into something she wasn't . . . as if she were trying to prove a point to her estranged husband or to herself. Odd how eager her sister was to change now; she'd been unwilling to so much as compromise when she and Tim started having problems. Gillian was looking for a tactful way to bring up that fact when the bartender set down their drinks. Vicky paid him and, moving away from the bar toward the dance floor, held out the glass of wine.

"To flirting and fun."

Taking the drink, Gillian made her own toast. "To being with the right man."

Now, if only her sister would realize *Tim* was that man...if only she would give her marriage another try.

Vicky asked, "So, is he?"

"Is who what?"

A wicked little grin curved Vicky's mouth. "John Slater." She erupted into giggles. "Is he the right man for you or not?"

Gillian had been foolish to think they could get through the evening without John's name coming up. "Absolutely not."

She had deep reservations about a man who'd gone through a messy divorce. The man she got involved with would be able to handle the compromises necessary to make a relationship work. She didn't want to end up in a situation similar to that of her parents.

"Hmm, you trying to convince me or yourself?"

That her sister might have a point made Gillian take refuge in her glass of wine. She feverishly thought of a way to change the subject when the guy next to Vicky invited her to dance.

"Hold my drink, would you?" she asked Gillian.

"Sure."

Great. Now she was stuck standing alone in the middle of a crowd. At least she wouldn't have to answer any more questions about John Slater. And Vicky would consider the evening a success. Looking for a place to set down the drinks, Gillian approached a ledged area, then spotted a couple leaving their stools. No sooner had she claimed one of the seats when a man slid into the other.

"Hi, there. You alone?" he asked.

"Actually I'm with my sister. She's dancing."

"Then you are alone. Good thing I came along to keep you company, huh?"

Gillian took a better look at the dark-haired man, who was at least five years younger than she. He was attractive and slickly dressed. There was something about the way he handled himself—his aggressive stance, his overconfident expression—that put her on guard. Remembering Vicky's claims that she was too picky, that she looked for a reason not to get involved, Gillian decided to give the guy the benefit of the doubt.

"I wouldn't mind having someone to talk to until she returns."

He edged closer. "Don't count on that. She might just get real involved with her partner and forget all about you. Know what I mean?"

"She just met the guy," Gillian told him, a little irritated at his assumption. "Vicky wouldn't forget about me just because she's having a good time."

He slipped off of the stool and slid an arm around her shoulders. "What about you and me doing the same?"

"You mean dance?"

"I mean go someplace quieter where we can get to know each other better."

Gillian stared. Of all the nerve! He was coming on to her and he hadn't even introduced himself or asked her name. Was it the thick blue eyeliner Vicky had applied or was he just forward? Shrugging free of his arm, Gillian said, "Maybe I don't want to know you better."

"You don't mean that." When she merely raised her brows, he lost his cool exterior. "Hey, are you kidding? You're turning me down?"

The way he said it, he must have thought he was doing her a favor. "I guess there's a first time for everything," she said calmly. "But don't worry, I'm sure you'll get over the rejection."

"You bet I will."

He straightened the lapels of his sports jacket and pushed his way through the crowd. When he disappeared, Gillian looked toward the dance floor but couldn't even catch a glimpse of Vicky. She had a moment's unease. How had she let her sister talk her into coming to this place? She'd had more fun the other night at the library...

With John Slater.

Just thinking about the man made her anxious to get out of Rochesters. But when Vicky did show up, Gillian didn't want to spoil her sister's mood, though Vicky did seem to be trying too hard to have fun. The guy she'd been dancing with was nowhere to be seen. Had he tried a come-on, too?

Gillian was relieved when, after finishing their drinks, Vicky suggested they leave.

Outside, they hugged and headed for their separate vehicles, Vicky shouting she'd call the next day. Gillian waved and climbed into her car. She was home within the hour.

Tired after an emotionally strenuous week and disappointing evening, she was nevertheless restless and so didn't go straight into the bedroom. The man in the bar had gotten to her more than she cared to admit. He'd made her think of all that she was missing in life.

She wandered through the living area to the small solarium in the turret where moonlight shone over the dollhouse that was not only her hobby, but her pride and joy. She had lovingly built and painted and was still decorating and furnishing the miniature Victorian house that was irreplaceable, too valuable to be a child's toy, even though Gillian fully planned on letting her daughter play with it someday.

More and more often she worried she'd never be given the opportunity to have a child, since she couldn't even find a man with whom she could have a lasting relationship. Trying not to let the fact worry her was impossible with that old biological clock ticking away.

Who in the world had ever come up with such a ridiculous—and trendy—way of describing a woman's fertility cycle, anyway?

With a flip of a switch, the dollhouse lit up from within. Gillian pulled up a stool and stared at the symbol of her youthful daydreams, many of which had been inspired on the roof of her family's home.

Climbing out of her second floor bedroom had been her way of being alone, away from all her sisters and brothers with their incessant noisy squabbling...not to mention her parents' arguments. She used to lie on the roof and stare up through the tree branches at the sky or read romantic tales. She had even imagined the kind of life she would have as an adult. There'd be a loving husband, two beautiful children—a boy and a girl—and a cozy home filled with harmony.

The roof had been her special place. She'd even kept her prize possessions in a drainpipe, away from the other kids. Her younger sisters, Rose, Ginny and Vicky, never could resist touching what didn't belong to them. So the drainpipe had been her vault, until her favorite doll and a book of poems had been ruined in a rainstorm. She'd been desolate at the loss of her only real personal possessions other than a tiny china tea set, the pieces of which had been broken except for the teapot. It now rested on the dining room sideboard of the dollhouse.

As she switched off the lights and left the turret, Gillian wondered why real life couldn't meet such simple expectations. John Slater had been correct when he'd said college studies weren't a substitute for real life experiences.

Neither were dreams.

"MR. SLATER, this is Russell Danton of Marks, Danton and Stein. I'm Katherine Webb's lawyer."

Immediately on guard at the mention of his ex-wife, John wondered what kind of legal action Kate had taken. That her lawyer chose to call him on a weekend didn't bode well.

"What can I do for you, Mr. Danton?" he asked cautiously.

"Your ex-wife decided to seek my legal advice because you're refusing to allow her to see her children."

"As much as I would like to deny Kate the privilege of seeing the daughters *she abandoned*, I haven't refused her anything. I told her I would leave that decision to the girls themselves."

"Mrs. Webb mentioned that conversation, but since you haven't gotten in touch with her, she's convinced you haven't kept your promise."

"Not yet, no, but it's only been a few days!" John told himself to calm down. Yelling at Kate's lawyer would get him nowhere. "I intend to tell the girls, but in my own way, when the time is right."

Danton paused momentarily before saying, "Mrs. Webb is trying to be fair about this, Mr. Slater. She asked me to speak to you directly so this issue doesn't have to be decided in court."

"Court? What the hell are you talking about?"

"If you won't allow her to see her children, Mrs. Webb will sue for her visitation rights."

Just what he was afraid of. "Listen, Kate had better be patient," John said, his anger building. "She kept Kim and Tracy on hold for five years. Now it's *her* turn to wait." And if she weren't careful, he'd be tempted to slow down the process.

"Mr. Slater, give this some serious thought. I know the situation may not be a pleasant one, but you will have to deal with it. Out of court or in . . . that's up to you."

"You'll hear from my lawyer."

"Is that what you want me to tell Mrs. Webb?"

"Tell her whatever you damn well please!"

John slammed the receiver into its cradle. His hand was shaking. How dare Kate threaten him? He waited a moment to cool down before he called Wayne Millikan at home. Not only was the man his lawyer, but a personal friend. When he got Wayne on the line, John quickly explained the problem.

"I would suggest you talk to Kim and Tracy as soon as possible," was Wayne's advice.

"Are you telling me Kate would have a case even though she abandoned the girls?"

"She abandoned *you*, John. You know she didn't file for custody because I made her realize she wouldn't stand a chance unless she moved back to Indianapolis. Now she has."

The word *custody* lit a warning in John's mind. Surely Kate wouldn't try to take the girls away from him.... "Sometime in the past five years, Kate could have found the time to come back to visit her daughters, but she didn't, not even once."

"I know that," Wayne said in a voice meant to soothe. "But that won't influence the judge when it comes to granting visitation rights. Kim and Tracy aren't small children, Kate is their mother, and she doesn't represent a threat to their well-being, so there would be no reason to stop her from seeing them."

"No physical threat, perhaps, but what about emotional?"

"A divorce always leaves emotional scars, John. I'm being perfectly frank when I tell you that I don't believe the judge would have reason to deny some manner of visitation."

That wasn't what John had wanted to hear. "So what am I supposed to do now?"

"Talk to the girls and to Kate."

"That's what I was going to do in the first place," John muttered. He rubbed the back of his neck, which had grown stiff with tension. "I even tried once. Damn. Part of me wants to fight her, Wayne, but part of me wants my girls to have a mother. If only I could trust Kate. What if she starts seeing them and goes off with some new man she meets?"

"Life is full of chances. Maybe you should give Kate the benefit of the doubt. I know you want to do what's right for your daughters."

"All right. I'll talk to them."

"Good. Let me know what happens. And if you get any more calls that you don't want to handle yourself, refer them to me."

"Thanks, Wayne."

John figured he'd better talk to the girls at the earliest opportunity. But, as usual on a Saturday afternoon, they were both out with their friends; Kim at a shopping mall, Tracy playing softball. They would be home for dinner, but Gillian was due to come over to work on the marriage project soon after. He'd wanted her to come to his place so Kim could see they really were studying and Tracy would realize he wasn't romantically involved. Even so, he had to admit he'd been looking forward to seeing Gillian all day. It would be nice to spend time with her in a more relaxed, personal setting.

GILLIAN FOUND JOHN'S HOUSE easily on Saturday, even though the address was difficult to read and the place was on the far outskirts of Greenville in an area that had once been open country beyond the town limits. The gabled, two-story, obviously renovated farmhouse, "looked" like him—a combination of traditional and modern, warmth and bold contrast.

As she parked in the driveway and ambled up the sidewalk, she admired the natural wood siding and bright turquoise trim. A skylight protruded from one part of the roof, and she figured John had also renovated the interior extensively.

He was waiting at the door as she mounted the steps and crossed the wide front porch. "Hi." His welcoming smile was warm, making her forget that she'd meant to keep her distance. "You'll be pleased to know I've finally got a notebook, and I've even done my homework."

"Wonderful."

John's eyes swept over her as if her simple sweatshirt and jeans were something special. Gillian remained fixed, staring at him until he gestured for her to come inside. She brushed by him quickly, as if that would negate the rising attraction she was feeling. The brilliant turquoise walls of the little entryway made her stop in her tracks.

"Wow! What a gorgeous color."

"Thanks. I wanted a cheerful hue to greet visitors... and myself when I trudge home from work every day. The rest of the place is more conservative—mainly your basic off-white."

She looked around curiously. "You renovated the whole house, right?"

"Actually I had to. I bought it at a bargain price, but it was in terrible shape. The place was built around the turn of the century, so it needed some updating. Also, it hadn't been lived in for a while." He led her beyond the entryway down the narrow hall. At the end, a large room opened off to one side of a staircase. "This is the living room. I put in the fireplace and new windows."

Gillian sighed with envy. She spent her spare time fixing up a dollhouse; he'd had the opportunity to work on the real thing. She stood in the doorway and admired the living room.

Large windows bordered a massive stone fireplace. The wood-work and thick moldings had been restored to a rich oak luster. The room contained a pleasant mixture of both modern and antique furniture—a brown velvet couch, a refinished antique rocker, an art deco bronze floor lamp, a Scandinavian area rug. Her sur-roundings made her feel as comfortable as John was managing to do as he led her to the doorway on the opposite side of the hall.

"This is the kitchen," he said. "I knocked out a wall to make it larger. We can work in here." He motioned toward the butcher-block table. "Or we can use the family room."

"Either would be fine."

"Then I'll opt for a nice soft couch."

He grasped her elbow gently and guided her past the open stair-case and down another short hall into a spacious room that had to be a new addition. The furniture was older and more casual, but one wall featured new floor-to-ceiling windows and a door that led out onto a deck.

John had indeed done a lot of work on the place, and Gillian wondered whether he'd purchased the house before or after his divorce. The thought of his broken marriage reminded her of her vow to keep her distance, but she couldn't seem to manage it. She was mesmerized by the warmth of his hand on her arm until she heard the thud of running feet on the stairs.

John let go and stepped to the doorway. "Kim? Tracy? Come in here, will you?"

"Tracy's upstairs." Kim approached, eyeing Gillian with an odd expression.

"Hello, Kim." Gillian smiled, hoping to put the teenager at ease. She sat down in an overstuffed chair.

"Hello," Kim murmured, carefully avoiding eye contact with her teacher. "What do you want, Dad?"

"We decided to use this room for a couple of hours," John told his daughter, "so you won't be able to watch television in here."

"That's okay." Kim took a step backward, her face solemn. "I could watch the one upstairs if I wanted. If I had time," she hastened to add. "I need to crimp my hair."

"You're doing your hair?" John stepped into the hallway after his daughter. "I thought you said you weren't going out tonight. Have your plans changed?"

"Uh, no...er, maybe...Laura and a couple of other people might be coming by," Kim explained.

Gillian realized Kim was definitely uncomfortable, no doubt because a teacher had invaded the sanctity of her home. The girl had said little or nothing in class lately. Gillian hoped the Scott incident wasn't still an issue.

"I hope you and your friends won't be making a lot of noise while we're trying to work," John said.

"Don't worry, we'll probably go out for ice cream."

"Hmm, if you're back in the next hour or so, how about bringing some back for us?" He glanced back at Gillian. "That is, if you'd like ice cream? Have a favorite flavor?"

Watching Kim, Gillian didn't think the girl looked too thrilled with the suggestion. But John was waiting for her answer. "Anything with chocolate and nuts," she finally told him.

"But we're not going out until much, much later, Dad." Kim backed away further. "And I really have to do my hair." She whirled around and rushed toward the stairs.

John looked disgruntled as he turned from the doorway. "Teenagers."

Gillian nodded, though she thought more was going on that met the eye. "I have several classes of them every day."

"How can you stand it?"

"They're at an interesting if difficult age—very intense, impressionable. I like them ... well, most of the time."

"You must have a lot of patience." He wandered over to the desk in the corner and picked up a spiral notebook, then sat down on the plaid couch across from Gillian. "I'm sorry Kim was rude."

"You don't have to apologize. Lots of teenagers wouldn't appreciate a visit from one of their teachers."

"But it's not that simple. Kim's afraid you and I might get ideas while we're working together."

"What kind of ideas?"

"The romantic sort." He smiled. "We were a hot topic of gossip at school last week, you know."

"No, I didn't know." Considering she'd had a few ideas herself, Gillian was a bit uncomfortable. She was also surprised. But now that she thought about it, there had been a lot of giggling and hushed silences whenever she entered the classroom. Warmth flooded her face. "I'm not used to being the center of speculation."

"I guess there's always going to be gossip of some sort in a small town."

"Uh-huh." Tongues had certainly wagged about Gillian's feuding parents throughout her childhood. Because of that experience, she'd always made it a point to ignore rumors and those who started them. Still, considering this gossip concerned her and John, she couldn't help but be curious. "So what were people saying?"

"A couple of Kim's friends saw us at the library the other night and made up their own scenario," John explained. "We were working so intently that they thought we were discussing something more personal than the Xerxes' marriage." He gazed at her closely, as if to gauge her reaction. "It was getting pretty personal for me. I'll be upset if I can't name that dog Attila."

She had to laugh. "Okay, okay. You can name the beagle."

He sighed dramatically. "Thanks. It means a lot to me." His eyes twinkled. "I take it the rumors don't bother you, then."

Despite her disapproval of gossip, the idea of someone pairing her up with him was titillating. Not that she was about to admit it. "Well, I don't want to make Kim uncomfortable."

He shrugged. "It looks like she's going to be mortally embarrassed no matter what we do. I thought inviting you over and letting her see us work would help, but she's determined to hide out in her room."

"Would it help if I talked to her?" Gillian offered, having dealt with a lot of teen problems through the years.

"At this point, I wouldn't bother. She'd probably get even more uptight."

"Dad?"

John's younger daughter was standing in the doorway.

"Tracy." His whole face lit up in a proud fatherly grin. "Come on in and meet Miss Flannery."

"Hi!" Tracy approached Gillian with a shy but eager smile that showed off all her braces.

Gillian responded warmly, "Hi, Tracy."

The girl was a welcome relief after the standoffish teenager. She gazed at Tracy's unusual hairdo, which was poufed out around her well-scrubbed, freckled face. She must have spent some time blow-drying it. Dressed in a bright lilac sweater and pants, the girl just stood in front of Gillian's chair and smiled.

"You're certainly all spruced up." John stared at his daughter. "Are you planning to go out with Kim and her friends?"

Tracy made a face. "Are you kidding? They'd kill me if I tried to come along." She plopped down on the arm of the couch next to her father. "I just wanted to look nice, okay?" She grinned at Gillian. "I saw you playing volleyball with Billie Taylor and his brother. You did pretty good."

"Well, thanks," said Gillian. "I can't claim to be the best, though."

"You could use somebody like me on your team. I can beat Billie at anything."

So Tracy was a tomboy. "I'll look around for you next time," Gillian promised.

John placed an affectionate hand on his daughter's knee. "And I hate to interrupt this conversation, Tracy, but Miss Flannery and I have work to do."

Tracy popped right up. "Oh, yeah, you probably want to be alone."

"We have to discuss the project I told you we'd be working on," he told Tracy, indicating his notebook.

The girl nodded knowingly. "You want to talk. Okay, I'll get lost."

"You can watch television upstairs," suggested John.

"Naw, I'm going to do my homework in the kitchen."

"Homework?" John seemed surprised. "On Saturday?"

"Some reading." Tracy bounced toward the door. When she reached the hall, she called over her shoulder, "See you later."

"Tracy is a devoted student, huh?" Gillian commented.

"Not usually devoted enough to work on Saturday night. But I'd be a fool to complain." He opened his spiral. "And now we'd better get back to the Xerxes, shouldn't we? I don't want to keep you here all evening."

She almost told him she hadn't made any plans, then thought better of it. He might think she was hinting she was available.

"Now, about the matter of your mother," he began. "I think I've come to terms with her upcoming visit."

"Really? Are we sending her to California or locking her in the basement?"

"Too extreme." He grinned. "I'm willing to let her stay in our second bedroom for a week as long as she pays some rent."

Hoping he was joking again, she laughed.

Admiring the way her cheeks curved sweetly with her smile, John went on, "Seriously, though, I've come to terms with your mother's visit. She won't have much time to bring up my job in all the excitement over her coming grandchild."

"I'm sure you're right. The baby will change things."

Her expression was so warm that John felt disappointed when she glanced away, though he knew they had to get down to business. Opening their notebooks, they worked together amicably for nearly an hour after that, the house quiet except for the muted ringing of Kim's phone upstairs and some muffled sounds coming from the kitchen. They quickly sketched out plans for the mother-in-law's visit and, after her departure, figured out how they could redecorate the second bedroom as a nursery. They also made up a weekly and a monthly budget along with a list of goals. John thoroughly enjoyed Gillian's camaraderie. They'd gone far since the initial tension of their first meeting.

"So we're setting aside money for the baby as well as saving for a down payment on a house," she remarked, making notes in her spiral.

"I think we can handle that." John jotted down the information. At least their fictional couple didn't have the financial difficulties that were an issue in his real marriage.

A few minutes later, he glanced behind him when he heard a soft noise in the hall. He caught a glimpse of Tracy before she disappeared into the kitchen. The twelve-year-old was obviously curious but had managed to remain quiet. The whole house was quieter than usual with Kim cloistered in her room.

Of course, the teenager was overreacting, though John wondered if his daughter had had a sixth sense about her father liking her teacher. He was certain the attraction was mutual and that it was growing stronger every time he and Gillian got together. He stared at her as she worked, her glasses sliding halfway down her pretty little nose. He was tempted to reach out and push them before she blinked, then focused on the doorway behind him. "Tracy."

He glanced over his shoulder to see his daughter sidling toward the stereo. "Are you finished with your homework?"

Her back to him, Tracy monkeyed with the buttons on the tape deck. "Most of it." Soft music drifted from the speakers.

"Turn that off, will you? We'll be done in a few more minutes. You can listen to music then."

"But I'm playing this for you," Tracy told him archly, with the same silly grin she'd had when she'd first met Gillian. Then she giggled and fled from the room.

"I guess she thinks we should be entertained," Gillian said.

"Maybe." Actually John had the feeling Tracy was up to something. "I'll turn the music down."

"Don't bother. It's not that loud and we're just about finished. Can I look at your notebook a minute? I think I missed something."

John handed over his spiral, wondering if he should check up on Tracy. He was sure he'd heard another giggle coming from the kitchen. "My daughters don't usually act like this, you know."

"Kim's not unusual in being sensitive about her peers' comments and behavior."

"Overly sensitive, you mean." He couldn't resist adding, "Maybe some of the kids—the boys, anyway—were gossiping because they have crushes on you themselves."

She handed his notebook back and smiled. "At least the ones who like older women."

He appreciated the curve of her lips, the lights dancing in her eyes. "You're not old."

"Thirty is pretty ancient for a teenager."

"But it's perfect for a man my age." Her expression told him that she wasn't put off by the idea. He leaned forward, reducing the space between them to a few inches. "Maybe we should explore that fact further."

She seemed a bit flustered but didn't look away. "Well . . . there is a problem with that. I don't want the students thinking romance is a natural outcome of the project. Scott already had the wrong idea. In a way, we're serving as an example for the kids."

"Example?" He leaned back in the chair. He'd totally forgotten about her sociology class. And he shouldn't have, since he was the one who'd instigated the PTA meeting. Now here he was, ready to ask the woman he'd put on the spot for a date.

He rubbed his mustache thoughtfully. "Scott was talking about hanky-panky, not romance. I wouldn't have been angry if Scott had asked Kim out for a hamburger or a movie."

She nodded. "I see your point."

The track lighting behind them suddenly dimmed.

Startled, John started to rise to investigate the problem.

"You can sit back down, Dad," Tracy told him, rushing into the room with a loaded tray. She giggled. "I turned down the lights." She placed the tray on the nearest end table and gazed shyly at Gillian. "And I brought you a snack."

Glancing from the loaded tray to John's daughter, Gillian was obviously taken aback, but she managed to murmur, "How fancy."

John just plain stared at the odd "snack." "Oysters?" Tracy hated them almost as much as anchovies.

"Smoked oysters," Tracy announced proudly, "on garlic toast points. I made them myself."

She removed a couple of candles from the tray and placed them on the end table along with two plates, napkins, a bottle of wine and a couple of stemmed glasses. What was going on? The oysters were from cans John had stored in the refrigerator, appetizers left over from a gala opening he and David had thrown for a land-mark building renovation. Tracy must have thought they would look fancy. The red wine was from the rack in the pantry.

"No one gave you permission to open a bottle of wine."

"I didn't drink any, Dad," Tracy assured him. "I just opened the bottle for you. I had a real hard time getting the cork out, though—there's some crumbs in there."

She was blushing and grinning from ear to ear. John finally put two and two together: his daughter was trying to play Cupid.

Tracy quickly lit the candles and giggled again. "Hope you enjoy your 'love feast.'" Switching off the lamp, she turned to go.

Love feast? "Just a minute, young lady," John commanded. "Turn that lamp back on."

Tracy stopped in her tracks, looking disappointed.

John reached over to switch on the lamp himself. "Come back here, right now." As she shuffled toward him, he tried to clarify the situation. "I told you Miss Flannery and I were going to be work-ing on a project, not having a date."

She looked down at the floor, her face now almost as red as her hair. "Uh-huh."

His daughter was so cute, he wanted to smile, but he forced himself to remain sober. "You've embarrassed me." At least he wanted Tracy to think so. Her action was inappropriate, if amus-ing and in tune with the gossip and his real attraction. Were there some kind of vibrations in the air? "Not that we don't appreciate the food."

"It's very tasty," added Gillian diplomatically, sampling a piece. "You're a good cook."

Tracy grinned, and John gave Gillian an appreciative look, wishing he could take advantage of the situation. A love feast didn't sound half bad, appropriate or not. But he thought it best to act extra casual for the moment. He didn't want his daughter getting carried away. He patted the couch beside him. "Why don't you sit down and help yourself, Tracy? Gillian and I were finished with our project for tonight, anyway," he said, emphasizing the word *project*.

Visibly relieved she was off the hook, Tracy plopped down. "I didn't mean to embarrass you, Dad."

"I'm sure you didn't. Just don't make assumptions again, okay?" He handed his daughter the plate of appetizers and she took a piece. "Where on earth did you get the idea for a 'love feast,' anyway?"

"From *Cosmopolitan*. It said oysters and champagne, though, not wine."

"*Cosmopolitan Magazine?*" John was concerned. A racy magazine for single women? "Where did you get that?"

Tracy looked uncomfortable. "Uh, it's Kim's." She hastened to add, "It doesn't have anything bad in it, honest."

"*Cosmo* is a lot more conservative these days," Gillian assured John, then went on to address Tracy, "but the articles are slanted toward older rather than younger women. I'm surprised you found them interesting."

Tracy nodded, obviously pleased at being called a woman. "They were pretty boring all right—all about jobs and men and dorky-looking clothes. The article on the food was the only one I liked." She scraped the oysters off her piece of toast and wolfed it down.

John exchanged smiles with Gillian. She really was being very nice. He would have to talk to Tracy later, however. He didn't want her to have any false hopes. Even though he was attracted to the high school teacher, nothing might come of the situation. He wondered if his daughter was longing for a mother and saw Gillian as a new candidate.

"Want some more?" After helping himself to the oysters, John offered the plate to Tracy again. He was amused she took another piece without wrinkling her nose. "Remember to give that magazine back to Kim." Though he didn't think he liked the idea of the teenager reading it, either.

"I'll throw it at her," Tracy promised.

"Laying it on her dresser would be a better idea." John told Gillian apologetically, "They argue too much."

She nodded. "That's only natural. My six brothers and sisters used to fight all the time."

"Six brothers and sisters?" Tracy whistled. "Geez, you must have had a crowded house."

"Plenty crowded. Two of my sisters and I had to share a room."

"Ugh, I wouldn't like that." Tracy gazed at her father. "They should have remodeled, right, Dad?"

John just laughed.

The doorbell rang a few minutes later, interrupting the small talk. While Kim ran downstairs to let Laura in, Gillian gathered up her belongings. "I should be going."

"I'll walk you to your car." John wondered if she had to leave because someone was waiting for her. And why not? She probably had better things to do than hang out with a divorced man with two half-grown children.

Tracy accompanied them as John escorted Gillian down the hallway. "Why don't you clean up the kitchen?" he suggested to the girl. "I bet it's a mess."

"There's just a few dishes and some broken cork."

"It needs to be straightened up," he insisted, wanting to be alone with Gillian. He nudged Tracy toward the kitchen doorway. She finally acquiesced.

When they got outside, John tried to make excuses for his daughters. "I'm sorry for the way both kids acted tonight. It was ridiculous. Kim hardly spoke to you and Tracy came on too strong."

"Don't be concerned. Kim didn't bother me, and I thought Tracy was sweet." She paused when she reached her car and took out her keys.

Was she in such a big hurry? "You probably have a real date this evening, right?" he asked a little too casually.

"No, I don't."

He was relieved but tried not to be obvious about it. "No date? That must be unusual."

"Why? Have you heard some other rumors?" Fingering her keys, she leaned against the side of her car and smiled. "Just because I'm quick-witted doesn't mean I'm fast."

He laughed when he realized she was teasing. And her smile looked flirtatious. "Really?" he said softly, teasing in return. "I'm sure you could have a dozen boyfriends if you wanted. Might be a pretty exciting life.''

"I appreciate the flattery, but I'll settle for one good man, someone who's mature as well as exciting.''

"Which means you haven't found him yet." At least he hoped not. As he stepped closer, he thought he heard her catch her breath. The very air seemed to sizzle between them, and the tension had little to do with the project they'd been working on.

She dropped the keys in her jacket pocket and assured him, "I'm still looking.''

"I'm glad.''

And with the way she was gazing straight at him, her expression as open and vulnerable as it had been the night he'd walked her home from the library, he wanted to offer himself as a candidate right there and then. Without thinking further, he leaned forward and gripped her shoulders, then planted a soft kiss on her lips. Her mouth parted, her warm breath mingling with his.

He drew her closer, deepening the kiss, cradling her tightly against him. Her arms slid about his waist. He nudged her glasses with his nose, setting them askew, but she paid no attention. The sweetness of the kiss, the light touch of her tongue as the tip brushed his lips, made his blood pound in his ears. He reveled in the warmth of the body beneath her light jacket and blouse. He ran his fingers through her silky hair, then grasped a handful to tip her head back. His nose and her glasses had another collision that pushed them in a different direction.

"Oops." She grasped at the glasses, giving them a whack that sent them flying through the air. They bounced off John's arm, then down onto the driveway.

"I'm sorry." He loosened his hold, intending to stoop down.

She pulled away completely. "Don't worry, I'll get them.''

The mood was ruined, he realized as she picked up the glasses and rose. The evening air felt cool against his heated face. She slipped the glasses back on. He peered at her closely, trying to decide if she was uncomfortable.

"Pretty awkward, huh?" he said with a short laugh, feeling uncomfortable himself. He was probably rushing things. "I don't usually knock off women's glasses.''

"It was as much my fault as yours." She smiled warmly.

That seemed promising. He relaxed. "So when can we get together again? Maybe we could meet for a drink next time.''

"Sure . . . when?''

"How about Monday?" And that would give him the additional benefit of a day or so to deal with the Kate problem. "I'll call you and we'll decide on the place and time."

"I'll be available all evening. School is out by four."

"Great."

John opened her car door for her, then stepped back when she started the vehicle and backed it out of the driveway. He stood and stared down the road until her car disappeared beyond a grove of trees. Despite his present problems, despite the complications of his divorce and children, he couldn't deny his need to further explore his attraction to his daughter's teacher. A whisper of guilt, a reminder of his supposed role-model status in the situation, put an edge to his desire, one that John promptly fought to forget.

CHAPTER FIVE

THE KISS LINGERED in John's mind all Sunday morning, and in the middle of church service, he began to imagine Gillian playing a personal and important role in his life. He could almost envision her sitting next to him as the choir sang and the minister addressed the congregation.

Though he'd dated a few women since his divorce, not one had made him fantasize such a simple, yet complex, thing. Maybe that was because none had been special enough or because all had seemed a little intimidated about forming a relationship with a man who had almost-grown daughters. And Kim and Tracy hadn't appeared ready to accept a woman in their mother's stead, either. If last night's performance were any indication, his younger daughter *seemed* to have come around... yet he wondered about Tracy's innermost feelings.

As much as he hated to admit it, John was sure both girls would have to resolve their anger at their mother before they could ever make a serious attachment to another woman. In that respect, their meeting with Kate would be healthy. But would they want to see her? Second-guessing his daughters in addition to his ex-wife was driving him crazy. It was time he found out exactly how Kim and Tracy felt about being reunited with the woman who had abandoned them.

And so, the moment they arrived home from church, John set out to do just that, despite Kim's rush to change her clothes and to join her friends for the afternoon.

"We have something important to discuss before you go anywhere," John said, leading the way into the family room.

"Like what?" Her tone ripe with suspicion, Kim hung back in the doorway. "This is about Miss Flannery, isn't it?" She made as if to leave.

"Don't take another step," John ordered. "Come in here and sit down."

Kim reluctantly complied. She flounced past him and plunked herself down on the sofa, leaving a large space between herself and Tracy.

"What's up?" the younger girl asked. She gave her sister a sly glance. "*I* like Miss Flannery. She's great." When she turned to John, her freckled face wore an anxious, somewhat expectant expression.

John hated to disappoint her. "Yes, Miss Flannery is great, but this isn't about her."

"Oh." Tracy's smile wavered.

Kim sighed loudly. "So what *is* the big deal?"

He didn't know how to give it to them but straight. "Your mother is in Indianapolis."

"Mom's here?" Kim brightened. "How long is she staying? When can we see her?"

A bit surprised by Kim's instant enthusiasm, John realized his younger daughter was having the opposite reaction. Tracy seemed to shrink back into the couch. She remained silent and grew so pale that her freckles appeared ready to spring from her face.

"Actually your mother has moved back to Indianapolis . . . for the time being." He just couldn't say *for good*. He didn't trust Kate to stay put and therefore wouldn't risk disappointing the girls. "And she would like to see you both. Soon."

"Today?" Kim asked, her eagerness vanishing. "But I made plans with my friends."

"Then you'll keep them," John assured her. "But you do want to see your mother?"

"Of course, Dad. Maybe tomorrow night."

John was already thinking he would have to postpone his date with Gillian—he meant to be present the first time Kate met with their daughters—when Tracy burst up out of her seat.

"I don't want to see her tomorrow night or ever!"

"Tracy—"

"No, you can't make me! I don't have a mother. She died five years ago."

John caught his daughter by the arm as she tried to brush past him. He steadied her shoulders between gentle hands. Tracy wasn't crying, but her eyes were wide and her slender body was shaking like a leaf.

"Your mother isn't dead, Tracy. You know that."

All the hostility that the girl must have been saving since Kate abandoned them seemed to spill out at once. "She is so! She didn't want us, so I don't want her!"

"Tracy, honey, let's sit down and talk about this."

"No!" Frantically she ripped free of her father's grasp and ran through the doorway, shouting, "There's nothing to discuss!"

"Tracy, wait."

"Aw, Dad, leave her alone. You know how goofy kids can be. Tracy is just more spaced than usual, but she'll calm down." Kim rose and gestured toward the doorway. "My friends are waiting, so I can go now, right?"

"You don't want to talk about your mother, either?"

She shrugged. "What's to talk? I said I wanted to see her. Don't you want me to?"

John hadn't realized how perceptive his older daughter could be. But he wasn't about to confirm her suspicion. "Kate is your mother, sweetheart. No matter how I feel, I think you should see her. Both of you."

"Whenever." She shrugged again. "Gotta go. Okay?"

"All right. Go."

Kim appeared absolutely normal as she left the room. But John couldn't quite believe she felt as blasé as she appeared. She was acting as if her mother had been gone five days instead of five years. Then, again, Kim wasn't willing to see Kate at the expense of her own plans. That might have worried John—the self-interest reminded him only too well of her mother's shortcomings—if Kim hadn't seemed somewhat protective of Tracy for once.

Teenagers. John shook his head. Soon he'd have two of them. In the meantime...

What was he supposed to do now? Tell Kate that Kim was agreeable to seeing her but that Tracy wouldn't even discuss the possibility? No doubt his ex-wife would blame him for their younger daughter's mulish reaction. Maybe he'd be wise to give the subject a few days' rest before broaching it again. Kate was determined to force the issue, but it would be best for Tracy if the girl agreed to see her mother without coercion.

Too bad he couldn't work out this problem as part of the marriage project. Thinking about it reminded him of Gillian and their date the next night. His enthusiasm of that morning had waned a bit. What incredibly bad timing! Handling a budding relationship while trying to resolve an old one was going to be tricky at best. He was afraid Gillian was about to get caught in the midst of a family feud.

For the rest of the afternoon Tracy stayed holed up in her bedroom. When John checked in on her, she acted fairly normal, if subdued. She was working on a jigsaw puzzle she'd bought with her allowance and seemed disinclined to talk to him at all. John tried to concentrate on paperwork he'd brought home, but he found himself brooding instead. His own mood bettered by early evening when Tracy insisted on making dinner despite his offer to take them out for burgers. She even watched television with him until bedtime.

But later, halfway through the night, the stress the twelve-year-old had been trying to hide exploded. John had barely fallen asleep when Tracy's screams propelled him out of bed. He rushed to his daughter's room and turned on the nightstand lamp. She was sitting up, hugging the covers to her chest, sobbing as if her heart would break.

John sat at the edge of the bed and gathered her in his arms. "Shh," he whispered comfortingly, wishing there was someone to soothe away his own anguish at his child's hurt. Gillian's image bedeviled him. "Another bad dream, huh?"

Tracy nodded and clung to him as if in desperation. "Hold me, Daddy."

A lump formed in John's throat. Tracy hadn't called him that in years. "I'm here now."

"But will you always be?"

He held her close and kissed the top of her head. "Of course I will."

"You won't leave me like you did in my dream?"

"I'm your father and I love you." And he wanted to protect her from all life's disappointments, but he was afraid that was impossible, as the past had already proven. "Don't worry. You'll never get rid of me, pumpkinhead."

"*She* left," Tracy sobbed. "And I thought you did, too. I was all alone and so scared."

"You're not alone. You have me and Kim."

Hearing a rustling behind him, John glanced over his shoulder to find his older daughter backing away from the doorway, her arms wrapped around her slender frame encased in a cotton nightgown. He would have sworn that she, too, had been crying. But before he could invite her into Tracy's room, Kim whirled around and ran back to her own.

John sighed, the responsibility of solo parenthood heavy on his shoulders. No, he couldn't shelter his daughters from physical or emotional harm. All he could do was kiss away their hurts after the fact. He held Tracy in his arms until she cried herself to sleep. Then he tucked the covers around her and went back to his own room.

Any sympathy he might have felt toward Kate as a mother who wanted to be reunited with her children had been washed away by his daughter's tears.

JOHN SUCCESSFULLY VANQUISHED the Kate problem from his conscious thoughts the next day as he supervised his work crew. Everything was going smoothly and his mood was decent when David showed up unexpectedly. As sometimes happened, projects overlapped. The younger Slater had been supervising work on a specialty shop in nearby Zion.

"Did you finish early?" John asked.

"Yeah, something like that." David ran his hand through hair the same brilliant red as Tracy's. "We should be wrapped up by the end of the week. Then we'll join you here."

John was sure that wasn't the reason his brother had stopped by to see him, however. The usually easygoing David looked as if a thundercloud was shadowing him. Wrapping his arm around the shorter man's shoulders, John steered David away from the workmen.

"Why don't we go into the office and discuss whatever's wrong."

He didn't mean the Zion store, and he was certain his brother knew *he* knew some other sort of trouble was brewing.

He'd hardly slid into a chair before David announced, "Kate called me."

Flying to his feet, John cursed. "Son of a—"

"I figured you'd be ticked." David shoved his hands in his pockets and leaned against the desk edge. "She begged me to talk some sense into you."

"About letting her see the girls."

"What else?"

"And?" John prompted.

"I told her I wouldn't do her dirty work. What did you think I'd say?"

"I wasn't questioning your loyalty." All the pain and doubts he'd suffered the night before surfaced, making John edgy. "Since she's already contacted me through her lawyer, I was just wondering what my charming ex-wife was up to this time."

David's brows furrowed into a single straight line. "John, you don't still care about Kate, do you?"

"No. Well, maybe as a human being." Acknowledging David's glower—his younger brother had never liked Kate because of her selfishness—John said, "I *was* married to the woman for twelve years. But that's not the issue here. I'm worried about Tracy. She didn't respond well to the idea of seeing her mother."

"Kid's taking it hard, huh?"

"That's putting it mildly. After insisting Kate was dead, she had another nightmare. She imagined I left her and she was all alone."

"Man, no one ticks me off like that woman," David muttered. "I should have hung up on the witch when I heard her voice."

David had disliked Kate so intensely that he'd tried talking John out of the marriage. There'd been many times over the intervening years when John had wished he'd listened to his younger brother. Then, again, if he hadn't married Kate, he wouldn't have Kim and Tracy....

"So what are you going to do?" David asked.

"What can I do when Tracy's near hysterical? Wait."

"One of the things Kate's not very good at."

"She'll have to learn."

"She's determined, John. I recognized the tone. You know better than I how she gets when she wants something."

John nodded. The only child of older, doting parents, Kate had been used to getting what she wanted all her life. Having been raised to expect a traditional marriage, John had also indulged his wife—perhaps with more and more reluctance as the years had gone by—until they'd come to the money issue that had spelled the beginning of the end.

For once he'd done what *he'd* wanted and had held firm on the matter. He could do no less when Tracy's emotional welfare was at stake.

GILLIAN FROWNED at her reflection and wondered if she was too dressed up, too eager for what might turn out to be another disappointment. The drapey rose cotton jersey could be viewed as casually dressed, she guessed. But there was nothing casual about the anticipation she was experiencing.

Her leather clutch rested on top of her notebook. Should she take both, or not? Not. If she were wrong about this being a date and John started talking about the project, she would just say she'd forgotten the darn notebook. Then she'd turn the conversation elsewhere! A woman had to take some responsibility for getting what she wanted.

The very thought of what John's kiss had made her want set her cheeks burning.

"Cool it, Gillian," she told herself. "You're just a little out of practice, nothing that can't be fixed."

Gathering her pluck along with her purse, she left her apartment before she could change her mind. John Slater was an attractive man with a good sense of humor and a stable home life. Yes, he was divorced—a fact that had seemed of major importance the other day—but his concern for Kim and the warm way he'd dealt with Tracy had convinced Gillian he was a man worth getting to know better.

By the time she reached the front porch, a gray Olds was pulling up to the curb. A good sign—John wasn't driving the pickup. And, when he got out of the car, she was surprised to see him wearing a pale gray suit. He'd gone all-out just for a drink. Warmth curled through her stomach as she realized he wouldn't have bothered to dress up to work on their pretend marriage.

Her long skirt swirled around her calves as she hurried down the steps toward him. When his glance traveled over her, she was complimented by the spark of male appreciation in his expression. An answering smile quirked her lips as she met him halfway up the walk.

"Don't you look fancy," she told him.

Actually he was hunk material whether dressed casually or in a suit, but she kept the thought to herself. Such a blunt observation might embarrass them both.

"My work clothes would be a little conspicuous where I'm taking you."

"Where's that?"

"It's a surprise."

And what a surprise the Indiana Roof Ballroom turned out to be. Gillian knew of the 1920s-vintage night spot located a few blocks from the State Capitol building in downtown Indianapolis. She'd heard the ballroom had cost six million dollars to renovate a few years before, but she'd never had the opportunity to see the place for herself. Entering was like taking a step back in time.

The orchestra was playing a nostalgic tune of the forties. A facade that exemplified Spanish-Moorish architecture surrounded the recessed stage. Light washed the stucco walls with a golden hue and made the tile roofs flame. Larger seating arrangements surrounded the dance floor itself, while tables for two dotted the second-floor balconies, which were bordered by black wrought-iron grillwork. Thousands of tiny lights studded the domed ceiling, simulating a starry night.

John had reserved one of these tables nearest the orchestra. After ordering large icy margaritas for them, he leaned back and grinned.

"Well? What do you think of the surprise?"

"It's breathtaking," Gillian said, trying to take in the architectural details, the music and dancers all at once. As far as she was concerned, this place had it hands down over Rochesters. The ballroom was undoubtedly more crowded on the weekends, but even so, tonight she would enjoy the ambience. "Thank you for bringing me here."

"I'm glad you like it."

She gazed at him curiously across the candlelit table. "Is that a hint of proprietorship I hear in your voice? Did you have anything to do with the renovation?"

"Only a very minor role. My company was subcontracted to work on some of the wood restoration."

"I'm impressed. Do you do that often? Subcontract on big jobs?"

John nodded. "Once in a while. It's nice to play a small part in restoring a historical building, though it's not my favorite type of job." At her questioning look, he explained, "I'd rather play a bigger role in a smaller renovation. I like having control of a project and developing my own ideas. Must be the artist in me . . . not unlike Mr. Xerxes."

Growing wary at the mention of John's alter ego, Gillian skirted the subject by personalizing the conversation even further. "Did you really want to be an artist?"

"Ever since I can remember. My parents are the practical type—they grew up during the Depression. So, under financial pressure from them, I enrolled in an engineering program. They were more lenient with my younger brother. They supported David's desire to go into architecture even though they considered it a less-certain profession."

Gillian couldn't help but sense some resentment in John's words, though she wasn't certain he was aware of it. "An engineer and an architect. Well, surely your degrees come in handy now. You and your brother must make the perfect team to head a renovation business. Whose idea was it?"

John shrugged. "Hard to say who actually came up with the original suggestion. David and I talked about having our own business for years before we finally took the necessary steps to make our dream come true."

"I admire you for taking such a chance. Giving up a steady job and heading out on your own must have been a difficult decision."

"There were a lot of problems in making the change," he admitted.

Again she sensed an undercurrent. John was feeling odd about something, but Gillian couldn't quite figure out what. Were he and his brother competitive? With a family as large as hers, she had lots of firsthand experience with sibling rivalry. But she had grown out of letting it bother her. She was wondering if he wanted to talk about it when their drinks arrived.

John made a toast. They had barely taken a sip of the margaritas before he continued, "Mr. Xerxes is better off than I was at his age. He's starting out his adult life working at what makes him happy. Maybe he can do more free-lancing, start a real business. . . ."

Uh-oh. Back to the X marriage. "John, did you want to get together tonight to work on the project?"

"No." He seemed a little taken aback. "What gave you that idea?"

Did he think *she* expected to work? Gillian wanted to disavow that notion immediately. "This place has such a romantic atmosphere." She gazed at him steadily, hardly able to breathe as she added, "It would be a shame to waste it on the Xerxes, don't you think?"

For a short moment she thought she'd said the wrong thing. She could swear a frown flickered across his expression. Swallowing hard, she tried not to let her smile look as if it were pasted on. Then John leaned across the table and covered one of her hands with both of his. His golden visage relaxed. Reflecting pinpoints of light from the candle, his eyes seemed as heated as they had before he'd kissed her.

"I'm more than willing to take advantage...of the atmosphere."

A thrill of anticipation shot through her. Gillian laughed nervously as lightning streaked across the simulated night sky.

"Atmospheric conditions seem to be against us. Does it rain in this place, too?"

"If it does, I can shelter you in my arms. We can practice on the dance floor."

He was teasing her, but this time Gillian didn't laugh. Her pulse beat unevenly as John rose and pulled back her chair. He placed a proprietary arm around her shoulders and guided her down the stairs.

Gillian felt as if she were gliding on air, especially when they reached the dance floor and John took his advantage quite nicely. His arm tightened around her back until she was levered against his chest. A few turns and they melded with the crowd of dancers. He dipped his head so their foreheads touched. His skin was warm, his breath tantalizing.

His mouth was but a whisper away.

She longed to taste him.

The orchestra was playing a rumba, the sound intimate and seductive as were their movements to the Latin rhythm. Clouds passed overhead, camouflaging the stars, and more lightning strobed through the dark. He gathered her closer. Their hips swayed and touched and played a mating game that was perfectly acceptable in public.

But Gillian's thoughts strayed to places more private, rhythms even more natural. By the time the slow dance was over, she was anxious to put some space between them.

After all, she hardly knew John Slater....

Then, again, the purpose of the evening *was* to get to know him better, her other self argued.

By the time they left the ballroom more than an hour later, Gillian was convinced she had a very good start on the endeavor. They'd talked, trading funny stories about their childhood. They'd danced, communicating without words. She was anxious to see where they would go from there.

The drive home was made in a silence that was at once comfortable and tension-filled. Gillian felt charged with stress. But it was good stress. She couldn't remember feeling so vibrant before.

When John parked the car and got out, saying, "I'll see you to your apartment," she didn't have the slightest objection.

She led the way up the inner stairs. "Would you like to come in for a cup of coffee?"

"Coffee would keep me awake if I drank it this late." She was disappointed and assumed he meant to leave immediately, until he added, "But I would like to come in."

Aware of his nearness behind her, she unlocked the door. She'd left the living area lights on low earlier and didn't move to change the dimmer. Her place looked better—softer—in semidarkness, anyway. While the furniture was comfortable and the apartment neat, Gillian had never taken the time to individualize the space. For some reason—maybe because John was so devoted to detail on his job and in his own home—she felt obligated to say something about her unpretentious living area, something she'd never before felt the need to do.

"The apartment itself has some nice touches," she said as he looked around. "Beveled leaded glass. Great woodwork, especially around the fireplace. My furnishings are pretty simple by comparison. While I appreciate antiques and bric-a-brac, I've never been a collector myself."

"Just because you live in a Victorian house doesn't mean you have to furnish it with period pieces. This is quite nice."

"My things are practical." Especially the workstation that took up one corner of her living room. "Except for my dollhouse."

"Dollhouse?" He lifted an auburn brow. "Aren't you a little too old to play with dolls?"

"Doll*house*," she stressed. "Even us older women need a hobby."

"So . . ." He gave her an arch look that told her he was teasing. "Playing house is your hobby?"

If he'd meant to titillate her, he certainly got the right response. Suddenly flustered, Gillian crossed to the turret to cover her reaction. Moonlight streamed in through the lace curtains decorating the five windows. The towering Victorian dollhouse was dark in silhouette.

"Come on. I'll show you what I've done with my hobby so far. It's an ongoing project. By the time I'm finished with the last two bedrooms and bath, I'll probably want to start redecorating from the ground up."

When John followed without objection, she flicked the switch that lit the large dollhouse from within. He bent over and studied each room carefully, his expression somewhat of a puzzle to her.

"Is something wrong?"

"Actually I was just thinking I'd finally found the woman who hides behind her computer printouts."

On the other side of the table holding the dollhouse, she bent as well and met his eyes through the master bedroom window. "Found her where?"

"In here. Come look."

Even knowing he was having fun with her, Gillian couldn't resist. Circling to his side, she said, "I don't see her."

"You must be blind. Here she is." He pointed to the gossamer curtains edged with lace. "Delicate. And look at the hand-painted wallpaper. Imaginative. And here." He indicated the bed with its mound of satin pillows, one heart-shaped. "Soft and romantic."

Gillian straightened. "You're sure of all that, are you?"

"Positive." He moved a needlepoint footstool from one end of the bed to the other before facing her and taking her in his arms. "Stop me if I'm wrong."

With one hand, he removed her glasses and set them down at the edge of the dollhouse. With the other, he pulled her into him as he had on the dance floor. Intimately. Seductively. Hip to hip. Thigh to thigh. His kiss began as a gentle exploration of her mouth, yet Gillian sensed stronger emotions simmering below the surface.

She felt them herself.

The man not only made her simmer, he made her smolder. He ignited a passion she had felt far too seldom in her thirty years. Letting go would be so easy....

His lips leaving hers was a disappointment. His words brought her back to her senses.

"What an example we'd make for your high school class right now, huh?"

Gillian blinked at his slightly out-of-focus face. "Example. The marriage project." She frowned at the reminder. "That's right. We shouldn't get too carried away."

"Shall we stop?"

Part of her wanted to say no. That is, one whole side of her wanted to say no. But the other side sighed in resignation. "I guess we'd better."

John let go of her but didn't move away. Gillian found her glasses, then bent over and moved the footstool back to its original position in the master bedroom. She switched off the doll-house lights and led the way out of the turret.

"I wish I had kept my big mouth shut," John muttered.

Gillian silently agreed. "It's probably best you didn't. You've been trying to convince your daughters we're not even dating and here we are ..."

"Where are we exactly?"

"I don't know." She looked at him furtively. "How about you?"

"I'd say that we're at the beginning of what could be a promising relationship. Unless the idea doesn't appeal to you."

"It appeals to me ... as long as we're honest about it."

"You mean as long as everyone—meaning my daughters—knows about it." When Gillian nodded, John asked, "Do they have to know *everything*?"

"I'm not always detail-oriented."

"We could just say we're dating."

"And keep anything else that goes on to ourselves," she agreed happily now that the moment of crisis had passed.

"I said it before and I'll say it again. I like intelligent women. Busy Friday night?"

"Not yet."

"Would you like to be?"

"Depends on the offer," Gillian said airily.

"How would you like to see one of my major renovation jobs?"

"Another surprise?"

"Why not?"

"Why not?" she echoed in agreement.

John kissed her again, quickly this time, then headed out the door. "We'll see each other at the meeting on Wednesday."

Two days away. She'd be counting the hours.

CHAPTER SIX

JOHN ENTERED the high school classroom early Wednesday evening in hopes that he could have a few minutes of Gillian's undivided attention. He was disappointed to find her deep in conversation with Elaine Parker and Wes Meyer, obviously helping them hash out some problem. Not wanting to disturb them, he slid into a seat toward the back and, fascinated, watched Gillian work.

She was so earnest—so intense—in her efforts to help Elaine and Wes resolve whatever was bothering them. He knew she would be as fiercely logical with them as she had been romantic with him the other evening.

John wondered what prompted her to separate the two sides of herself—the logical and the romantic. He'd been lucky enough to glimpse the soft, dreamy woman she could be. Her dollhouse was a treasure, a true reflection of the woman he wanted to know in more depth. But how strange that she'd furnished her apartment in a way that was at odds with her inner self—comfortable but undistinguished—as if she saved all her creativity for an ideal rather than for the real thing.

It was almost as if she were trying to keep that part of herself separate. Inviolate.

Yet Gillian had suggested they not waste the ballroom's romantic atmosphere on the Xerxes. Her comment had gotten to him for a moment. He'd been reminded of Kate's complaints during the final few years of their marriage. But it had been difficult then to be romantic. He'd been worried about money, hassled at work and filled with resentment because his wife was too self-centered to understand his gut-level need to change his professional situation. Romance had been the last thing on his mind.

His darkening thoughts were interrupted by the entrance of the Bigsbys.

Sarah led the way, her trademark sunny smile replaced by a clenched jaw. She hurried to a seat, not waiting for her husband who ambled along, as usual—except that his face was set in a belligerent grimace. John had never seen either of his neighbors look so sour. Despite their differences, they normally seemed happier than most couples. He stood up to face the other man.

"Uh, Calvin, how's it—?"

"Don't ask." Calvin shook his head and rolled his eyes. "Let's say things around our place are a little out of hand at the moment. I'll be glad when we're done with this experiment and life gets back to normal."

John bit his lip to keep from smiling. Obviously the project was shaking up the Bigsbys' home life. They must be taking their made-up problems far too seriously.

"Don't worry, Calvin. Whatever's bugging Sarah, she'll cool off as usual."

"Can't be soon enough for me," Calvin grunted. He made his way down the steps. Though he entered the same row as Sarah had, he left an empty seat between him and his wife.

When another couple arrived, John figured he might as well join Gillian. Just finishing with Elaine and Wes, she looked up as he approached.

"Hi," she said softly. "Been here long?"

"A while. I was hoping to catch you alone for a minute."

Her brows popped up above the frames of her glasses, and her expression made his blood race. He wanted to take her off in a corner and greet her properly, with a long, lingering kiss. But that, of course, was impossible.

"I guess being alone will have to wait until after class," Gillian said with a grimace. "Can I buy you a cup of coffee later?"

"You can do whatever you want with me," John assured her in a low tone.

Gillian smothered a laugh and whispered, "I'm beginning to think we're not the only ones who are getting more than a working relationship out of this project. Elaine and Wes seem to be on the same wavelength, too." Her eyes shifted over his shoulder. "The Talbots just came in. Everyone's here, so we'd better get down to business."

John nodded and sat in the first row. Trying to get her mind off their promising personal relationship and back where it belonged,

Gillian quickly went through the envelopes to make sure everything was in order before she started the meeting.

When everyone was seated, she cleared her throat and announced, "I have your new set of problems here. Let's take a few minutes to go over them in case you have any questions. Then we'll have a progress report."

Gillian handed out the envelopes, smiling at each couple, even at the Bigsbys who not only appeared unhappy but who refused to look at each other. Uh-oh. Was their pique due to the project?

When she joined John, her mind was only half on their own assignment. She kept looking back at Sarah, who read each slip, then handed it to Calvin. The Bigsbys weren't discussing anything.

"Don't worry about them," John said. "We have our own complications to consider."

"Right."

They concentrated on looking over their new set of problems and discussing them in general terms. Nothing seemed earth-shattering. They decided to meet on Saturday to work on the assignment.

Gillian figured the other couples had had enough time to go over their materials, so she rose and asked, "Any questions?"

Arlene and Derek Talbot raised their hands immediately. Gillian nodded that they should begin.

"What do we do if we don't like one of the complications you've given us?" Arlene asked.

"Can you be more specific?"

Derek waved two strips of paper at her. "These say that I not only lost my job, but that I made a bunch of bad investments in the stock market."

"Yes . . ." Gillian waited for further explanation.

"Well, this just isn't realistic. I've never lost a job in my life, and I've been working since I was sixteen."

"And Derek is a whiz in the stock market," Arlene added.

"The problems assigned to your marriage aren't supposed to be based on your real life, but on possible situations for your particular marriage," Gillian explained. "Losing a job is an everyday problem."

"Not for Derek or for me," Arlene insisted. "We can't live like this—without money. Can't we just decide he finds an equivalent job by next week?"

"I'm afraid not. You'll have to be a little more creative than saying the problem just doesn't exist."

"So what *am* I supposed to do?" Derek asked.

"You can make a list of available jobs from the Sunday newspaper," Gillian suggested. "Maybe work on a new résumé. And you can apply for unemployment."

"Unemployment? Great." He looked disgusted. "Don't you think that's a little humiliating?"

Wes spoke up. "There's nothing humiliating about collecting unemployment. I've lost a job before myself. Sometimes it can't be helped. You do what you have to do to survive."

"Besides, Arlene is still working," Elaine added, "so it's not like you're going to lose your condo or starve to death."

Derek Talbot simply shook his head and subsided into an uneasy silence.

Gillian cleared her throat. "Are there any other questions?" No one raised a hand. "Then why don't we go on to our reports."

She went around the room in order. While other couples gave their updates, she warily eyed Sarah and Calvin Bigsby, who didn't seem inclined to speak to each other, nor to an audience of their peers. She decided to skip over them and leave them until last. When it was her and John's turn, she let him do the talking.

"We've solved the mother-in-law problem and have started saving for a house." He paused dramatically before announcing, "And we're pregnant."

"Congratulations, you old dog," one of the men said to titters of laughter.

"The group's first pregnancy. You two work fast," teased another. "Must be inspired."

Gillian felt a flush creep up her neck at the good-natured ribbing. Not that some of the other couples didn't already have "assigned" children. "See what I mean about the unforeseen? My partner threw me a curve by adding problems I hadn't expected."

"You're expecting now," Elaine said.

Gillian laughed. "And learning to deal with it."

"Some things are easier to deal with than others," Sarah said, giving her husband a brief glower.

"Like a bossy wife," he returned.

"You were supposed to paint the house, not find reasons to avoid the project, Calvin Bigsby. Your real-life procrastinating is bad enough, but I can't even get you to change in this pretend marriage!"

Before the argument could get rolling, Gillian interrupted. "I'm glad to see you're so involved—if not exactly happy. That's the interesting thing about this project. Sooner or later, people's real-life personalities show through even in a pretend situation. If you can learn to resolve your problems within the class structure, your outside problem-solving becomes even more effective."

"This may be one problem that will never be solved," Sarah stated.

"Maybe the two of you can approach this from a different angle," Gillian suggested. "Try to work on finding some satisfactory compromise instead of expecting complete change from the other partner."

Sarah muttered something under her breath and Calvin merely grunted. Gillian figured she'd better give the subject a rest and let the Bigsbys work things out on their own. At least she hoped they would.

"Anyone have anything else they'd like to discuss?" When no one answered, she said, "Class dismissed. See you in a week."

The couples dispersed more quickly than they had the previous week, no doubt due, at least in part, to the tension exhibited by the Bigsbys and Talbots.

"A few people were really wound up," John murmured as he picked up her case. "Mixing up the project and reality again."

"Hopefully they'll work things out as they have in their real marriages. After all, they've stayed together long enough to have kids in high school."

"I'm sure we'll never take our problems so seriously," John said with a grin as they headed for the auditorium doors. "I have a feeling we'll find a way to work things through."

Gillian was absolutely serious when she said, "Sounds good to me." In her opinion, fighting never got a relationship anywhere positive. "By the way, did you tell your daughters about us... dating?"

"Last night. Tracy was delighted and Kim horrified. I asked her what she expected when *she'd* given me the idea in the first place."

"She must have loved that."

"She moaned and groaned all the way to her room about how she'd never live this down once her friends found out." John held the door open for her. "So we're still on for Friday night, right?"

"I'm primed for that surprise you promised," Gillian agreed. "Sure you wouldn't like to give me some clue as to what to expect?"

"Absolutely not. Make 'em laugh, make 'em sigh, make 'em wait, I always say."

She raised her brows. "I think I'll keep that motto in mind when dealing with a certain man...."

"Uh-oh. I think I'm in trouble."

They laughed together as they left the school and headed for the coffee shop. That was the way a relationship should be, Gillian thought. Love and laughter went hand in hand.

And she was ready for a good dose of both.

KATE HAD DECIDED to take things into her own hands. Who could blame her? It was her prerogative to see her daughters, and she'd given John every opportunity to do the right thing. But obviously he intended to let their lawyers negotiate some kind of decision about when and how often. And until then he was leaving her out in the cold.

Knowing how long lawyers could take to accomplish anything, she wasn't about to wait.

Kate tapped her lacquered nails on the steering wheel and peered out at the big old house John had bought since the divorce. The building's size was appealing, and he seemed to have fixed up the place, but she would have insisted on a new home, one with all the modern conveniences. Not that her wishes would have mattered . . . They never had.

Remembering the day he'd told her that *he'd* used *their* savings to go into business with David, Kate shook her head. That's when she'd realized John didn't really love her and would never give her what she wanted—needed—from a man. That's when she'd started rethinking their marriage.

But all that was history. Right now, all she wanted was to be reunited with her girls. She'd pleaded illness to get off work early this afternoon so she could wait for them to come home from school. So where were they? She checked her watch and tapped her nails on the steering wheel some more. It was Friday. Maybe they'd made after-school plans.

Morose that she might have given up an afternoon's pay for nothing, Kate refused to leave. She would sit in her car until dark if necessary. Or at least until she saw John coming home. If Kim and Tracy didn't show before then, she would leave. She didn't want John to spot her; he might think of some way to foil her.

Her anxiety level had risen considerably before she spotted the girls coming down the street with some friends. The other teenagers went on while her daughters headed toward the house. Kate's heart just about stopped. They'd grown so much. Kim was a real beauty just as Kate had known she'd be. And Tracy...Tracy looked like the most huggable kid on earth.

Kim was saying something her younger sister obviously didn't like. Tracy tried to punch her, but Kim danced out of range and ran up the porch steps, Tracy in hot pursuit. When Kim unlocked the front door, they shoved their way through the opening together.

Tears slid down Kate's cheeks and froze her to her seat for a while longer. They couldn't see her like this. She wasn't one of those women who looked more appealing when crying. She had to get herself under control. Producing tissues from her purse, she blew her nose, patted her cheeks dry and checked her eye makeup in a mirror. She stared at her image for a moment.

Would her own daughters even recognize her?

She had to find out some time. She got out of the car. Her heart—beating in her breast—urged her to race to the front door. But she forced herself to slow down, to take deep breaths, to keep her composure.

She stood on the front step and had barely pressed the bell when the door swung wide and she was face-to-face with her older daughter.

"Kim!" Kate held out her arms.

"Mom."

Though Kim seemed glad to see her, she didn't respond to the silent request for an embrace, merely stepped back to let her mother in the house. Kate entered, nerves suddenly attacking her once more. She heard Tracy's girlish voice float down the hallway from the back of the house.

"Yeah, Dad, don't worry. I told you I would listen to Kim."

"Dad just called to make sure we were home," Kim explained.

"Oh." Kate stood staring at her daughter, wishing the teenager would break down and rush into her arms.

"He didn't tell us you were coming tonight."

"He doesn't exactly know. We were trying to work out a schedule, but, uh, I thought I would surprise you girls and take you somewhere nice for our reunion. Anywhere you want to go."

"Really?"

They stared at each other for a moment, and Kate sensed some other emotion hidden behind her daughter's smile.

"Da-a-ad, you don't have to be late for your date just to check on us," Tracy was insisting from the other room. "We're not babies, you know."

Kate realized John wasn't coming home until later. She could spend more time with her girls than she'd thought!

"Uh-huh. Okay. Bye, Dad."

"I've got a really great idea, Mom," Kim said. "Why don't we all go shopping, like we used to. There's this really radical blouse I've been wanting—I know you'd love it—but I already spent my allowance."

"I'll buy the blouse for you," Kate said quickly, relieved that Kim was accepting her so easily.

"Great! Then it's settled."

But Kate realized nothing was settled when she heard a choking noise at the other end of the hall. She whipped around to spot Tracy standing there staring at her. The girl's freckles were stark spots against her chalk-white face.

"Tracy, honey? It's me, your..." Her words trailed off when her daughter turned and ran to the staircase. "Tracy, wait, please."

The younger girl didn't even pause as she flew up the steps and down the hall. By the time a door slammed with a loud bang, Kate was already following, Kim skirting her to take the lead.

"Don't mind her." Now Kim was looking at her oddly, too, even if her words were meant to be reassuring. "Tracy can be a dorky kid sometimes, but when I tell her we're going shopping, she'll come out."

Kate wasn't so sure, but she didn't hesitate until she reached the second floor landing. "Which room?"

Kim went straight to Tracy's door and banged on it. "Hey, come on out. Mom's going to take us shopping. You can get that new skateboard you wanted."

"I don't have a mother!" Tracy shouted. "But I'm going to have one real soon when Dad marries Miss Flannery."

Kim hit the door with the flat of her hand—hard. "Don't be stupid. Take advantage of what you can get. If Dad remarries, he'll have another kid. Maybe more. He'll be too busy for anyone else."

Kate grabbed her daughter by the arm. "Kim, how could you say something so cruel to your sister? Your father will never stop loving either one of you, even if he does remarry."

"A lot you know about it," Kim said belligerently as she stared at her mother's hand. "You haven't been around."

Stricken by her daughter's sudden attack, Kate let go and thought about the ramifications of Kim's prediction. No, John would never stop loving his daughters. But what if her daughters turned to their new stepmother instead of to her?

"Tracy," she said in her sternest voice to hide the way her stomach was shaking. "Open this door right this minute."

A moment of silence was followed by a shuffling sound. Then Tracy opened the door, but her expression remained closed.

"That's better."

Kate breathed a sigh of relief. She just had to reassert herself and do whatever else was necessary to reclaim her daughters' love before she lost them to some stranger....

"TIME FOR YOUR SURPRISE," John murmured into Gillian's ear. "You can look now."

Having shut her eyes as instructed during the last few minutes of the drive through one of Indianapolis's older neighborhoods and having kept them closed while John had helped her out of the car, Gillian was happy to be able to see again. Before her sat a red brick mansion on a huge lot lined with trees and bushes. Three stories high, the turn-of-the-century building had a slate roof marked by numerous chimneys.

"Wow, this is some place. Your current renovation project, I assume?"

"One of them. David is handling a smaller undertaking in Zion. But this is my baby. Come on. I'll give you the grand tour." He took her hand possessively, swung open the black iron grill gate and led her up the brick walkway. "Notice that we've brought the front doors back to their original wood finish. Decades ago, someone decided they should be painted."

Climbing the stairs, Gillian looked over the massive carved panels. "What a crime to hide such natural beauty."

John nodded in agreement. "When we stripped the paint, we found coats of white, beige, blue and even pink."

She ran her hand down along the grain. "You did a wonderful job."

"Thanks. We had to do a bit of woodworking as well. Some of this trim had been destroyed," John told her, pointing out the section. "We had to replace it."

"An amateur like me would never know the difference."

"I'm pretty happy with the calibre of the repair myself," John admitted. He unlocked the door. "We just replaced the front windows and reinstalled the stained-glass trim. Much of the glass work was broken years ago. Luckily David and I have contacts with experts in every area of restoration, so we always have someone to turn to, no matter what our problem."

Gillian was pleased that John seemed so proud of his work, as though he'd seen to every detail himself. He probably had, if only in his supervisory capacity. As they entered the house, she realized why he'd told her to dress comfortably—she'd worn a pair of soft, faded jeans and a fancy sweatshirt imprinted with pale pink roses—and why he, himself, had not bothered to change out jeans and a flannel shirt.

The inside of the mansion was in a state of chaos. Wooden horses and building materials of every kind sat in the middle of the great hall. The marble floor was covered with sawdust, and the ornate banister looked to be in the final stages of restoration.

"I hope you don't mind if your hair gets a little crushed." John proffered a yellow hard hat. "You'll need to wear this for safety if you want the complete twenty-five-cent tour."

Putting it on, Gillian felt engulfed in the thing. She tilted her head back and peered out at him from under the front lip. "I must look pretty silly."

"Cute," he corrected, wrapping his arms around her and kissing the tip of her nose. "You do things for that hat that none of my men do."

She feigned indignation. "What? No women on the crew?"

"I was speaking generically," John said, pulling the hard hat down to the bridge of her nose. "Actually I do have a woman on this crew, and we use others from time to time."

"Whew!" Gillian righted the hat. "Glad you're not sexist."

"I don't know." His auburn brows arched. "I've been told I'm a pretty sexy guy."

"I'm not about to argue with that."

She sighed when John bent toward her. But he merely teased her lips with a brush of his mustache before letting go. She was inordinately pleased when he kept a hand at the small of her back, however.

"Let's start downstairs with the main parlor, formal dining room and kitchen," he said, leading her to the left, away from a room that remained closed off from the hall. "That's my current office—a former cloakroom."

The large, high-ceilinged rooms were lined with tall windows equipped with inside shutters that had been stripped and refinished. Although paper covered most of the floor for protection, she noted the quality of the parquet where it peeked out here and there. Both parlor and dining room had massive marble-manteled fireplaces over which were suspended great mirrors in gilt frames. From the ceilings hung original brass and glass chandeliers that had been wired for electricity. In the dining room, a massive buffet lined one wall, but its doors were missing.

"They're still being worked on," John said, "as are the sliding pocket doors that separate the dining room from the main parlor."

"I'd love to see this place when you're done."

"That can be arranged, but it'll be awhile."

The warmth in his statement made Gillian's stomach curl. He made it sound as if he had no doubts they would still be seeing each other for months to come. The idea didn't displease her, and a happy little grin curved her lips as they went on to the kitchen, which turned out to be in a state of near-demolition.

"This kitchen—if you can believe it—is going to be a gourmet cook's dream when we're done with it," John said.

Remembering the love feast, Gillian smiled. "I'll bet Tracy would appreciate that."

"You're right. My younger daughter has got a head start on most girls her age."

"Must have something to do with her father's influence," Gillian said, wondering about Tracy's mother. How could any woman be content with no more than occasional contact with her children?

"When it's finished," John was saying, "the kitchen will have a center island with counter space and a stove top with six burners and a grill. In that wall, we'll install built-in microwave, convection and conventional ovens—top-of-the-line appliances all around."

Suppressing her curiosity about Kate, Gillian said, "Sounds like your budget is unlimited."

"Just about. It's nice to have a client who can afford the best. This is the most ambitious project we've ever done."

She could well imagine that to be true when he gave her a tour of the rest of the house. The third floor was totally gutted, while the second was in various stages of completion. Altogether, there were fourteen rooms and six baths. John's favorite area was the master suite—bedroom, sitting room, two dressing rooms with a shared bath and nursery.

The nursery reminded Gillian of her pretend pregnancy and the teasing she'd taken from the other adult class members. Wandering through the small room, she could imagine an old-fashioned crib like the one she had in her dollhouse as the centerpiece. She'd add a modern mobile to hang over it—something stuffed and soft, easily grasped by a tiny hand. Gillian hoped she would have the opportunity to have children of her own. But she was barely thirty. She had another dozen or so years to start a family, so there was no real reason to worry about it. Right?

Maybe it was the company she was keeping....

Already a father of two, would John even want to have more children? Then she quickly pushed the inappropriate thought aside. They were only dating, for heaven's sake.

John led her back downstairs and stopped in front of the room that had remained closed off.

"I guess you might call this the ladies' parlor," he said as he slid open the door.

The first thing she noticed was the incredible parquet floor. Inlaid with woods of various colors from pale to dark, yellow to red, it was designed in the style of a "carpet" with a flowered border. She hesitated to step on such beauty.

"Go on in. You won't hurt the floor."

"How did you know what I was thinking?" Gillian asked.

"Maybe we're just on the same wavelength."

Entering the room, she noticed the fireplace with its wooden mantel carved with three-dimensional flowers. And the Tiffany-inspired ceiling fixture represented a stained glass garden. She peered through the double doors leading to the side yard and the real garden outside, still visible in the soft evening light. A white, wrought-iron gazebo was surrounded by a tangle of bushes and flowers.

"Looks like the garden has grown wild for years," Gillian said, enchanted by nature's loveliness. "It will be a shame to tame it."

John's arms slid around her waist. His cheek found and nuzzled hers. "Hmm, that's not the very organized Miss Flannery I hear speaking. It's that other woman. You know, the romantic."

She leaned back into him and sighed. "You have a way of bringing out my secret self."

"At least you're admitting you have one."

"I never denied it."

"No, you just do your best to cover it up."

"Speaking of covered up," Gillian said, having spied an odd-shaped mound on the floor covered by a quilt, just a few feet away from the garden doors. "What's that?"

"Another surprise." He let go of her as he explained, "Tonight, you get to eat dinner without any of the comforts of home. I'm glad you like the floor so much—" he lifted the coverlet with a flourish "—because we're going to eat sitting on it."

Under the quilt was an old-fashioned wicker basket surrounded by two stacks of pillows. John flipped the quilt onto the floor and quickly arranged the pillows in charming disarray.

Gillian knelt before the basket and lifted the lid. "Did Tracy make dinner for us?"

"Actually I am solely responsible for the contents of this picnic basket . . . with a little help from my local supermarket."

The repast was simple—French bread, Brie cheese, roasted chicken and lemon crunch cookies—but Gillian thought it one of the best meals she'd ever had. After they ate, they leaned back against the pile of pillows and sipped at the blush wine John had included. Twilight had descended over the garden outside. The interior was growing dark, but neither made a move to turn on the room light.

Tucked into John's side, Gillian felt a special glow of warmth and security that she hadn't often experienced as an adult. She was comfortable enough to want to know more about John's personal life. The name Kate almost tripped over her tongue, but for some reason she changed her mind and held it back. At the moment, she didn't want anything to disturb her tranquillity, especially not the reasons for John's divorce.

"So, how did your daughters take the news that we were going on a date tonight?" she asked instead.

"As expected. Kim sulked while Tracy cheered. I talked to Tracy a little earlier—I was running late so I called in to check on them—and she said to say hello for her."

Gillian couldn't help the bittersweet smile that crossed her lips. "She's a neat kid. I'm just sorry that Kim doesn't like me, as well."

"Don't take it personally. Kim's just not fond of being the object of teasing from her friends. To make things worse, I told her she couldn't go out tonight because I wanted her to stay with her sister. This is kind of a difficult situation. Tracy would have fits if I mentioned the word baby-sitter. She thinks she's so grown up."

"Twelve is a difficult age."

"As is thirteen and fourteen and fifteen and sixteen," John said, making them both laugh. "To think I'm going to have to go through those teenage years again."

"Does it really bother you?"

He shook his head. "Not at all. Parenting can be burdensome, especially when it's solo, but the experience has its joys as well. I wouldn't have missed one minute of my daughters' lives."

Gillian took another sip of wine and snuggled closer. John was such a caring man . . . one of the things she liked best about him. He made her feel warm and wanted and a little on edge.

Good stress, she told herself.

Stimulating.

"Mmm, this is nice," she murmured, noting that her entire side tingled everywhere they touched. "Being alone in this beautiful room, watching darkness fall as the house's first owners must have done a century ago. It makes you realize that the most special moments are still the simple ones."

"Ah-hah, I hear the romantic speaking."

"Wine tends to submerge my practical side," she admitted.

He picked up the bottle and refilled her glass. "Then have some more."

"Are you trying to get me drunk so you can take advantage of me?" The thought was more than stimulating. It was downright titillating.

"Would it work?"

Not wanting to make things too easy for him—that would take away the fun of the courtship—she primly said, "Wrong answer."

"What's the right answer?"

"I don't know." Gillian sighed and then, very dramatically, said, "Something like, 'I want you clearheaded so you can fully enjoy every kiss, every touch, every attempt at seduction.'" Then she giggled at her own silliness.

"Okay, you're cut off."

John took her drink from her. He set both glasses down on his other side, out of her reach.

Wide-eyed and feigning innocence, Gillian asked, "Does that mean you're going to kiss me now?"

"Unless you kiss me first."

"A challenge, huh? All right. I'm up to it."

She made such a hokey production of physically preparing herself for the embrace that John started laughing. That's when she attacked. Throwing her arms around his neck, she shifted and pressed him back into the pillows.

"Wipe that silly grin off your face, mister." She could still see his handsome features though the room had begun to grow dark.

"Think you can make me?"

Tracing the silver streak in his hair with one finger, she whispered, "I sure as heck can try."

Gillian stroked his mouth with her own, keeping the touch light, unfulfilling. Then she traced the inner curve of his upper lip with the tip of her tongue. A groan rose from his depths.

"Are you sure that smile's not gone?" she whispered against his mouth.

"It's even bigger," he claimed. "You'll just have to try harder."

Kissing him fully, Gillian savored the wet warmth, the taste of wine, the hint of lemon and spices. Their mouths meshed, breaths mingled, tongues dueled until she was light-headed. She took a deep breath, and his male scent, musky and seductive, assaulted and aroused her. The edge grew sharper as she became aware of his body, fit and taut, snug under hers. He opened his legs. Her lower body dropped between his thighs and pressed snugly against his groin.

John moaned again and took over, kissing her with a passion that felt barely repressed, as if, with the slightest urging, he would take her right there on the floor. The very thought was almost as titillating as his hands sliding up under her sweatshirt, his fingers finding the clasp of her bra and unhooking it. He explored the fullness flattened against the wall of his chest. Her flesh quivered under his expert touch. Her nipples hardened. Her thighs quaked.

The room seemed to spin as if out of control, as did her insides. She wanted to let go but she couldn't. Fighting her way out of the dreamlike embrace, Gillian abruptly ended the kiss. This was going too fast. She wanted too much. She had to slow down. She had to think. She pushed herself away from John and, shaking, settled at his side. He was breathing hard. They both were. And her glasses were steamed up.

"Still smiling?" she murmured weakly.

"My whole body's smiling now."

She redid her bra with hands that shook. "Mine, too."

Gillian expected a protest, a "then why did you stop" kind of comment. He gave none. A relief. Silently John put his arm around her and pulled her against his shoulder. She lay against him stiffly for several minutes before he offered her the glass of wine he'd confiscated. Gillian gladly accepted, happy to have a reason to put some distance between them.

And yet a building discomfort grew as the lull lengthened, as they drank their wine in silence, but she waited until her limbs took on some semblance of normality before trying to make conversation. One of them had to. But what could she say after stopping something both of them obviously wanted? Especially when she wasn't sure why she had?

The surroundings prompted her to ask, "How long ago did you and your brother start your renovation business?"

John sounded a little strange when he said, "Almost six years."

He shifted and rearranged himself on the pillows—almost as if the topic made him even more uncomfortable than his physical frustration. Gillian remembered his similar response at the ballroom and again wondered if he and his brother were friendly competitors.

"It seems as if you've done pretty well for yourselves." She felt obliged to keep up friendly chatter, more desirable than silence at the moment. She was starting to feel a little weird. Maybe some kind of accusation from John would have cleared the air. She wished he'd said *something*. "Any ambitions to expand?"

"Not really. Part of the attraction of having our own business is being in charge of everyday decision-making, giving attention to details. If we grow too much, that won't be possible."

John's voice had taken on a more relaxed tone as he talked. Gillian tried to relax, too.

"So which one of you actually does the supervising?"

"David and I take turns. Actually we usually have more than one site in the works at a time. Ventures tend to overlap. Once in a while we get in a situation where we have three or four things going at once."

"That must be pretty hectic."

"It can be. Usually the jobs are of different size and in different stages of completion. We're careful not to take on too much, yet we have to make up for those slow periods . . . although we haven't had any down time for more than a year. The work has been constant. I guess I've been pretty lucky. How many guys get paid to help preserve the past?"

"That's a nice way of thinking about what you do. You save the past for the next generation . . . while I try to enrich the future." Gillian rolled the stem of her glass between fingers that were still a little stiff. "We're lucky. We get paid for doing things we enjoy."

"Too bad everyone doesn't think that's important."

She didn't miss the note of fervor in his tone and wondered where it had come from. "Well, they should. Work is the next most important thing to love."

The comment made her think about the past and the future, made her face what was wrong, what was making her uneasy. Suddenly it occurred to her that she was thinking about John as her own future.

Startled, half happy, half frightened by the implications, Gillian wondered if she was, indeed, falling in love.

CHAPTER SEVEN

GILLIAN SEEMED SUBDUED the next afternoon when John dropped by her apartment to work on the Xerxes' marriage. For a moment, he wondered if she was regretting getting so close, then dismissed the idea. Though she might not be as comfortable with their attraction as he was just yet, he was certain she'd had a wonderful time on Friday night. Maybe she was tired. He was a little tired himself, having gotten home long after midnight.

Not that a date with a lovely woman wasn't worth some loss of sleep. Grinning at the memory of Gillian's warm body pressed against his own, John gazed toward the kitchen where she'd gone to fix them some coffee.

She appeared in the doorway a few seconds later with two steaming mugs. "I hope this isn't too strong. I put an extra tablespoon in the coffee maker."

"It'll be fine. I need to wake up."

She approached and set the mugs down on the long table that served as her workstation, then pulled up a chair. "We've only got a few things to discuss today."

He nodded. "Like this little fender bender Mrs. Xerxes had. I assume our car insurance will pay for it."

"After we take care of the deductible."

"How much is that?"

"Oh, a hundred dollars, maybe two—whatever you think is average."

"Let's make it one hundred." He quickly jotted down the amount in his notebook, then took a sip of coffee. "You weren't hurt, were you?"

She glanced up from writing. "In the accident? Of course not—the slip would have said so."

"Are you absolutely sure?" He leaned forward and solicitously covered her hand with his own. "These whiplash cases can sneak up on you. I'll be happy to massage your neck...or any other part of you that hurts.''

She laughed, her voice low and husky. "I'll keep that in mind."

Great, now she was warming up. He grasped her hand and drew her toward him, rubbing her fingers lightly. "We can start with your fingertips. Feeling better already, right?"

Her lids lowered slowly. "So good, I'm in danger of ignoring our project."

"Do we have to work on the project right now?" he teased.

"I suppose we'd better."

"At least you sound reluctant." They exchanged smiles and he released her hand to pick up his coffee cup. "Actually we should be happy we have the project to bring us together."

She nodded. The project was a great excuse for them to get together more often than they might otherwise—and without seeming too eager.

They forced themselves to get down to business after that, comparing budgets and dealing with the usual small problems. They talked about naming the baby and how soon John would have to quit his job.

"Speaking of jobs," he said, turning to another section of his spiral, "I came up with a great idea the other day. I even worked out the financial details. Mr. Xerxes could be working on newsletters while he stays at home."

"Newsletters?"

"They're very popular nowadays with organizations and businesses." John showed her the figures. "I think we could invest in a laser printer and one of the smaller computer systems to begin with. I could hire someone to write and edit and use my own commercial art ability on the graphics. With your contacts in the financial world, you could help drum up some business. I'd have an independent and lucrative career in two years' time."

She raised her eyebrows as she scanned the figures. "Six thousand dollars?"

"Most of the money is for the printer, plus I'd need the right kind of software."

"This is very costly." She gazed at him unsmiling. "We're already dealing with the expense of the baby and saving toward a house." There was a definite edge to her voice.

"Maybe we should wait on the house, then," he went on. "But don't worry, these expenses will be repaid." He flipped to another page of figures. "See, this is from our savings account—with hard work and luck, I can pay it back completely in two years, then start building up a tidy profit."

"Our savings?" Still unsmiling, she tapped a finger on her coffee cup. "You've spent our money without my input?"

He couldn't believe she was taking it so seriously. "I haven't really spent anything. You know that. I just worked it out on paper."

"But you should have discussed this with me before you went that far."

"You weren't around when I was reading the computer magazine." He closed the spiral and slid it in place in front of him.

"But our savings belongs to both of us," she said accusingly.

To both of them. Oops. Suddenly John was experiencing déjà vu. In vivid detail, he flashed back on the day he'd told Kate he'd spent their savings on a new business, over her objections. He could hardly believe the situation was repeating itself.

Quickly he tried to extricate himself. "Look, I'm sorry... this was just an idea. And we don't have to carry it out," he said sincerely, then went on to explain, "I guess I'm the independent type who's always looking for ways to succeed on my own."

"But we're supposed to be working on the problems in this project together," she continued peevishly. "Not that your career was such a big problem. And you were the one who added the baby in the first place...."

"All right, do you want me to tear up the pages of figures?" Would that soothe her?

"No." She took a deep breath, obviously realizing she'd gotten carried away. She fingered her spiral.

"I wasn't trying to pull a fast one."

"I guess I'm taking this project too seriously now."

"You just misinterpreted my idea." He conceded, "Not that you don't have a point. And I've conjured up an old nightmare. One of the reasons my ex-wife and I split was because I insisted on investing our savings in my own business, rather than in the new house she wanted. I should have learned something from that."

Her face softened a little. "You couldn't agree on a compromise?"

"Kate isn't...wasn't the sort of person who compromises. And I was desperate to get out of a job I hated. When David approached me with the idea, I jumped at the chance."

"So that's how your business got started." For a moment, she seemed lost in thought. "You do tend to come up with unique yet practical ideas," she went on finally. "And you've proven you can succeed." She gestured to their notebooks. "It's difficult to keep the individual person from creeping into these projects whether we like it or not. Your idea for the newsletters was pretty good. I'm sorry if I jumped to conclusions."

He shrugged. "You had good reason to object."

"But I'm willing to consider the newsletter idea."

"It's really not necessary."

"No, seriously..."

He had to laugh. "If we don't watch out, we're going to get into another argument."

She looked offended. "We weren't arguing. We were having a discussion."

He sobered. "Okay." Whatever she wanted to call it. As for himself, at the moment, he'd like to fling the notebooks out the window, then throw her on the couch and love her into a better mood. He tried to joke to break the tension, "You know, it's so easy to spend money with pen and paper—reminds me of the way some people deal with credit cards. Maybe you should give each couple a wad of Monopoly money with their computer printouts...and little bankbooks and tiny checks. Then fools like me might be less likely to get carried away."

"You're being silly, all right." But the corners of her lips turned up. Elbows on the table, she rested her chin on her hands.

"And you're smiling." Grinning, gazing into her eyes, he leaned over to run a light finger along her cheek, eliciting a chuckle.

"You really don't want to start a newsletter business for Mr. Xerxes, then?"

"Nah, he's got enough to do keeping Mrs. Xerxes happy."

"You make her sound like an ogress."

"It's a tough job but old Xerxes enjoys it." He rose to kiss her lightly on the forehead. "Haven't we done enough work for today? Let's talk about recreation."

"Do you want to go out?"

"Today?" Sunlight was streaming in the apartment's windows. Too bad he wasn't free. "Unfortunately I have to pick up some equipment at four o'clock. And go over to David's later." He thought fast—he also wanted to spend some time with the girls this weekend. "But how about getting together tomorrow? How would you like to join the whole family for pizza and a movie?"

She stacked the coffee cups before rising from her chair. "Don't you think Kim would be upset?"

"She'll be okay," he promised. Actually the teenager would rather go out with her friends than with her family any day, but she could spare her dad a few hours. "And Tracy will be delighted."

Gillian smiled. "All right, why not? Sounds like fun."

"We could have fun doing just about anything." Though one thing in particular had been on his mind since the night before. But he was determined not to rush her. He slid his arms around Gillian's waist and kissed her gently. "Do you like apples? Next time we work together, I'll bring one for the teacher."

"I'm more of a participant in this project than a teacher," she insisted with a smile in her eyes.

"So much the better. It's best to experience life firsthand."

Pushing aside his thoughts of experiences to come, he kissed her again before turning to leave, resolutely heading for the door, then hurrying down the stairs to the street. Gillian was an intelligent, capable, vulnerable . . . and sexy woman. She also had a refreshing, down-to-earth sense of humor. She'd probably laugh if she knew that right now he was imagining her as a tempting siren.

GILLIAN HAD BEEN PLEASED when John asked her to spend time with his family. He was definitely taking her seriously. How flattering. However, she was also feeling a bit dizzy from jet lag. The relationship was moving extremely fast, creating the kind of friction that had made her react so intensely to his newsletter suggestion.

Of course, a wife had every right to object to her husband spending their savings. It must have been a bitter battle. That's why John still had an edge to his voice when he spoke of starting his business.

After mulling over the problem John had had with Kate, though, Gillian decided to give him the benefit of the doubt. He'd dropped enough clues—he said they'd married too young, that his ex-wife hadn't been willing to compromise—to show that he now understood the problems he'd encountered in the past. Everyone had a few skeletons hanging in the closet. What if John knew about Edwin and wondered why she'd broken up with the man?

At least Gillian didn't have children to complicate the new relationship. John's two girls were quite enough.

By the time they got to the movie on Sunday, Gillian was very aware of Kim and Tracy. Despite John's reassurances, the teenager was cool and sat on the far side of her father, while Tracy clung to Gillian as if she were a lifeline. Gillian's resulting discomfort took the edge off the comedy they watched.

They stopped at a pizza restaurant afterward for dinner. The place was packed since it was Sunday night. As in the movie, the adults sat next to each other in the U-shaped booth, with Kim on her father's side, Tracy on Gillian's. The teenager slid down in her seat.

"Don't worry, none of your friends will see you," John told Kim, glancing up from the menu. "That's why I drove to another town for both the movie and dinner."

Kim didn't respond, so Gillian decided to try to put her at ease. She'd been admiring the silky black shirt the teenager was wearing. "That's a beautiful blouse. Where did you get it?" A little sophisticated for a sixteen-year-old, but very nice.

Kim shifted her gaze, refusing to meet Gillian's. "Um . . . some boutique in the mall."

So much for finding something to talk about, Gillian decided.

"Is that blouse new?" John asked his daughter.

"Sort of. What does it matter?" Kim replied, then got even more defensive. "I do my own shopping. I didn't think I had to show you everything before I wore it."

"Mm-hmm." Maintaining an amazingly neutral expression, John just raised his brows slightly and reached under the table to squeeze Gillian's hand.

Grateful for the warm clasp, she squeezed back and smiled. She knew he was concerned with the way things were going. Well, she would try to do her part by being friendly and appearing relaxed, even if it was a facade.

He gazed around the table. "So what do we want on the pizza?"

"Sausage," Tracy suggested immediately. "What about you, Miss Flannery?"

"Sausage is fine."

Kim wrinkled her nose. "Yuck, sausage is greasy and spicy." She glared at her sister. "Hamburger's better—and it doesn't come from filthy pigs."

Tracy raised her chin stubbornly. "Who says cows are so clean?"

"Relax," John cut in. "All the animals took long showers before agreeing to be pizza topping, all right?"

Gillian was the only one who joined his laughter.

"Guess I wouldn't stand a chance of winning the stand-up comic award on *Star Search*," John told Gillian with a wry grin. "We'll have to go half and half with the hamburger and sausage. And let's have extra cheese and some mushrooms."

"Do you like mushrooms?" Tracy asked Gillian.

"I love them."

The girl beamed happily. "So do I."

"Except for oysters and anchovies, you like just about everything, don't you?" John reached across the table to tweak Tracy's ear. He told Gillian, "She has unusually wide-ranging taste for a kid her age."

"I hate mushrooms," Kim cut in. "You didn't ask me if I wanted them, Dad. I just want hamburger and cheese."

"You can pick the mushrooms off, as usual," John informed the teenager. He stared around the noisy restaurant. The hostess and a party of eight wandered by. "Excuse me, but where's our waitress? We'd like to order."

While the hostess turned to assure John he'd have service soon, Tracy leaned toward Gillian. "Do you like kids?"

Startled, Gillian wondered where that question had come from. "Of course I like children."

"Do you want to have some of your own?"

Was Tracy feeling her out? Gillian was surprised. Her relationship with John hadn't gone far enough to seriously think about it. "I want to have children someday."

"But what if you adopted kids? Would you love them, too?"

The question was so plaintive, Gillian was touched. Tracy had to be thinking about what it would be like to have a stepmother. Gillian wanted to reassure her. "Absolutely. I would love adopted kids just as much as my own. Who wouldn't?"

Tracy smiled tremulously, and John, who'd been listening, remained silent. If he took a second wife, would he want to have more children? Since he'd told her he enjoyed fatherhood, Gillian probably assumed so.

Kim's gaze moved from her father to Gillian. "People should be married before they have kids, though," the teenager stated.

A little taken aback, Gillian finally nodded. "I agree." Now what? Was Kim concerned about out-of-wedlock, teenage pregnancies? Good. She was being sensible.

"I mean, for Pete's sake, you ought to know someone for a while before you just up and have a baby with them," the teenager continued. John frowned. "Is one of your friends, uh, having problems?"

Kim drew back. "No."

"Then what are you talking about?"

"Oh, nothing."

The waitress's arrival put an end to the strained conversation, though Gillian, too, wondered if one of Kim's friends had gotten herself in trouble. She hoped it wasn't anyone from her class.

John ordered a large pizza, a salad to split and drinks. Before the woman left, Kim tapped her arm.

"Leave the mushrooms off the hamburger side, will you?" The teenager turned pleading eyes to her father. "They ruin the flavor of the cheese, Dad. There's always too many of them."

"Okay, put mushrooms on the sausage side only," John finally told the waitress. The woman walked away to place the order.

Though his expression was resigned, Gillian could tell John was irritated. And why not? Kim was being ridiculously picky about pizza ingredients, more than likely because she resented Gillian's presence and Tracy's attention to her teacher. Would Kim be angry if the others ate some of the hamburger side? If so, too bad, Gillian thought irritably. The teenager couldn't expect to hog it all to herself.

Tracy reached for the crayons in the container near the center of the table. The white butcher-paper table covering was meant for scribbling. The girl drew an orange heart near Gillian's place setting and muttered, "Phooey, I wanted mushrooms on everything."

Kim immediately responded, "You know, you've really got sick taste. Mushrooms are fungus...like mold."

Tracy scowled. "Oh, yeah, how would you like your lips to be moldy green?" She grabbed a green crayon.

"Settle down, will you?" John said, his voice low but full of meaning. "This is no way to behave around a guest."

"I'm sorry." Tracy touched Gillian's sleeve.

"That's okay."

Kim said nothing and deliberately examined her silverware.

"Mushrooms are full of vitamins and minerals," John told the teenager.

"I still hate them."

Gillian felt even less comfortable than she had in the movie. John had obviously brought her along too soon. Though she'd always heard there were difficulties with men who had ready-made families, Gillian had never before experienced the problem herself.

She picked up the orange crayon Tracy had left by her fork and quickly colored in the center of the heart. Then she drew dots around it as John discussed the movie with his daughters, obviously trying to make peace with conversation. She herself didn't want to get involved in case tempers flared once more. When the waitress delivered the salad, everyone helped themselves.

"I liked the part where the scout leader fell in the swimming pool," said Tracy, still discussing the movie. "I thought the skunk in the camping part was funny, too, except I didn't like it being killed and made into a hat."

"Luckily they didn't kill that skunk for real," Gillian told the girl. As a child, she'd worried about the fate of movie animals herself. "The hat was just a fake. And that was a 'stunt' animal you saw, a trained skunk."

Tracy stuffed her mouth with salad. "Wow, I bet it would be fun to have a job where you trained animals for movies."

Kim snickered. "Especially skunks—and you should know exactly how to do it, since you're a stinker yourself."

"You stink!" Tracy threw her napkin at her sister and started to rise from her seat.

"Stop it, right now," John commanded. Tracy immediately plopped back down. He glared at the teenager. "What is your problem, Kim?"

Kim looked stricken. "Why are you picking on me?"

"Because you've been picking on your sister."

Laying aside her fork and the salad for which she now had little appetite, Gillian picked up the crayon again, sketching another heart by her water glass, some dots, then lines, then more dots. If this bickering didn't stop, she was going to be tempted to leave. Then maybe everyone else could enjoy themselves, because she certainly wasn't having a great time.

John had turned to Tracy. "And you've been saying nasty things back to Kim. Cut it out."

"Okay, Dad," Tracy agreed quickly. "Sorry."

Kim mumbled, "All right, I'm sorry, too." She sighed deeply and nibbled at her salad.

The waitress delivered the soft drinks—a diet cola for Kim, a root beer for John and two lemon-limes for Gillian and Tracy. Gillian noticed that, so far, Tracy had ordered exactly the same thing as she.

Tracy took a sip of her soda. "You know, the camping in the movie looked pretty neat. I love tents and fires. I wish we could have camped more times this summer."

"I hoped we'd have a chance to go more often," said John. "But it's not too late. We can go camping one weekend in October if you want."

"Can we?" Tracy enthused. "Won't it be too cold?"

"I don't think so. We can just take extra blankets."

"Great!" Tracy turned to Gillian. "Would you like to come with us, Miss Flannery?"

John voiced no objections and Gillian didn't want to reject the girl. "I like to camp," she said nebulously.

"It would be more fun with more people," insisted Tracy.

John merely nodded. "Sounds good."

Did that mean he wanted her to go or not? Gillian wondered. Did *she* want to go? This dinner didn't make the outing seem attractive.

Kim sipped at her soda and pulled a face. "This isn't diet cola, it's regular. I don't want anything with sugar in it. It's too fattening."

John shrugged and waved at the waitress. "You aren't too fat."

Gillian almost opened her mouth to say that it wasn't a bad idea to cut out extra sugar in one's diet, then thought better of it. If she supported Kim's choice, the teenager would probably do a turnaround and insist she wanted sugar. Gillian would have ordered a diet drink herself if the restaurant had served one that had no caffeine.

As if guessing her thoughts, the teenager stared at the lemon-lime sodas in front of Gillian and Tracy. "You should drink diet soda, too," Kim told her sister.

"Are you trying to tell me I'm fat?"

"I didn't say any such thing," the teenager claimed with an innocent expression. She glanced at her father. "I'm not picking on her, Dad."

"Why don't you concentrate on your salad and chill out?" John told both of them.

Gillian took a blue crayon from the container and sketched stars between the hearts and among the dots and lines. The girls' squabbles were reminding her of the many quarrels she'd witnessed between her siblings...and between her parents. Stuart and Carolyn Flannery had been terrible role models in that area. As soon as she reached her teens, Gillian had participated as little as possible in disputes and had learned how to retreat into herself when other tempers were riled.

While the girls continued to eat, John leaned closer to Gillian. "I bend over backward to have a nice evening and they have to fight. But this is only a little worse than usual, you know."

She nodded understandingly. "They aren't used to being with a stranger."

He stared at the scribbling she'd been doing. "You've created some nice patterns there."

She had to smile.

"Didn't you say that you and your sisters and brothers went around and around a lot?"

"We fought quite a bit when I was a child." Not that she enjoyed it.

"Must have had some family outings. You all went to restaurants together, right?"

"Actually we didn't go out very much. My father didn't make a lot of money. And when we did go to the local pizza parlor or a hamburger place, they had to pull two or three tables together to seat all nine of us."

He laughed. "A crowd of nine—how did you ever agree on pizza ingredients?"

"We didn't have the luxury of disagreeing over the kind of food we ordered—that was useless. Instead, everyone competed for second and third helpings, especially my brothers."

"A real circus, huh?"

"Some people might have found it entertaining."

She knew he didn't mean to offend her but wasn't pleased by the comparison. What would he say if she told him the loudest battles were between her parents, over whether her mother was keeping tight-enough control on the smallest kids or whether her father could have a second beer?

"How on earth did your parents maintain discipline?"

"By yelling at us." Very loudly.

"And cracking heads, I bet." He grinned. "I'm sure the older kids bullied the younger. You must have been able to play both roles, since you were born in the middle."

"I tried to avoid problems whenever possible." By the time she was older, anyway.

"Really? How on earth could you stay out of trouble in a family of seven kids?"

"I tuned out."

"Oh." He nodded knowingly and pointed at the table covering. "You drew stars and hearts and dots and lines?" He squinted and leaned closer with mock earnestness. "Hmm, nice execution there. It's a wonder you didn't become . . . an abstract symbolist."

His humor was infectious. Feeling better, she picked up her fork and pushed at the lettuce in her salad bowl. "Abstract symbolism? Was that a real art movement?"

"No, you'd be the originator."

"Mr. Xerxes is the artist, not me."

"But Mrs. Xerxes has her own kind of symbolism." He used one of the crayons to draw money symbols next to the stars and hearts.

She shook her head and laughed, meeting his twinkling gaze. "I think you'd make a good stand-up comic."

She felt even better by the time the pizza arrived a few minutes later. Kim and Tracy dug in with relish. Except for a couple of snide comments, they refrained from any more fighting. And John didn't bring up Gillian's family again. He wasn't aware of just how much the Flannerys' constant battles had bothered her or he wouldn't have asked all those questions.

At least the Flannery siblings—if not the adults—had had the excuse of being immature. As were Kim and Tracy. Though John must have been exaggerating about his daughters behaving only a little worse today. They were as nervous about being with Gillian as she with them. Hopefully everyone would grow beyond that with time. Gillian would be counting the days.

CHAPTER EIGHT

"WE OUGHT TO EAT TOGETHER more often, Gillian," Rose Flannery told her older sister on Monday. Four of the Flannery siblings had gotten together for dinner at Rose's Indianapolis apartment and were now taking a stroll through a nearby park. "You're a good influence. Tonight was the first meal the three of us have shared in weeks."

"You call take-out Chinese food a real meal?" Gillian was surprised. "Doesn't anyone cook?"

"No, but I would if I had my pots and pans," said Vicky, who seemed to be in an unusually irritable mood. She'd moved in with Rose and had slept on the couch since separating from her husband. The apartment's second bedroom was already occupied by Ginny, who was going to school and waitressing part-time to pay her share of the rent. "I left the household stuff with Tim." She sighed. "I get so tired of snacking and eating junk food."

"What's the matter with my pans?" asked Rose.

At twenty-seven, an editor for a local trade magazine, Rose was more freewheeling than conservative Gillian but a bit more established than twenty-four-year old Ginny and, at the moment, far more together than poor mixed-up Vicky.

"Your two—and I emphasize the word *two*—pans are disgusting. They're not even lined with Teflon," complained Vicky. "They're impossible to clean."

Dark blond curls bouncing as she strode along, Rose rolled her eyes skyward. "Well, excuse me, I'll make sure I outfit the kitchen for you the next time you move in."

A little tense, Gillian rubbed the back of her neck. Her sisters had bickered throughout the meal. "Why are you all so testy? I came to visit you to relax."

Otherwise, she'd be wandering restlessly around her apartment and thinking about John. She could usually count on her siblings to be diverting, if not always supportive. Excluding their competitive oldest sister Hillary—who was married, working and the owner of a small building with three flats—the Flannery girls were fairly close.

"I'm thirsty. Too much monosodium glutamate in that food. Is there a water fountain around here?" Vicky asked, changing the subject.

"There's one near the shelter in the center of the park." Ginny removed a hand from her baggy pants' pocket to motion in that direction.

"I'll be back." Vicky took off.

As soon as Vicky was out of hearing range, Gillian asked, "Has Tim called?"

"A few times," Rose told her, "but I don't know what they talked about."

"Vicky was angry at him after he phoned last week," added Ginny. She ran a hand through her cropped short brown hair. Very thin and narrow-faced, she looked least like the other Flannerys. "I eavesdropped for a minute, and she accused him of not taking her seriously."

"Do you really think they'll get a divorce?" inquired Gillian.

"Who knows? I just hope she'll get into a better frame of mind," said Rose. "She makes a big show of going out dancing and flirting around but she's not happy."

The subject of Tim and divorce was dropped quickly when Vicky came running up. "Wow, there are some great-looking guys playing volleyball on the court by the shelter. Want to check it out?"

"I suppose so." Rose raised her brows at Gillian. Though single, Rose had a steady boyfriend she'd been seeing for more than a year.

"Yeah, let's take a look," agreed Ginny. "I don't usually have time to ogle men, what with classes and working at night."

They stepped off the sidewalk and headed across the grass toward the shelter.

"What time do you get home from your waitress job?" Gillian asked Ginny. She didn't get to talk to Ginny very often because of her crazy schedule.

"One or two o'clock."

"And she's so noisy she always wakes me up," said Vicky.

"That's not true, I'm quiet," insisted Ginny.

Vicky wasn't appeased. "Last night you slammed the refrigerator door at least ten times." She pouted. "And I bet it was you who ate my cookies."

"There were only two left."

Feeling tense again, Gillian massaged her neck as her sisters continued to give each other a hard time.

"But they were mine."

"Uh-huh," Ginny said. "Like the panty hose you stole out of the bathroom this morning."

"I didn't know they were yours. I have several pair of black ones, also. Don't accuse me of stealing unless you want me to move out...and I never said you could borrow my bat earrings, either."

"Oh, come on," Gillian broke in, thoroughly annoyed. "You sound like children."

"You'd argue, too, if you lived with Rose and Ginny," Vicky snapped.

"You should work harder to try to get along," Gillian insisted. She'd roomed with the two when she was a kid.

Ginny threw an arm around her younger sister's shoulders. "Nobody is asking you to move, Vicky. Relax. You must have gotten up on the wrong side of the bed."

"The wrong side of the lumpy couch you mean," said Vicky, shrugging off Ginny's arm. But she seemed calmer.

Rose just laughed. "Doesn't this remind you of the good old days, Gillian?"

"Unfortunately, yes."

"Aw, we had fun. Remember when Ginny borrowed our doll carriage and left it in the middle of the road and it got hit by a truck?"

"It was *my* doll carriage," Gillian corrected her.

Rose shrugged. "I thought we were sharing it."

Her sisters had always thought they could share everything of hers, Gillian thought, though she didn't voice the opinion. That would probably start another argument.

When they got to the cement slab that was serving as a volleyball court, the sisters lined up against the fence. There were four men in jeans and sweatshirts tossing the volleyball back and forth. The youngest—probably a college student—turned around and grinned at them.

"See, isn't he cute?" Vicky waved, then sidled up beside Gillian. She leaned closer and lowered her voice. "Rose's apartment is too crowded."

"But it's only temporary," Gillian told her. "You're working every day for that secretarial agency, aren't you? It won't be long until you've saved up enough money for your own place." Unless—as they all hoped—Vicky went back to Tim.

"Uh . . . you have a little more space, don't you?"

Gillian suddenly realized what Vicky was leading up to. She tried to be diplomatic. "This isn't the greatest timing . . . John has been dropping by a lot lately. We need to have some privacy."

"You've gotten to that point, huh?" Vicky said knowingly. "And you can't stay at his place because of his two daughters. That's a little inconvenient. Do you get along with the kids?"

"Fairly well," Gillian exaggerated hopefully. She'd confided in Vicky a couple of times after deciding to date John. "We all went to a movie and out to eat last night." Then she told the whole truth. "John's younger daughter was very friendly, the sixteen-year-old was cold and crabby. They kept fighting with each other. I'm sure Kim feels weird about her father dating one of her teachers."

"Hmm, a father dating a teacher. I can see why she'd be uptight." Vicky leaned on the fence and smiled when another of the volleyball players turned to look at her. "You know, John's not the only man in the world. There are lots of others, many of whom come with no complications."

Great, Vicky was changing her tune after weeks of egging her on.

"Are you talking about that divorced guy?" Rose had overheard and added her two cents, "You aren't getting serious about him, are you, Gillian?"

"It's too early to even think about it." Gillian kept her response noncommittal. Rose was always trying to fix up her sisters.

Rose nodded toward the volleyball court. "That's Ty Spencer out there."

Not having recognized anyone, Gillian asked, "Should I know him?"

"He's the neat psychologist I told you about. You know, the one I met at a neighborhood block party. He's single—never been married—and owns a town house a few blocks from here. I see him around. When I mentioned you one time, he seemed interested."

Gillian was about to say she didn't remember any psychologist when one of the volleyball players came running over to the fence.

"Hi, wanta play a round?" the young, dark-haired man joked. The other men laughed at his innuendo. "There are four of us and four of you. It'd be even."

"Sure," Ginny agreed immediately.

"But that still wouldn't be fair—men against women." Another player, a tall blond, approached. "We should mix the teams. Don't you think so, Rose? How're you doing, anyway?"

"I'm fine." Rose smiled. "These are my sisters, Ty." She pointed. "Ginny, Vicky and Gillian."

"Nice to meet you." Grinning good-naturedly, Ty reached through the fence to shake their hands. "You're certainly a good-looking family." Probably in his early thirties, Ty was very personable and not at all bad-looking himself.

"So let's get this game going," the dark-haired young man urged. "I'm Dean, that's Brad and Adam. Let's choose up teams and get out on the court."

"I want to be on your team," Ty told Gillian when the women came around the fence to join the men.

"Fine."

From the way he was looking her over, Gillian figured that he must have remembered Rose mentioning her. If it weren't for John, Gillian might be tempted to flirt with him. As it was, she'd concentrate on the game to make sure she didn't encourage him. Gillian, Vicky, Ty and Dean took one end of the court, the other four, the opposite. Batting the ball back and forth, they were soon involved in a laughing, if competitive, battle.

"You're blind—that ball was in!" Ty yelled to his opponents. He stepped closer to Gillian, his eyes dancing. "We'll psych them out. Make them question every move."

Gillian grinned. "Going to use your skill as a psychologist?"

He laughed. "It'd be one of the few times I've worked with people since I left school. I collect reams of data at my job."

"You're in research, huh?" she commented, appreciating that Ty wasn't full of himself. His Ph.D. hadn't made him lose his perspective.

"Pay attention to the ball!"

At Dean's shout, Ty and Gillian jumped apart. Vicky came running forward to hit the ball over the net, but the other team sent it hurtling back. Everyone played fast and furious. At one point, Gillian collided with Ty and he helped her up. When he held her hand too long, she smiled and moved away.

Twenty minutes after it had started, the game wound down, Dean objecting to the other side's victory. "You cheated! That last ball wasn't out of bounds. We get another try!"

"You'll have to play by yourself then," Ty told the younger man. "I'm tired."

So was Gillian. Wiping the sweat off her face, she ambled off the court a few paces behind Vicky. At least the exercise had reduced the tension she'd been feeling.

"Wait." Ty hurried to catch up with her. "Would you like to go out for a drink?"

"Um, no thanks."

"Some other time, then? Can I have your phone number?"

Oh, great. It was just her luck to be approached for a date when she didn't want one. "I appreciate your interest, Ty, but I'm seeing someone."

"And it's exclusive, huh?" But he seemed unabashed. "If your situation ever changes, I'm in the phone book—Ty Spencer. Ask Rose for a recommendation."

He didn't press her any further. Bidding goodbye to the men, the Flannery sisters walked back toward Rose's apartment building. Once there, Gillian got in her car and headed for Greenville. Though it made her feel a little guilty, she had to admit Ty was quite attractive. And he had the additional advantage of being unattached—no ex-wife, no children.

Of course, John's experiences had shaped the mature man he was. Gillian had never dated anyone who was so special. She'd just have to have faith that Kim would come around and that Tracy would learn to trust her enough to be less clinging. It was a difficult situation, one that Gillian wouldn't have chosen on purpose. She only hoped she would have enough strength to handle it.

On Wednesday afternoon, Gillian received a note from the principal's office saying that the Fosters were dropping out of the marriage project. Wonderful. If they had been unhappy about something, why hadn't they told her personally? And no one answered when she phoned the couples' home after her classes were over.

Eating a quick dinner by herself, Gillian hurried back to the high school that evening. She rushed into the classroom a few minutes early, looking forward to seeing John, only to find that he hadn't yet arrived. Her spirits sank. She desperately needed a warm smile from someone supportive. It seemed like eons since they'd been together—the pizza outing hardly counted. She'd wanted to hear his voice so badly today that she almost called him at work.

The Talbots were seated in the front row. "Hello, Derek, Arlene," said Gillian. Arlene smiled faintly while Derek merely nodded. They both were glum, as if a dark cloud were hanging over them. In the back of the room, Wes and Elaine pursued a heated discussion. They sounded angry. Nearby, another grouchy-looking couple added cryptic comments. Was the whole world in a sour mood?

Gillian sighed and dropped her purse and the folder of envelopes she was carrying onto the teacher's desk. She'd heard too much arguing the past few days. She was beginning to feel like a taut wire humming with pressure.

The other adults wandered in as seven o'clock neared. Late as usual, the Bigsbys arrived a few minutes after seven, John on their heels.

"Hi, beautiful," he murmured as he passed by Gillian to take a seat.

Ready to start the initial discussion, she turned to meet John's gaze, pausing to let his smile wash over her. Thank heavens. She could almost feel the positive energy flowing from him.

"Has anyone had any special problems this week?" Gillian asked. She glanced around the room, wondering whether she should ask if anyone had talked to the Fosters. But then she'd have to tell the group that the couple had dropped out.

Derek immediately spoke up. "I have a problem."

"The same one he had last week," Arlene explained, sounding annoyed. "But you're just going to have to get a job, dear."

Derek looked stubborn. "Not for minimum wages, I'm not."

"You're still receiving unemployment," Gillian told the man. "Did you make a list of jobs from the employment ads?"

"Yes, but there were very few in my bracket."

"So I suggested he take a lower-paying job to supplement the unemployment," Arlene said rather defensively. "I don't see anything wrong with that. We bought a lot of furniture before he lost his job and could use the extra income."

"Sounds practical," Gillian agreed, but she could see Derek hated the idea.

"I'm not working in a fast-food joint," he stated. "And you can forget about the car wash and the janitor job as well. How would that look on a résumé?"

"Don't be so stubborn," Arlene said. "Who says you have to list those sorts of jobs?"

Derek folded his arms. "If you don't list them, you have to admit you're unemployed. That looks bad, too. And I would appreciate it if you would quit nagging me."

Arlene's brow furrowed. "I'm sure we can work this out—"

"Not unless the next slip we draw says I'm getting a decent job," Derek interrupted.

"But if it doesn't, you'll have to find something else to do," Gillian explained, fearing a new job wasn't an option for the Talbot's marriage until the end of the project. "How about fixing up the condo your couple owns?"

Derek frowned. "I'm not good at home repair."

"You could paint the walls," Arlene suggested.

"I'm really bad at painting."

Becoming uncomfortable, Gillian hastened to change the subject, "Does anyone else have any feedback before we go on?" She got the envelopes from the desk. Although she figured the Talbots wanted to continue their discussion, she was determined not to be in the middle of another argument.

Sarah Bigsby smiled and raised her hand. "We have good news."

"Wonderful," said Gillian, noting that Calvin was bright-eyed for once.

"My husband's doing a lot of home repairs," Sarah told the class.

Calvin grinned. "I'm getting into this thing now. I made a big list of tasks I've accomplished."

"He painted the porch," Sarah said proudly. "He's rewiring a circuit for the laundry room. He's going to sand the living room floor."

"My, my." Gillian was impressed. But it was her job to make sure everyone's homework was both logical, given their marriage's circumstances, and feasible, as well. "Are you sure you have enough time to do all that within the project's time span? We have to be realistic."

"I'm being realistic," Calvin insisted. "I worked it all out in my notebook, the expenses and everything." He laughed. "And it sure is easier to do paperwork than the real thing, let me tell you. When I realized just how easy it was, I really went to town."

Sarah nodded in agreement. "He filled out six or seven pages."

"That's great," said Gillian.

Everyone smiled and murmured except the Talbots. Hoping that couple would get the right idea from the Bigsbys' example, Gillian passed out the envelopes. But Derek was openly disappointed when he didn't find a new job on his slip, while Arlene looked impatient. Wishing they could just relax, Gillian took her place beside John, pulling her desk close to his.

John leaned over to whisper, his breath feathering her ear. "The Talbots are being impossible."

"I wish I could help them," she whispered back.

"Save your energy. Derek's not going to listen to anyone at the moment."

As the project coordinator, however, Gillian still felt responsible. What if a second couple dropped out? She had to push the worry out of her mind as she and John discussed the newest change for the Xerxes. Their slip announced that Mrs. Xerxes had been promoted at the bank.

"Speaking of realistic, I'm wondering if a bank would really do this." Gillian frowned. "They'd have to know that I'm going to be out for weeks on maternity leave."

"Maybe we'd better draw another slip," suggested John.

"You're drawing another one?" asked Derek, obviously having overheard. "Then we want a new slip, too."

"That's against the rules," explained Gillian, not allowing herself to get upset. "We just have a special problem here."

"Oh, sure, you can change the rules for yourself but not for anybody else."

John intervened. "This isn't Gillian's fault. I insisted on adding a baby to our original setup and she was nice enough to compromise. She shouldn't have—I realize now that the purpose of this project is defeated unless you work with what you're given."

"And we're not going to draw another slip," Gillian said quickly. "John was merely wondering if that were possible."

"All right." Sounding pacified, Derek turned back to his notebook and Arlene.

"So Mrs. Xerxes is going to get a promotion, right?" John said loud enough for the Talbots to hear.

"She can receive work at home by messenger service," Gillian agreed, writing that down in her spiral.

John lowered his voice. "Interesting how the project brings up psychological patterns, don't you think? I bet this will be good for Derek in the long run. He may have had it too easy in real life."

"I appreciate any positive feedback."

John thought Gillian looked a little frazzled. There were tiny lines beside her mouth and her skin was paler than usual. "Had a rough day?" He was more than willing to be sympathetic.

"The Fosters dropped out of the project. They sent me a note."

"And you're assuming they were unhappy with it?"

"I tried to call them to find out, but they weren't home."

"Don't jump to conclusions. There are lots of possible explanations. Maybe something came up. Six weeks is a long commitment for most people."

"I hope you're right."

He engulfed her hand with his own. "I know I'm right. This is a great experience. I love everything about it." Including Gillian.

Love? Was he actually in love? Yes, John realized, in a moment of silent revelation. He gazed into Gillian's eyes, searching for her response. She smiled and blinked, seemingly uncomfortable with his intensity. But a classroom of noisy people was no place to talk about feelings. And Gillian might not be ready to deal with them yet.

Behind him, John heard Elaine chuckle at some remark Wes had made. He glanced back at the widow and her partner and caught them staring. They ducked their heads and chuckled again, obviously having noticed the way John was holding Gillian's hand. Considering how cozy those two were getting, however, they had nothing to talk about.

Reminded of the potential for gossip by a recent clash with Kim, John told Gillian, "You know, we should be completely honest here."

"Honest about what?"

"We should tell the people in this group we've been going out."

"Think so?" She adjusted her glasses.

"Otherwise, they'll just make up their own stories. They know something's going on, anyhow."

She sighed deeply. "I hate rumors."

Wait until she heard the newest from Kim. Deciding he'd tell her when he got her alone and that he'd save the announcement about their dating until the end of the class, John went back to work.

Gillian concentrated on her spiral until the Bigsbys asked her a question. She turned around to talk to them, then tried to encourage Derek, assuring him that his unemployment wouldn't last forever. John couldn't believe the man was so uptight about it.

The remainder of the two-hour meeting passed quickly. Near the end, Gillian rose to gather her materials together while the rest of the group got ready to go. John saw it as his chance to make that announcement.

He stood up. "Hey, everybody, just for your information, I want you to know that Gillian and I are dating."

"Wow," teased Wes. "One week, you're expecting, the next you're dating. Kind of a reversed process, don't you think?"

John laughed. "Gillian and I have gone out a couple of times." He gazed about. Most faces showed no surprise. He was looking directly at Derek and Arlene when he added, "And there's nothing wilder or crazier going on—I give you my word. I'd appreciate your stopping any rumors."

He didn't glance toward Gillian until he'd finished. He noticed her adjusting her glasses, a sure sign that she was uncomfortable.

"I think it's great that you're bringing your relationship out in the open," Sarah said, distracting John from Gillian's reaction. "You might as well inform people yourself."

Wes feigned innocence. "But there's seldom any rumor-mongering in Greenville."

"Sure, and the sun doesn't come up in the east," said Sarah. "Gossip is a small town's most enjoyable extracurricular activity."

As the group filed out, Gillian stayed behind to turn out the lights. She adjusted her glasses again as she and John walked through the empty halls.

"You're uncomfortable," John observed. "Don't tell me my announcement embarrassed you."

"I was a little embarrassed," she admitted. "I hope the principal doesn't have a fit when he hears about this."

"He'd have a fit over a teacher dating a single parent? That would be close minded." And he felt she was overreacting.

They went down the stairs, and he opened the door leading outside.

"I had a good reason to talk to the group tonight," he went on. "It seems Laura Talbot overheard her parents talking about our 'baby.' Arlene and Derek must have been discussing our surprise announcement and Laura took them seriously. She told Kim, and she's been worried sick. Remember when she made those mysterious remarks about pregnancy on Sunday?"

Gillian stopped in her tracks, startled. "She thought that we…"

"Uh-huh. I straightened her out, though."

Gillian let out her breath. "Oh, great, the gossip's probably all over the high school. Of course, Kim would jump at anything that would make me look bad."

John frowned. "You make it sound like she hates you."

"Well, we both know she isn't exactly thrilled with the idea of you and me dating. She treats me like I'm a poisonous snake."

John couldn't help feeling annoyed. "She's just a teenager. You of all people should know what they're like. Kim's defensive and hypersensitive, not to mention a little mixed-up because of my divorce."

"I realize that, but I'm only human. You haven't gotten the cold treatment from her like I have."

"Wanta bet? Kim is always cold when she's angry. As her father, I just happen to have enough power to demand she talk it out with me."

"Power over curfews and allowances." She nodded. "I see."

"And I also have power from longtime emotional commitment. Kim will straighten out one of these days. You have to give her time." Plus, he should try to be extra understanding of the pressure on Gillian, he told himself.

"All right. I only hope Principal Fowler won't be on my back in the meantime."

He draped an arm around her shoulders. "Has Fowler got it in for you or something?" He noted that she didn't cuddle into his side as she normally would.

"Principal Fowler's secretary was the person who brought me the news about the Fosters. That's why I'm so aware of what he might or might not think." She gazed at him seriously. "And Principal Fowler is the man you approached when you first became concerned about my questionable project."

"So it's all my fault if he flips out? Are you really that concerned?" He couldn't believe she was acting so prickly. "I'll talk to Fowler if you want."

She drew away. "No, please. Just let the matter lie. I don't think I can take any more confrontations . . . or announcements."

John dropped his arm, becoming annoyed once again. "I seem to remember you encouraging honesty and communication. I was trying to be up-front with the group."

"But being honest doesn't mean you have to get on a public platform."

"Come on, I didn't call a town meeting."

"I just thought we were going to let anyone who was interested know individually. I didn't think you were going to shout something so personal from the rooftops."

"You really are overreacting." As she'd done with the newsletter figures. "I suppose you thought we should have a major discussion about how, when and where we were going to let people know."

Couldn't he do anything on his own? Although Gillian was far more down-to-earth than flighty Kate, he was beginning to wonder if all women got their noses out of joint over what a man said or did not say, and when.

"That would be better than blurting it out the way you did."

"Look, there was no harm done." He'd be damned if he was going to apologize.

"Okay." Her voice was tight. "It's too late to do anything about it, anyway."

But obviously she was still displeased. He cleared his throat, then asked half-heartedly, "Want to go out for some coffee?"

"I'm really not in the mood for coffee at the moment. . . ."

"All right," he cut her off, not caring to hear any alternatives she might offer. "I'll call you."

He turned and walked toward the parking lot, glancing over his shoulder to see if Gillian was staring after him. If so, he might have headed back. But she was walking firmly in the opposite direction, her carriage stiff.

Damn! John strode to his car, got in and slammed the door, fearing he'd made a big mistake. He'd let himself fall in love with a woman who not only wasn't comfortable with his kids but who didn't even want to admit she was dating him.

CHAPTER NINE

IN A FUNK over the way she and John parted company the night before, Gillian got through the school day by rote. Normally focused, she found her mind wandering . . . and her students giving each other strange looks when they caught her at it.

When the last period began, she was relieved. Less than an hour and she would be able to go home. Working on her dollhouse always picked up her spirits, so maybe she'd spend some time painting one of the bedrooms. If only she didn't have to teach her junior sociology class first. More specifically, she wished she didn't have to face Kim Slater, who sat in the third row—a vibrant reminder of her own foolishness.

For foolish was exactly how Gillian was viewing her falling in love with a man who had too many complications in his life.

Three too many to be specific: Kim, Tracy and the mystery ex-wife, Kate. Gillian could do without them and the arguments they were sure to instigate.

And yet, shutting out his daughters would mean shutting John out—assuming he still wanted to see her. And she not only cared about him, she had to admit to a growing affection for the younger girl. Poor Tracy was so confused, so needy. She even felt sorry for Kim, who was being as impossible as she could manage. Despite Gillian's abhorrence of the conflict they aroused, her heart went out to both girls. She still remembered the effect her parents' separation had had on her.

Somehow, Gillian made it through the first two-thirds of the class the same way she'd gotten through the rest of the day. But when she handed back corrected and graded homework assignments, Andy Bigsby shook her out of her complacency.

"You didn't hand mine back, Miss Flannery."

"How could I when you didn't turn one in?"

"I turned it in."

"Andy, why don't you just be honest—"

"I *am* being honest," he insisted. "I handed in my assignment on Monday with the rest of the class."

"I'm sure I never saw it," Gillian said, reaching for her record book. She flipped to the correct page and found his name. "I keep very careful records. I always use one column to check work in, and a second to enter the grade." She slid her finger to the correct column. "I'm sorry, but I don't have a check indicating you turned in your work. Would you like to see for yourself?"

"I don't care what your dumb book says," Andy stated, crossing his arms over his barrel chest. "I know I did my homework. My mother even saw me doing the assignment. If you can't find it, then it's *your* problem."

Gillian was appalled both by his statement and his tone. As if she didn't have enough problems with John and his children, now a student was contradicting her! No matter which way she turned, she couldn't get away from arguments. And this was one she couldn't tune out. The other students were watching her carefully, waiting for her response.

"Andy," she said firmly, sounding more in control than she was feeling, "if you would like to discuss this with Principal Fowler, I'll be happy to give you a hall pass so you can get to his office." She noticed the teenager's jaw tightened, but he didn't say anything more. "Now please sit down so the rest of the class can go over the assignment."

Gillian experienced a moment's unease as Andy took his seat. The teenager didn't seem to be bluffing—his scowl looked genuine. Andy had never failed to turn in an assignment before. But if he had turned it in, she would have recorded the fact, Gillian assured herself. She couldn't be mistaken.

Still, a healthy doubt plagued her for the rest of the class, and as she left the school, she decided to search her workstation as soon as she got home.

The telephone ringing as she climbed the stairs to her apartment made her forget everything but John. They hadn't set another study date. Perhaps he was calling to make one. Or maybe he was just calling because he missed her and was sorry they hadn't spent time alone together the night before. She prayed he wouldn't lose patience as she unlocked the door and rushed into the living room to pick up the receiver.

Her "hello" was a tad breathless.

"Gillian?" came a familiar voice. "Did we catch you on the run?"

Her spirits plummeted when she realized it wasn't John, after all. "I just got in from work, Mom."

"We can call back," her father told her from a second telephone.

"No, it's okay." Gillian tried to temper her disappointment and sound cheerful. She didn't want them to know anything was wrong. "Just let me catch my breath." She took a deep one and asked, "How are you?"

"We're doing just fine," her mother said.

"Carolyn might be doing fine," her father amended, "but I'm bored stiff. This taking it easy thing because of some dumb blood pressure problem isn't all that it's cracked up to be."

"So he takes it out on me by hanging around the house and finding things to complain about."

"I'm not the only one who complains...."

Gillian's stomach clutched. Her parents couldn't say two words to each other without getting out of sorts.

"Maybe you need to get involved in a hobby, Dad. Or some sport."

"Like what?"

"You enjoy bowling."

"I'm already in two leagues."

He went on to tell her about the great scores he'd gotten during his last league night. Then her mother started grumbling that he wouldn't consider taking up candlelight bowling with her, making Gillian sorry she'd brought up the subject in the first place.

"So-o-o," she interrupted. "What's up? Did you call about something special?"

"We don't need a reason to call you," her mother said. "We just miss you."

"You're not around nearly enough," her father added. "We see your sisters and brothers all the time."

"Well, not all the time, Stuart."

"Vicky and Rose spent Sunday with us. We sort of hoped you'd have time to come with them."

"I was, uh...busy," Gillian told them, avoiding the word *date*. Strictly speaking, she hadn't been on one, anyway. It had been a family outing.

Carolyn Flannery switched to her most effective "neglected mother" tone. "You've been busy since before school started. We haven't seen you once. You don't suppose you could spend this weekend with us?"

"This weekend?" Gillian echoed.

"Or do you already have plans with that divorced man you've been dating?"

Great. She didn't have to wonder how her mother knew about John. Vicky never could keep anything to herself. "John Slater and I have the marriage project to work on. I told you about that the last time I called."

"Uh-huh, the *marriage* project." Her mother was using her slightly disapproving, "mother knows all" tone now. Despite her own marital problems, Carolyn Flannery was always worrying about the status of her unmarried children, and she didn't sound convinced that John was a good prospect. She probed, "If you make plans ahead of time, I'm sure your...John will understand."

Her John? If only! Gillian wasn't about to make any statement that would encourage her mother's curiosity. Besides, she didn't know how things were going herself and certainly didn't want to admit she was in love with the wrong person.

"Next weekend will be great," she said. "I'll be at your place mid-morning Saturday and stay until after dinner Sunday."

"You couldn't come Friday night?" her father asked.

"All right. Friday night," she agreed, bringing the conversation to an end.

She only hoped she could make it through two-and-a-half days with her parents without getting on edge, Gillian thought as she hung up. Not that she didn't want to see them. But she spent much of the time under tension because of their bickering. And often they got into major arguments. She remembered the old days when her mother chased her father across the lawn, both of them yelling at the top of their lungs. Talk about gossip fodder for the entire neighborhood....

Gillian brought her schoolwork to her desk. If her parents started in on each other, she'd just have to tune out as she'd learned to do as a child. Find something to distract herself with so she wouldn't have to listen and take the disagreements personally as she had once done. She'd had enough of arguing and feeling responsible lately. The go-around with Andy was still vivid in her mind. As she'd vowed to do earlier, she searched her workstation for the missing homework assignment.

She found it mixed in a stack of papers from another class.

"Just great," she muttered, sinking into her chair.

Something else to blame herself for. She'd collected the assignments on Monday, the day after the pizza date from hell. Distracted by Kim's presence in the room, she must have been careless when she'd shoved the pages into her briefcase. And she'd blamed Andy for not turning in the homework in front of the entire class. Now she'd have to apologize. How embarrassing! She only hoped she wouldn't get a call from Sarah Bigsby.

Her relationship with John Slater was shaking up every facet of her life. What in the world was she going to do about it?

JOHN HEADED HOME from work early, leaving the renovation site in David's capable hands. Both brothers would be working on the mansion for the coming few weeks until David took over the next scheduled project.

Now regretful that he hadn't tried to smooth things over with Gillian the night before, John was determined to see her in person to straighten out any awkwardness between them. He could hardly believe that his announcement about their seeing each other had snowballed into a disagreement. He supposed he'd have to chalk up his heated reaction—and probably hers as well—to the uneasy if exhilarating insecurity of falling in love. Gillian wasn't really ashamed of dating him. She'd merely been embarrassed by the way he'd announced their relationship. And she'd had real reason to complain about Kim.

But John wasn't going to let Gillian get away. For the first time since his divorce, John was forming a serious relationship, and he didn't want anything—or anyone—coming between him and the woman he loved. Not Principal Fowler, not other members of the group, not Kate. Neither predictable nor convenient, love was too precious to waste.

That thought uppermost in his mind, he knocked at Gillian's door. He was a man who went after what he wanted. Part of him was convinced he would win Gillian's heart no matter what he had to do, but a less-certain part was making his palms sweat. After wiping his right hand on his jeans, he pulled an object from his pocket and hid it behind his back. A moment later, when Gillian opened the door and couldn't hide the pleasure that instantly brightened her gloomy expression, John felt more in control.

"What are you doing here?" Gillian asked, doing her best to shutter her elation behind a stiff mask.

She's merely being cautious, trying to protect herself, John told himself. The thought was encouraging. That must mean he'd been right—their feelings for each other were mutual.

"I brought you a present." He took his hand from behind his back and offered it to her.

Gillian stared at the apple that he'd promised her on Saturday. "We didn't make a study date." She sounded uncertain when she glanced up at him. "Did we?"

"No. Consider this a peace offering."

"I didn't know we were at war."

"We aren't. We merely had a minor skirmish last night." He placed the apple practically under her nose. "Aren't you going to take it?"

"Sure." She did so without looking at him directly. "Thanks."

John studied Gillian briefly. Her face flared with a becoming color, a slightly lighter shade than the rose-colored sweat suit she wore. Her expression had softened, revealing the underlying vulnerability he too infrequently encountered. It was nice to know she wasn't always so sure of herself.

Reaching out, barely preventing himself from pulling her into his arms, John coaxingly stroked a flushed cheek instead. "It's such a nice afternoon I thought we could go out for a walk and talk things over."

She met his eyes but didn't smile. "Shouldn't you be at work?"

"I'm the boss, remember?" He let his hand drop. Okay, so she wasn't going to make it easy, but he wouldn't let that discourage him. He'd keep at her until he broke down her defenses. "I can't get into trouble for leaving early. So, what do you say? Will you come?"

"I guess I have some free time." She held up the apple. "Let me put this down somewhere and get my keys."

Since she hadn't invited him inside, John leaned against the doorjamb while Gillian crossed to her desk, where she traded the fruit for her key ring and a couple of tissues that she stuffed into a pocket. She hurried back.

"Ready."

"A woman after my own heart." At her questioning look, he added, "I hate being kept waiting."

He thought she might come back with some smart remark, but she merely said, "Why don't you go on down. I'll lock up."

John did as she suggested. Gillian caught up to him on the front porch. Talking about unimportant things—things that weren't in the least personal—they walked to a nearby ice cream shop, then headed for the park. There they slid onto adjoining swings and finished their cones. It wasn't until she'd licked the ice cream from her upper lip and pushed off so the swing started moving gently that Gillian allowed her curiosity to get the better of her.

"So, what did you want to talk about?"

"Us."

"Can you be more specific?" she asked in her schoolteacher voice. But John knew she was protecting herself.

He watched her intently as he said, "I want there to be an 'us,' and I want everyone to know it. I'm not sorry I told the group, but I am sorry that you were upset and that I let you go home alone last night. I should have explained how I was feeling."

"What do you mean? How were you feeling?"

"Like a man who'd just discovered he was in love."

She stilled her swing. "Love?"

"Love," he said with certainty. "And I would like to shout it from the rooftops, but I won't if you don't want me to."

"The way gossip spreads in this town, all you'll have to do is whisper," she murmured.

"And you wouldn't mind if everyone knew?"

"I—I'm not sure."

He tried to read the mixed emotions flitting across her face. "I told you how I feel. What about you? Don't you feel the same? Or could I be wrong?"

"It isn't that simple," she said, skirting a direct answer and starting the swing moving again.

So she wouldn't have to look at him?

John was determined to get to the heart of the matter...her heart. Whether or not she was ready to admit her feelings for him, he couldn't let the subject drop.

"Does that mean you don't care about me?" he asked.

"Of course I care."

"You're just not sure about being in love, is that it?"

She pushed off again, swinging higher. "This relationship is developing too fast."

"If we were Kim's age, I would agree with you. But we're not. We're adults. We know our own minds. Don't we?" John prodded.

"Sometimes. But this situation is so complicated."

"By my daughters?"

"Well . . . yes."

John stilled the feeling of defensiveness that quickly rose to the fore. If they weren't honest with each other, their relationship wouldn't have a chance. He set his swing in motion so that it kept up with hers.

"Are you saying that your regard for me depends on how Kim and Tracy respond to you?"

"You have to admit they could be a problem," Gillian said, avoiding a direct answer. Her brow was furrowed, giving her a decidedly unhappy expression. "Kim's attitude isn't going to change fast."

"Kim will have to come around. I'm sure she doesn't dislike you underneath. And on the positive side," he went on, "Tracy is crazy about you."

"She's trying to adopt me because she can't deal with the fact that her real mother walked out on her."

John tried to reassure Gillian. "Once Tracy feels some sense of permanency in our relationship, I'm sure she'll settle down and give you some space."

Or once Tracy accepted Kate back into her life, she'd feel more secure, John thought.

"In the meantime, they'll keep fighting with each other because of me."

"Hey, is that what's been bothering you?"

"Of course it's been bothering me. I hate fighting!" Gillian said vehemently. "There was too much strife in the Flannery household."

"All families fight."

"Not like mine did." Her voice held a tinge of old hurt. "It was a horrible way to grow up. And I certainly don't want to be the cause of more stress in your life, John. Your daughters have suffered enough."

"You're right, but that has nothing to do with you. That's Kate's fault."

John remembered thinking Gillian was going to be smack in the middle of a family war. Realizing how much she would hate that—perhaps to the point of calling off their relationship—he grew desperate to reassure her. He brought his swing to an abrupt halt.

"Gillian, I'm sorry if my daughters or my situation with my ex-wife affect you adversely. I never meant that to happen. You came into my life at a tough time. I wish I had met you long before Kate decided to come back or after she and the girls were reconciled, but fate doesn't always treat us the way we would like. I refuse to give you up merely because things are a little rough right now. Give Kim and Tracy enough time and things will work out."

"I hope you're right."

That sounded more positive, but John wanted to encourage Gillian even further. She couldn't help having doubts about their relationship. He was the one with the ready-made family with all its inherent difficulties, so it was up to him to soothe her fears away. He rose, reached over and brought her swing to a stop with a jerk.

"Look, I'm not going to give up a wonderful relationship because my daughters have to work out some problems. See, I just can't seem to do anything about my emotions." He pulled her up and settled her against his chest, then wrapped his arms securely around her back. "I wasn't looking for love, but you walked into my life and there it was."

Splaying her hands flat against his chest and looking around as if nervous, she said, "You mean you walked into mine."

Was she afraid someone might be watching? John didn't care who saw them. He caught her face with a gentle hand and tilted it so she would have to meet his eyes.

"So I did," he said softly. "And to think that if Scott hadn't been teasing Kim about having sex, we might never have met each other."

If Gillian's emotions weren't responding, her body certainly was. He could feel the rapid beat of her heart against his chest, the expression in her eyes was soft and yielding, and her face was flushing with color again. He couldn't prevent his own quickening.

"Would you have preferred that we never met?" he asked.

Gillian shook her head. "No. Don't ever think that." Touching his face, she took a deep breath and whispered, "Because I love you, too, John, and I wouldn't give up that feeling for the world."

John felt as if his whole body were smiling at her admission. "Took you long enough," he murmured before capturing her mouth in a kiss.

Gillian felt as if she were drowning in John's kiss. Everything but his lips, his touch, his love, faded from her mind for a dizzying moment. When he finally lifted his head and ended the embrace, she felt disoriented, unable to readjust herself to the real world for a moment.

He was grinning. Her lips responded in kind, as if smiling were the most natural thing in the world. With John, she thought, it was.

"I don't want to give up on us, either," she told him. She ran a fingertip along his mustache and down to his chin. "I never really did. Our relationship picked up such speed that it made me a little nervous. I've never been in love before, not like this."

His grin grew even broader. "Then I'm glad I'm the one who has opened new experiences to you. The good ones, anyway," he amended.

"You know, I think, subconsciously, I've not only been blaming myself for the rocky date with the kids, but I imagined you wouldn't want to see me again because of it." And of course, he'd reinforced that idea the night before when he'd let her go home alone, but she wasn't about to voice that opinion. She was happy to be in his arms, connected once more.

John gave her a reassuring squeeze. "You know that's nonsense, I hope."

"I do now."

Gillian imagined the emotions that flowed between them were almost tangible. She wanted more. Much more. Enough to require privacy. She was in love and exalting in the fact that John loved her in return. They should be allowed to celebrate as two people in love had the right to do. But they were in a public park, for heaven's sake. Several passers-by had already given them long looks. By nightfall, the entire town would know of this little tryst.

"Are you expected home soon?" she asked.

"Nope. Both girls are at friends' houses. I told Tracy to be home at nine, Kim at ten. So I have the evening to myself." Letting his hands slip lower to cradle her hips, he asked, "What did you have in mind?"

She tried to match his sexy tone. "Maybe we should head back to my place."

"Homework?"

When she said, "I have something more personal in mind," his auburn brows raised.

"What are we waiting for?"

Grabbing her hand, John started running, and Gillian was hard-pressed to match his longer stride. Other than slowing a bit to cross streets, he kept up the pace. They were both breathing hard when they stumbled up the steps to her apartment. She'd hardly gotten the door open before John had her in his arms and was kissing her once more.

He kicked the door shut, twirled her around and backed her across the room to the couch, where he pressed her into its welcoming length. He straddled her, let his weight lightly cover her, all without breaking contact. His mouth dominated and caressed, his tongue explored and teased. And his hands . . . once he had her at his mercy, his hands did wicked things to her outside which in turn did even better wicked things to her insides.

When John finally came up for air, she was breathless and ready for more. Her glasses were so fogged up she couldn't see. . . .

Gillian giggled.

"What's so funny?"

"You're real hot stuff, Slater. Hot and steamy."

She giggled again when he removed her glasses and drew a heart in the steam on each lens. Then, without removing himself from where he had her wedged against the couch, he set them on the coffee table.

"Better?" he murmured.

"I wasn't complaining."

"How about if I try to fog up your eyeballs?"

"Maybe I'll fog up yours instead."

"Do your worst," he said encouragingly.

Taking up the challenge, Gillian inched her face closer to John's. She stroked his mustache with the tip of her tongue, tightened her

buttocks and tilted her hips so she was pressed hard against him.
He stirred, and the sensation took her breath away. The room
seemed to spin and tilt crazily. Wanting nothing more than to close
her eyes and give in to the exquisite feelings, she continued with her
seduction. She drew her fingers along his neck, caressing the
corded muscles that told her of John's strength and rising passion.

After running the tip of her tongue along the inside of his
mouth, she caught his lower lip with her teeth. Her hands slid along
his shoulders and down his arms to his waist. She tugged at his
workshirt, pulled it and his undershirt free of constriction, then slid
her hands up his naked back.

John stiffened as though he were hanging on to his control with
difficulty, but he couldn't stifle the groan of satisfaction that
started deep inside him. Gillian was hard-pressed to keep from
groaning herself. His flesh was warm and vibrant under her
searching hands.

"Tell me what you want," he whispered seductively.

"You. I want you. I want you to touch me," she said, taking his
hand and sliding it between their bodies. He allowed her to guide
him, to draw his hand down inside her sweatpants and below the
lace-trimmed bikinis she wore. "Here." Her breath came as ragged as her pulse when he found her.

John pressed and stroked and kissed and murmured sexily until
waves of pleasure rolled through her. A drumming in her ears made
everything seem so unreal. And yet John was the most real, most
earthy man she'd ever been with. Her man. The man she loved. She
pushed his collar out of the way, bit his neck lightly, felt goose-
flesh form under her fingertips. She nipped him again, harder.

"I want you to make love to me."

No sooner had she said it than he was removing her sweatpants.
The sweatshirt followed suit. She undid his buttons and unzipped
his jeans, then explored him thoroughly while he cupped her
breasts and stroked her nipples through her bra's sheer fabric.

"Lacy underwear. Who would've guessed."

"Let's discuss my underwear later," she urged, pulling his over
his hips.

When they toppled onto the bed, Gillian somehow ended on top.
He stripped her of the fragile underwear and Gillian slid back,
stroking his hips and thighs. She created patterns of love with her

mouth, not stopping until John shuddered and caught her hair, pulling her up over him into position. He cradled her hips with his hands, arched and impaled her, at the same time capturing one of her nipples between his teeth. The urgent softness of his mouth stripped her of control. Her world went spinning.

A moment later, Gillian cried out, the sound of her ecstasy echoed by one intensely male.

"I love you," she whispered.

"I love you."

They lay entwined for what seemed like an eternity. When John shifted restlessly, Gillian rose and grabbed his hand. She tugged and he followed.

"Where are you taking me?"

"To the shower. Lots of steam in there."

John's laughter was soon replaced by intense sounds and a fierce desire they satisfied in diverting ways.

Afterward, happy, satiated and hungry, Gillian suggested they raid the refrigerator and freezer for an impromptu dinner. The sun had set and the air had grown chill, so John volunteered to build a fire. He set about the task, whistling happily, while she broiled pork chops and made stir-fry vegetables. Once again, they shared a meal sitting on the floor.

Gillian was beginning to think this was the best way to eat.

That reminded her of a less-satisfying meal, one they'd discussed earlier. Worried about John's younger daughter, she asked, "How's Tracy doing?"

"Terrific, considering."

"She's a pretty spunky kid, but she must be hurting terribly." Gillian wrapped her arms around her knees and stared into the fire as John quickly took their empty plates to the kitchen. "Why else would she cling to a woman she barely knows?"

"Seeing Kate would be healthy for her, but she won't even stay in the same room when I bring up the subject," John said. "I've tried a couple of times. Kim seemed anxious to see her mother when I first asked her about it, but she hasn't mentioned it since."

"Maybe she's being careful of Tracy's feelings."

"Possibly." Back at her side, he threw another log onto the fire. "A couple of times I've noticed Kim has taken Tracy's feelings to heart. That's certainly unusual."

"Hey, even if sisters fight, they can still love each other." She was the voice of experience speaking.

"True. But neither Kim nor Tracy would admit it."

"They will when they're older. Give them time."

"Exactly what I suggested you do," he reminded her. "Give them time...and another chance. I'm taking the girls camping this weekend. We leave tomorrow night and come back Sunday evening." He stroked her cheek lovingly. "Want to be part of an outdoor adventure?"

Remembering how she'd avoided answering Tracy when the girl had asked her to go, Gillian hedged once more. "I haven't had much experience with the great outdoors."

"So what. None of us are experts, but we always manage to enjoy ourselves. Say you'll come." He took her hand. "Please." Squeezed it. "For me." Kissed it. "For us."

When he put it like that, she could hardly refuse. Despite her reservations about spending a few days back-to-back with his daughters before they'd had a chance to get used to her, she agreed. "All right. I'll come."

"Hmm. Is that Freudian phrasing?" John immediately asked.

He had a gleam in his eyes that made Gillian shiver with anticipation. It was getting late—he had to get home before Tracy—but they might just have enough time....

"Take it any way you want," she said.

"What I want right now is dessert."

"You already had ice cream."

"That's not exactly what I had in mind." Leaving her side for a moment, John walked to her workstation where he picked up the apple he'd brought her. He threw the piece of fruit a few feet into the air and caught it, took a bite and offered it to her. "Does this give you any ideas?" he asked.

Gillian began stripping.

CHAPTER TEN

"KIM!" John hollered from his position at the stove. "Breakfast is ready. If you don't hurry, you're going to be late for school."

The sound of feet running down stairs was followed by Kim's return shout. "Coming, Dad." A few seconds later, she rushed into the kitchen. "But I really don't have time to eat. I'll just grab a piece of toast."

"You know how I feel about starting the day right with a good..."

John's words trailed off into shocked silence as he turned toward her with the pan of scrambled eggs in hand. He could hardly believe his daughter's garish appearance. Dressed in Day-Glo lime green—a better name would be *slime* green—that clashed with her wildly gelled auburn hair and made her skin look sallow and jaundiced, Kim seemed more appropriately dressed for a rock concert than for school. No matter the destination, her knee-length spandex pants hugged her maturing curves far too tightly for his peace of mind. And the matching crop top left two inches of her stomach exposed!

From the table, Tracy made none-to-subtle gagging noises she pretended to smother behind her hand. Kim was about to lay into her younger sister when John stepped forward and intervened.

"You'll not only take the time to eat, young lady, you'll change your clothes, as well."

"Da-a-ad, don't be so uptight." In a fit of pique, Kim threw the unfinished piece of toast onto the table. "I can't wait for Laura and my other friends to see my new outfit. We'll be gone on this dumb camping trip all weekend, so if I can't wear this to school—"

"I didn't give you money to buy another new outfit." And if he had, he certainly wouldn't have allowed her to buy this one.

Kim avoided his eyes. "It's not that new."

"Then why haven't your friends seen it before?" Frowning at her uncalled-for nervous reaction as well as at her protest—she'd said the black blouse she'd worn on the pizza date hadn't been so new, either—he ladled eggs into the three plates already on the table. "You always go shopping with your friends, anyway, don't you?"

"Yeah, sure. Usually."

"Well, then?"

"Well, they haven't seen it *on* me."

An unpleasant suspicion taking root in his mind, John set down the frying pan and faced her, fists on his hips. "Kim, exactly *when* did you buy this outfit?"

Avoiding his eyes, Kim spun toward the doorway. "Dad, if you want me to change, I will. Okay?"

"Stop right in your tracks, young lady." She froze and muttered something under her breath, but John wasn't about to let her off the hook. "I'm waiting for an answer about this mysterious shopping trip."

For a moment he didn't think he would get one. Then Kim turned, and, arms crossed over her chest, she said, "Last night." But she still wasn't looking at him.

"You told me you and Laura were going to study." The flush on her cheeks was more revealing than words. And he didn't remember her carrying any package into the house. She must have stuffed the purchase into her book bag. "You lied to me, is that it?"

"I didn't mean to."

"Yes, you did," Tracy piped up from the table. Now it was she who seemed out of sorts. She slapped down her orange juice so hard it sloshed over the side of the glass. "Why don't you just tell Dad the truth and get it over with?"

Kim traded scathing looks with her younger sister. "Big mouth!"

"I'd like to hear the truth, Kim," John said, waiting for his suspicion to be confirmed. "Just who bought you that outfit? I know you didn't have the money for it earlier this week since I declined to give you an advance on your allowance like you wanted me to."

Her mumbled answer was unintelligible, yet it made the hair rise on the back of his neck. "Who?" he demanded.

Kim lifted defiant eyes to his own. "Mom. Mom bought me new clothes. Okay?"

Exactly what he'd been afraid of. "No, it's not okay. You've seen your mother and you didn't tell me?"

"She said not to. She said you'd be upset. And she was right."

"Of course I'm upset." Not only because Kate had forced the encounter in her own inimitable way, but especially because Kim had lied to him on her mother's orders. Great values Kate was passing on to their daughters! "I thought I taught you to be truthful, Kim."

She skirted the real issue. "You told me I could see Mom if I wanted to."

"But not until things were settled around here." John glanced at Tracy, who'd gone very white and still, her expression mulish. A bubble seemed to expand in his chest and he couldn't do a thing to make it recede. With effort, he softened his tone. "Tracy, honey, did you see your mother?"

Nodding her head, his younger daughter looked as if she were about to burst into tears. "I didn't want to, but she followed me up to my room and—"

"When?"

"Last Friday when you took Miss Flannery on a date. She made me go with her, but I told her she wasn't my mother anymore and I wouldn't let her buy me anything," Tracy stated as if trying to assure him of her loyalty. "When she got us home, she said I had to keep her secret—" she glanced nervously at her older sister "—and Kim threatened to cut off my hair when I was sleeping if I told."

"Kim!"

"I was only kidding, Dad!"

"No she wasn't!"

No wonder the girls had been at each others' throats all week. He had Kate to thank for the chaos in his household. And Tracy's clinging to Gillian made sense now. In her own way, Tracy was denying her mother the affection Kate thought her due. What a mess!

Was there no end to the havoc his ex-wife was willing to wreak to get her own way?

"So you both saw your mother again last night?"

Again while he was with Gillian, John realized, suddenly feeling guilty for what had been one of the most special nights in his life. Rather than making love with Gillian, he should have been at home where he could protect his family. With no one else to look out for their best interests, his daughters had to be his priority.

"Mom took me shopping, but Tracy refused to go," Kim admitted. "She was at her friend's house like she said. But I didn't do anything wrong," she added defensively. "I just took what Mom owed me."

Hoping that he'd misunderstood, John asked, "You what?"

"Buying us a few nice things was the least Mom could do after walking out on us." Kim's eyes filled with tears. "Not that new clothes can make what she did okay. But at least it's something."

Not knowing what to say, John stared. He hadn't realized how negatively Kim had been affected by Kate's unexpected return. Her expression revealed all. What a dolt he was! He'd been so worried about Tracy, who'd shown her emotions in a more forthright manner, that he hadn't even noticed his older daughter was suffering as well.

Another thing to feel guilty about.

"So what are you going to do?" Kim asked. "Cancel the camping trip?"

That she actually sounded hopeful made John more determined than ever to pull off the weekend without a hitch. He and his daughters needed to spend time together... and with Gillian. The more they saw of the woman he loved, the more comfortable both Kim and Tracy would be with her. He was determined to make their relationship work.

And getting the girls out of town where Kate couldn't get at them for a few days was the best move he could make in that direction. In addition to their getting to know Gillian better, Kim and Tracy would have a chance to cool down. And maybe now that he knew about their mother's visits, they could open up to him. He would try to convince them to open up to Kate, as well, if only to tell their mother how they really felt about her leaving them.

If nothing else, a few days away would give them all a short vacation from stress, John assured himself.

"The camping trip is on," he stated firmly. "But those clothes are coming off right now, young lady... and going back to the store."

From Kim's crushed expression, he could see that was punishment enough. Besides, he couldn't really blame her for reacting to her mother's return as she had. Not that he would let her think her actions were acceptable.

"I'm going to forget about your lies this time, Kim," John told her. "But I hope you won't disappoint me again."

"I'm sorry, Dad. I'll go change now."

As his daughter ran from the room, John hoped Kate's influence wouldn't follow them throughout the weekend. He dreaded bringing Gillian into the midst of any more turmoil. And before Kate could do further harm, he was determined to meet his ex-wife in person and tell her exactly what he thought of her selfish, misguided actions.

JOHN WANTED TO SEE HER! He'd called her at work early and had made a luncheon date to discuss the girls. Kate had marveled over the fact all morning. Soon, she thought victoriously, soon she would have her visitation rights and could see her daughters any time she wanted. Several days a week at least, she thought as she walked from the Circle Center shopping mall to Union Station where they'd agreed to meet. She could hardly contain her excitement.

Her stubborn ex-husband was finally coming around to seeing her point of view. If only he could have done that more often when they were married....

Not that she wanted John Slater back. As a matter of fact, after her last disastrous relationship, Kate wasn't sure she wanted to get too close to any man ever again. The ones she'd been involved with so far hadn't been worth all the energy and love she'd poured into those romantic alliances, nor the heartache she'd taken away with her.

But Kim and Tracy wouldn't try to end their relationship with her. They were her daughters, her flesh and blood, and would be forever. She could never lose them.

Now was the time to make sure she had some stability in her life. She deserved so much more emotionally than she'd ever gotten from a man. Surely her daughters wouldn't begrudge her future happiness because of a mistake she'd made in the past.

Kate frowned as she remembered Tracy's reaction to her unannounced arrival. Her daughter's claims of being motherless had nearly broken her heart. But Tracy would get over her feelings of betrayal and resentment, Kate vowed. She would make up every one of those five years of separation if it was the last thing she ever did. All she needed was time with her daughters, and John was obviously ready to give her that.

Her step was confident as she entered Union Station and made her way through the lunchtime crowd to Hobos, a small but popular eatery new to the renovated complex. The place was quaint, decorated like a railroad car, its walls strung with photographed portraits of hobos in railroad yards and in train cars. John was already seated, drumming his fingers on the table and checking his watch.

Kate stopped. Her stomach fluttered, especially when she noted the expression distorting his still-handsome face. Unaware of her presence, he was scowling. She checked her own watch and realized she was ten minutes late. No doubt he wanted to get this over with as much as she did. Forcing her lips into a smile he would read as confident, she approached.

"John, good to see you again."

She offered her hand. For a moment, she thought he might not take it. But, as he'd always been in the past with strangers and acquaintances, he was too much of a gentleman now to make her uncomfortable. He stood and, politely if briefly, grasped her hand.

"Kate."

His nod was as curt as the handshake. No words of welcome. Her stomach fluttered again as she slid into a chair opposite him. Within seconds, a friendly waiter dressed like a tramp descended on their table and took their order. If Kate had imagined she and John might spend a few minutes chitchatting—catching up on the past five years—she was mistaken. Also as always, her ex-husband was unnervingly direct.

"I hear you've seen the girls behind my back."

Kate lifted her chin and held his gaze. "Yes. I got tired of waiting for your permission." As if she needed it to see her own daughters!

"And you told them to lie to me about it."

"I did no such thing!" At John's raised eyebrow, she explained, "I merely told them there was no reason to mention my visit if you didn't ask."

"Well, that makes all the difference in the world," he said, his voice laced with sarcasm. "You're merely teaching them to lie by omission."

"John Slater, don't you dare judge me." Kate allowed her hurt to show through. "You have no idea of what my life has been like for the past five years."

"No, I don't. You saw to that when you left us for the world of romance and adventure and honest communication with what's-his-name."

She tried to ignore her ex-husband's hostile tone, but it ate away at her already-raw emotions. "All I could think about was the time when I'd get to see my babies."

"That's a load of garbage, Kate." His scowl deepened, and she could almost feel his disgust with her. "You could have seen the girls if you'd wanted to. All you had to do was come back to Indianapolis."

"I'm back now."

"A little late."

"Better late than never." Kate gave him a beseeching look. "John, please let's stop this."

The argument reminded her of the last months of their marriage. Only then *he* had been the one on the defensive after using their savings to start a business with David. *John* had been responsible for the demise of their marriage, not she, Kate reminded herself. But that had been a lifetime ago, and she was willing to forgive and forget if he was.

"Can't we start fresh?" she pleaded. A woman at the next table was staring at her, making her uncomfortable. This meeting was not going as she had imagined. She curled her hands into each other as if the action would give her strength. "That's what I'm trying to do by coming back here. I've finally learned how to support and take care of myself. I've accepted being alone. Without a man," she amended quickly.

And that had taken such courage . . . but John would never understand even if she tried to explain. He'd always been so sure of himself, so sure of what he'd wanted, even though he'd been as young as she was when they'd married. He had no idea of how feeling dependent and helpless could cripple a person, no matter her good intentions. She drew the conversation back to the purpose of their meeting.

"Right now, reestablishing a relationship with our daughters is the most important thing in the world to me."

"Is that why you're trying to bribe your way back into their lives?"

Kate's mouth dropped open at the accusation. "How dare you!"

"I dare speak the truth." She could tell John's temper was on a tight leash when he continued. "I don't know what else you would call taking a teenager shopping and buying her anything her heart desires, no matter how inappropriate."

While Kate had disliked the Day-Glo pants and top Kim had chosen so enthusiastically, she knew teenagers had their own fashion code—an expensive one that she could ill afford on her modest salary. "There was nothing inappropriate about Kim's outfit."

"I'll decide what's appropriate for my daughter."

Good intentions be damned! "Kim's my daughter, too." He couldn't take *that* away from her...though he'd been doing his best. "As is Tracy."

"Even if the poor kid doesn't want to be."

"And exactly why does she claim to have no mother?" Kate demanded, her throat tightening. The pain she'd felt when she'd tried to get close to her younger daughter still haunted her. Why would Tracy turn against her so completely that she could wish her own mother dead? "Maybe because you poisoned her mind against me."

"Don't be ridiculous."

"Thank you so much." Her own anger burning brightly, Kate wondered how she could ever have loved this man. "Now you're adding ridiculous to my other shortcomings."

"Kate..." John shook his head and furrowed his brow. "This isn't getting us anywhere."

She wondered how she could have fooled herself into believing he meant to be reasonable at last. "You're damned right it isn't."

"I know we have to come to some compromise about the visitation rights, but Tracy is feeling too insecure for me to push it. I'll try to talk to her, but you've got to be reasonable—"

"Reasonable? Visitation rights?" Kate rose so quickly her chair teetered behind her. Backed into a corner, she was ready to come out fighting. "I was willing to settle for crumbs a week ago, John Slater. But not now. *Now* I intend to sue for joint custody."

"Over my dead body!"

"Anything is possible," she said, her voice steadier than she was feeling.

As she turned her back on her ex-husband and pushed her way past the waiter who'd arrived with their order, John yelled, "Kate, come back here," just as if he were speaking to a child.

Kate continued on right out the door and around the corner, where she leaned against the building for support. Never having done anything that took so much guts before, she was shaking and her knees were threatening to collapse.

Joint custody?

As much as she would like to think it possible, Kate knew her chances of succeeding were slim, if not nil. But she was getting desperate. Now that John knew about her furtive visits to their daughters, he would be on guard to thwart her if she tried to see them again. What was she going to do?

Before she could crumble under the emotional pressure, Kate took herself in hand, straightened her spine and left the support of the building. Kim and Tracy were her daughters. She would do whatever was necessary to get them back into her life.

"HOW MUCH FARTHER IS IT?" Kim asked irritably from the back seat of the car.

Trying to ignore everything but thoughts of a cozy fire and roasting marshmallows, Gillian stared blankly out the front window and counted oncoming cars.

Two hundred and fifty-six, two fifty-seven...

They were well on their way to Turkey Run State Park, and since they'd left Greenville earlier that evening, Kim had barely stopped complaining long enough to pick on her sister. They hadn't gone far before Gillian had adopted a childhood method of removing herself from the bickering.

When the teenager didn't get a response from anyone, she added, "I'm going to scream if I can't stretch my legs soon." The threat was followed by her shifting and cry of displeasure.

"Relax already," John ordered. "We're almost there."

"I can't relax."

Two hundred and fifty-eight.

Gillian was having a difficult time loosening herself up. Not only were the back-seat squabbles getting on her nerves, but John had been acting kind of weird ever since he'd arrived at her place. Rather than taking her into his arms for a serious embrace as she'd expected, he'd hardly taken the time to brush her lips before grabbing her bag and marching back out to the car.

What in the world had happened in the last twenty-four hours to sour his mood?

"Ki-i-im, move over, would you?" Tracy suddenly complained. "You're hogging the whole seat."

"I can't help it. It's too crowded back here."

Two fifty-nine.

John made a sound that indicated he was exasperated himself. "You shouldn't have brought so much stuff that we couldn't fit everything in the trunk."

"We never had this problem before," Kim whined. "This car is perfect for *three* of us."

Gillian stiffened and let the next few sets of headlights go by without counting. The teenager wasn't even trying to hide her resentment at her teacher's presence. Then Tracy slid forward and put a hand on Gillian's shoulder.

"But it's going to be so much more fun with Miss Flannery along."

"Yeah, right."

"Kim, *enough*," John growled.

The teenager subsided into a hostile silence, and John slid his right hand over the seat to find Gillian's. Comforted by his fingers lacing through hers, she glanced his way and smiled wanly. Not that he could see her. The sun had set long ago. Setting up camp in the dark was going to be a challenging experience—more fun, she hoped, than the drive. At least everyone would be able to stretch their legs and backs....

She should have known she was being too optimistic, Gillian realized after they arrived at the park and pulled up to their tree-lined campsite set in a small valley. The girls couldn't even help unload the car without getting in each others' way. Heads buried in the trunk, they were hip-to-hip, pushing at each other.

Tracy lost her footing and almost fell. "Hey, what do you think you're doing?" she demanded of her sister.

"Looking for my jeans. My legs are cold."

"Only a dope would wear shorts in October."

Maybe she should start counting stars, Gillian thought. That could keep her busy until bedtime.

John placed himself between his daughters. "Before you two start World War III, has anyone seen the ground cloth?"

"Tracy must have put it someplace," Kim replied.

"Baloney, Dad. Kim probably threw it under the car or in the bushes when she was trying to get at her stupid ghetto blaster."

John began rifling through the trunk himself, and Gillian began counting stars. Too bad she couldn't really shut off Kim's whine.

"My *stereo* is important."

"Oh, sure, you really need it on a camping trip," Tracy said sarcastically. "I thought we were supposed to be able to hear nature."

"What? You mean crickets? Of course, *you* would like to listen to a bunch of disgusting bugs rather than a hot group."

"Crickets aren't disgust—"

"Enough, already," John thundered. Having found what he was looking for, he stalked away from them and spread the ground cloth several yards away from the picnic table. "Can't we get a little campground spirit around here? We need to set up the tent, get a fire going and warm up the chili. I'm sure we'll all feel better after having something to eat."

"I have to change first," Kim said, holding up her jeans.

"Hurry." When the teenager headed out of the camp area, John asked, "Wait a minute. There's some bushes right there."

"Forget it Dad. I'm not stripping out here. I'll change in the facilities."

He waved her on and turned to Gillian. "Actually I rather thought some bushes would do just fine, but my insisting wouldn't go over too well right now."

"Teenage girls like privacy," Gillian said, remembering her own desires for that hard-earned commodity. In a lower voice, she added, "Adult women like privacy, too."

John caught her drift and sighed. "I'm afraid we won't have much of that this weekend. If the girls don't make you so crazy that you hitch a ride with someone else, maybe we can sneak off alone somewhere tomorrow."

"I won't run away, though spending time alone is a nice thought."

One that made Gillian relax a little. The girls must have started irritating John the moment they left home. Obviously his negative mood had nothing to do with her—thank goodness! Working as a team, they drove stakes into the ground and set up the tent while Tracy cleaned out the fire pit and carefully arranged logs in the middle of the ring. Only after all the major work had been completed and the camp fire started did Kim come waltzing back to camp.

She dropped her shorts on the picnic table bench and asked, "Isn't the food on yet? I'm starving."

Gillian was relieved when both John and Tracy let the comment pass.

"Get the sleeping bags and set them up in the tent," John told Kim.

Unbelievably Kim headed for the car without complaint. While John went through the stores of food he'd brought, Gillian wandered over to where Tracy tended the camp fire, which was now flaming brightly. She ruffled the girl's hair.

"That's a great fire."

Tracy looked up and gave her an impish smile. "Thanks. Dad taught me how to set the bigger logs on the bottom and put smaller stuff on top to get the fire going right. Now when we go camping, it's my job." She nodded toward her sister, who had just removed a single sleeping bag from the car and was poking along. "Kim's supposed to help set up the tent."

Not wanting to encourage the younger girl's resentment, Gillian said, "I was happy to help your dad. It's been a long time since I've had the opportunity to camp."

"*I'm* glad you came."

"And so am I," John added, hunkering down next to them. He indicated the coffee can he was holding. "This is Tracy's secret chili recipe. Wait until you taste it. She always makes the chili ahead of time when we go camping. Then we load an empty two-pound can and set it directly over the flames." He placed the chili on a small section of grating at the edge of the fire pit. "Dinner will be ready in five minutes, and there'll be no messy cleanup because we throw the can away."

"Clever," Gillian murmured.

"Makes for some happy campers," he said knowingly.

They could use one more of those, she thought. Kim was now carrying another sleeping bag to the tent. The coverings were so light, she could have made one or two trips instead of four. And she certainly could quicken her pace. Was she trying to make an all-night project of setting up their bedding?

Just about. The teenager didn't join the others until the table was set, the chili was hot, and they were ready to eat. The adults sat on one side of the table, the two girls on the other. Chili was heaped on styrofoam plates and topped with chopped cheddar cheese and sour cream.

"Delicious," Gillian told Tracy after tasting it. "Is the recipe really a secret?"

"Sort of. I like to take recipes from books and magazines and add my own stuff." The younger girl's face beamed in the lantern light. "But I can tell you how to make it if you want."

Gillian was touched the girl was willing to share her secret. "I'd like that. Maybe I can make a big pot sometime soon and invite my three younger sisters over for dinner. They're always complaining about not having the time to share a good meal."

"Yeah," Tracy said, giving Kim a sly glance. "Some sisters don't want to know how to cook."

Kim's elbow made contact with Tracy's ribs. The younger girl whacked the older with her spoon.

"Ladies," John said, his tone warning.

Kim was inspecting her sleeve. "You crud. You got chili on my new T-shirt."

"It'll wash off," an unruffled Tracy told her before resuming eating.

Gillian was thankful Kim didn't pursue the argument. For the rest of the meal, she stewed in silence.

John sneakily kept Gillian's attention off the girls and on him by rubbing his leg up against hers under the table. He even brushed his hand along her calf when he reached down to pick up a fallen pop can. Furtively responding in kind, she was grateful for their dark surroundings. Not only did their actions go unnoticed, no one would be able to tell she was blushing by lantern light.

If only there was some way she and John *could* be alone...but, of course, it was impossible to be *that* alone this weekend and they both knew it. Having to put lovemaking on hold was one of the problems of dating a single parent.

After dinner, John said, "I'll find the marshmallows. Tracy, how about getting the skewers. And Kim, you can clean up the table."

"No assignment for me?" Gillian asked softly.

He gave her a penetrating look. "Yours can wait until later."

Reading his expression, Gillian sighed. Much later. Days later. Still, a thrill shot through her. Anticipation would make their being together all that much sweeter when they finally were able to arrange a night alone.

For the next half hour, all four enjoyed themselves roasting and eating marshmallows. Tracy managed to get the sticky stuff all over her face and hands. A cleanup trip to the facilities was in order. They set off together, Tracy in the lead with the biggest flashlight, Kim bringing up the rear several paces behind the others.

Once in the women's room, Gillian tried to form a friendly bond with the older girl. "Want me to help you get that chili out of your sleeve?"

Kim actually looked grateful. "Yeah, thanks."

Using the bar of soap she'd brought along, Gillian did her best, but when she was finished, a light stain remained. "I'm sure the rest will come out in the wash."

The teenager gave her sister a resentful glare. "It'd better."

"If it doesn't, it's your own fault," Tracy spat.

The twelve-year-old grabbed Gillian's hand and huddled into her side, which made Kim back away. Great. She could be allied with one or the other of the girls, but not with both. Tight-lipped, Kim took her own flashlight out of her pocket and rushed outside where John was already waiting for them. He grasped Gillian's free hand, and the three followed the teenager back to camp.

They were within yards of the tent when Kim stopped dead in her tracks.

Gillian heard a rustling noise.

"Hey, what's going on?" Kim whispered, focusing the beam of the flashlight on the picnic table.

Green eyes glowed in the dark and a startled-looking animal stuffed a marshmallow into its mouth and flew to the ground.

"Raccoons!" Tracy whispered excitedly. Turning on her own flashlight, she swept the area. Another animal froze near a tree and stared. "Neat." She drew closer. The raccoon scampered away and joined a third. "We're surrounded."

"Think they'll attack?" Gillian joked. "They're wearing their masks."

"They're thieves, all right." John lit the lantern on the table. "Doesn't look like there's too much damage."

"Oh, yes there is," Kim suddenly wailed. "My best shorts!" They were lying on the ground. Picking up the garment, she inspected a gaping hole. "They're ruined!"

"Why would the raccoons be interested in clothing?" Gillian asked, puzzled. "They were looking for something to eat...not for something to wear," she added, trying to lighten the atmosphere.

"She probably had a candy bar in the pocket," Tracy offered. "She's a chocolate freak."

"You're a freak, and those rotten raccoons are dead meat! If one of them comes any closer, I'm going to bash it over the head with a piece of firewood."

"You better not!" Tracy cried.

"I will!" Kim insisted, her voice growing shrill. "And I'll throw its lifeless body into the fire and roast it, too!"

With a scream, Tracy jumped her sister, fists flying. The two girls hit the dirt before anyone could get between them. Appalled, Gillian could only stare at the free-for-all that had been building up all evening. As they traded punches, John reached down and grabbed them both by the scruff of the neck.

"If you don't stop *now*, I'm going to roast both of you!" He let go and the girls backed off. "Thank you. Now, I think we should clean up and go to bed. Obviously you two needed naps today."

Neither girl said a word. Not while cleaning up and not while crawling into the tent and setting their sleeping bags at opposite corners, as far away from each other as they could get. Gillian was tense and uncomfortable. She wished she had refused John's invitation to come on the family outing. Though he tried to reassure her silently—with looks and comforting touches—she couldn't help but be dismayed by the bad vibrations that seemed to cling to the walls of the tent.

If only she could see those stars to count them....

Within minutes, the others were asleep. Gillian lay awake, listening to the even breathing. How could they sleep so easily? Her head was spinning. She was convinced that if she hadn't been along, the girls would never have gotten into such a serious fight. How did other women who dated single fathers handle such antagonism? How could anyone last long enough to become a stepmother? And, then, what if there were additional children? Gillian didn't even want to think about the complications, but she couldn't help it. If only she could run away from the unwelcome stress as fast as her legs would carry her.

A rustle in nearby bushes caught her attention. Another raccoon raid? More rustling was followed by agitated animal voices and then a screech that split the quiet. Heart pounding, Gillian flew straight up and sensed everyone else in the tent doing the same.

Tracy cried, "What was that?"

"Yeah, what's going on?" Kim demanded, sounding confused while John unzipped his bag as though he were going to check.

"Even the raccoons are arguing," Gillian muttered.

An ominous omen for the days ahead.

CHAPTER ELEVEN

"Aw, c'mon, Dad, Miss Flannery." Tracy stood at the top of a cliff and peered down at the two adults. "You guys can make it up here if you try."

"What do you think?" Gillian asked a bit breathlessly.

The rest of the uphill climb on the boulder-strewn path looked like more of a challenge than she cared to face, but if John were willing . . .

"I think an old man shouldn't be required to have as much stamina as his kid," he returned loud enough for his daughter to hear.

"You're not old, just well-seasoned," the girl argued.

Gillian laughed and John whispered, "She probably picked that up from one of her sister's magazines or a nighttime soap opera." To Tracy, he yelled, "Give us *well-seasoned* folks a break, honey. Why don't you go exploring without us? We'll wait for you and rest for a while."

"All right."

"You meet us back here in half an hour."

Tracy checked her watch. Her "Got it" held not a tinge of disappointment.

"I don't want you getting lost," John warned. "So make sure you stay on the trail."

"Da-a-ad, I know the rules, okay?"

"Okay. Have fun."

With a grin and a wave, Tracy turned her back on them and immediately disappeared.

"Whew!" Gillian gratefully sank back against the stone wall. "Saved from extreme torture."

"Hey, I thought teachers were supposed to be able to keep up with kids."

"Just as much as parents are. I have a notion that by tonight, we're *both* going to have tortured muscles we didn't even remember we owned."

Their laughter companionably coalesced and echoed along the rocks. Gillian realized she was having a pretty darn good time despite the negative start to their minivacation.

Magically, or so it seemed, the girls had mended fences while sleeping. They'd both risen in good spirits. Kim hadn't complained when Tracy asked for her help finding twigs and pine cones for the fire that morning. And the teenager had been the one to discover the object of the raccoons' loud dispute of the night before. The chili can, which must have contained enough leftovers to be choice pickings, had been discarded several yards behind the tent.

To Gillian's further surprise, the girls had actually fixed a hearty breakfast of gooseberry pancakes, scrambled eggs and sausage. They'd worked together and hadn't gotten into a single squabble.

As a matter of fact, Kim had been civil, if quiet, all morning. While she hadn't actually warmed up to Gillian, at least she'd been polite. No more snide remarks, no more references to what the trip might have been like had there only been the three of them. John had been right about giving the girl some time to get used to the woman her father was dating. Perhaps Gillian just needed more patience.

Kim's enthusiasm for the outdoor adventure had really sparked when she'd met a couple of teenagers from another campsite—and John had granted her permission to go hiking with them.

Gillian had thought Tracy might feel left out, but the younger girl had seemed perfectly happy to be on her own for a while.

Who could blame her? Turkey Run was made up of more than two thousand acres of virgin woods. Within the unique slice of Indiana were trails that took the hiker through deep, rock-walled canyons, along cliffs, across winding streams and through quiet forested areas. Fearless, good-natured Tracy would have a great time exploring.

And she and John would have a great time "resting" in a secluded area, Gillian thought with mounting anticipation when he placed a hand on the stone's face beside her head. She didn't have to be clairvoyant to know what he was up to. Her lips quirked and parted as he leaned closer. Her pulse picked up a beat; her quickened breath and flushed skin no longer had anything to do with the uphill hike.

John tucked her glasses into her hair, brushed her mouth with his mustache, then drew back slightly. "Are you a happy camper this afternoon?"

"Very."

"Good."

She reached up and touched his brow, ran seductive fingers along the vein of silver that slashed through his auburn hair. "Only one thing could make me happier."

"What?"

"More."

He gave her an innocent expression and nuzzled her lips with his mustache. "That?" he murmured, removing his mouth mere centimeters from hers.

"That."

Again he complied, this time seeking entrance which Gillian gladly gave. His tongue slid inside the smooth fold of her lips, skirted the sharp edge of her teeth and teased the uneven roof of her mouth. A small sound escaping the back of her throat triggered his like response.

Without freeing her mouth, John plucked her from the rocky wall, gathered her in his arms, and deepened the kiss. She was helpless to resist the pull of sensuality that enveloped her from top to toes. Encircling his neck with both arms, she felt light-headed, floated on air.

And then when John pressed and circled his hips against hers, she began to burn with desire. . . .

Calling up a reserve of inner strength, she freed her lips. "Forest fire!" she gasped.

"Huh?" Frowning, John froze and sniffed the air.

"You're going to start one if you don't watch out," she teased in an attempt to lighten the smoldering atmosphere they'd so quickly ignited.

John smiled and raised an eyebrow. His eyes held a hint of mischief. "And who are you supposed to be?" he asked, sliding his hands to her sides. "Smokey the Bear?" Not waiting for her comeback, he tickled her ribs.

"Hey!"

Gillian giggled and slapped at his hands until John caught her to him and trapped her arms securely within the fold of his. Their gazes meshed; laughter died in her throat. He kissed her again, as thoroughly as the first time.

She was helpless to stop him, but just then they heard the excited screams of young voices.

John freed her just as a half-dozen kids and a young woman trudged by them and continued up the path. The kids were giggling and whispering to one another, and every eye seemed to be glued to the couple.

Or so it seemed to Gillian when she set her glasses back in place.

Made to feel silly by the flush of embarrassment that swept up her neck, she moved away from the trysting spot and looked around for a comfortable perch. She spied a flat-topped boulder that would do.

"Break time," she said in a low, humor-filled voice. She climbed onto the rocky surface and settled down with a sigh. The noisy kids had already forgotten about them and were making their way up to the cliff. "We'd better take it easy. Tracy will expect us to be rested when she comes back. If we're out of breath, she'll wonder what we've been up to."

John didn't seem ready to give up, however. "We wouldn't want to disappoint her." A gleam in his eyes, he scrambled across the rock. "Tracy was the one who made us the love feast, remember?"

Gillian put out a hand to stay him. "But think about it logically for a minute. If we continue, we'll have to be disappointed ourselves."

Groaning, he settled down a few inches away from her. "Do you always have to be so logical?"

"What's wrong with being logical?"

"Nothing," he quickly said, obviously not meaning to censure her. "Can I at least hold you?" he asked in a lost-little-boy voice that made her laugh.

"Sure." She scooted closer and settled into his side. "How's that?"

"Better."

It was better than better, Gillian thought. It was wonderful.

A breeze sighed through the shady canyon, ruffling the broadleafed trees that were dressed in their bright autumn colors. Red, gold and yellow contrasted with the less-vibrant stone. A nearby stream gurgled as it mysteriously made its way through rock to the earthen floor, and a sparrow called to its unseen companion. The fresh scent of fall surrounded and soothed them.

Gillian was content to relax against John, pleased to be connected to his warmth. She closed her eyes, stretched, took a deep, satisfied breath. The night before, she wouldn't have believed she could be this happy.

"How different everything seems in the daylight, surrounded by such beauty," she murmured.

As if he'd been thinking about the bad start to the camping trip as well, John said, "Kate has a lot to atone for."

Not wanting to instigate a discussion of his ex-wife, and yet curious as to how Kate was involved, Gillian merely murmured a noncommittal "Hmm."

"You don't want to hear about her."

Sensing he needed to talk even though he was giving her a way out, she asked, "What happened?"

"Kate not only saw the girls behind my back—twice—but she tried to bribe them with new clothes. It didn't work with Tracy...."

"But it did with Kim?"

"Sort of. Kim felt her mother owed her something for walking out on her." John remained relaxed, but his vexation was clear in his tone. "I should have realized she was just as upset as Tracy over their mother's return, even if she didn't react negatively when I told her the news."

"Kids just express themselves in different ways." Coming from a family as large as hers, Gillian knew that for a fact. "You're not feeling guilty, are you?"

"A little," he admitted. "Not enough to condone Kim's actions, however. I told her she had to take back the outfit." He shifted as if he were uncomfortable. "I have a confession to make. She's probably viewing coming along on this camping trip as sort of a punishment, too." He hastened to explain. "She suggested I would probably cancel because of her lies, but of course I knew that was what she wanted...."

Gillian wasn't sure she liked the sound of that. Maybe under the circumstances, John shouldn't have pushed her and Kim together.

"No wonder she was so out of sorts last night."

Although, she hadn't seen Kim in a really excellent mood since she'd started dating the girl's father. But which bothered the teenager more? Gillian wondered. Her dating John or Kate's return?

Her stomach knotting at what she considered a very natural question, she asked, "John, you don't think Kim resents me because she thinks there's some chance of your getting back together with Kate, do you?"

He shrugged and gave her a reassuring squeeze. "Who knows how a teenager thinks? But don't worry, as much as I love my daughters and would do just about anything to make them happy, getting back with Kate is not a viable option."

She took a deep breath and relaxed a little. "Well, at least Tracy seems to be in a better place than last week. She's not as clingy."

"That's why I wanted you to come along this weekend. Tracy is already feeling more secure about our relationship. She thinks you're great."

She tilted her head to look at him. "Like Dad, like daughter?"

"Uh-uh. Dad thinks you're better than great. Try hot stuff." He nuzzled her neck, sending shivers down Gillian's spine. "Just remember that."

"I'll try."

It was easy to make such a promise when they were feeling so in tune with nature and with their relationship. That was the problem. This idyll was the exception rather than the rule, and Gillian felt the need to point out the fact.

"We don't exist in a vacuum, you know."

"I know. If we want our feelings for each other to grow, we'll have to work hard to overcome the real everyday obstacles that plague any couple—just like the ones in your marriage project," he added, crooking his eyebrows. "Kim may continue to have her irritating moods and we'll continue to deal with them. Just remember that you're not to blame, so don't take it personally."

Deep down, Gillian knew that any man's kids would probably resent her at first. The problem with Kim had been exacerbated not only by Kate's return but by their teacher-student relationship. Yet it was impossible not to take Kim's outbursts personally, and she couldn't help wondering if she wasn't contributing to the family strife. If she caused irreparable damage between John and his older daughter, she would never forgive herself.

This, added to the other doubts she had about their relationship, put her under incredible stress. John nuzzled her neck once more, coaxing Gillian to try to be more optimistic. She could win over Kim with patience, she told herself. Time would soften all their problems . . . time and true love.

With that happy thought in mind, she surrendered to another smoldering kiss.

GILLIAN AND TRACY were sound asleep when John woke the next morning, but Kim's sleeping bag was empty. Pulling on a long-sleeved sweatshirt against the morning's chill, he left the tent and found the teenager sitting Indian-style on the ground in front of the fire ring. She'd built a small fire and was staring at the dancing flames, which she fed with twigs. Her pretty face was set in a frown. Obviously brooding, she didn't notice his presence until he stood directly over her.

"Trouble sleeping?" he asked.

Kim shrugged. "Not really. I just woke up early."

John seated himself next to her with a grunt. He'd just found a few of those muscles Gillian had been warning him about. They sat in silence for a few minutes, listening to the crackling flames and the call of birds out for an early morning meal. He tried to relax, but he sensed something was wrong. How to find out what? Teenagers were so sensitive, and Kim had been touchier than usual lately.

Even so, she'd straightened out her act the day before—to his everlasting thanks. And to Gillian's, as well, he was sure. They'd had a peaceful and companionable dinner, and there'd been no more talk of roasting raccoons when the bold rascals had dared to skirt the campsite at dark, waiting for the opportunity to get their little paws on human food. Kim had joined Tracy in throwing them half a box of wheat crackers.

Hearing the girls laughing together had been reassuring. For weeks he'd wondered if they'd ever be close again.

Wanting to be close to his older daughter himself, he wrapped an arm around her shoulders.

"Sweetheart, you don't usually get up this early without a good reason. I have the feeling something is wrong. Want to talk about it?"

Kim merely shrugged and pitched a small piece of branch into the fire. The flames greedily licked, then devoured the wood.

John tried again. "Does that mean nothing is wrong or that you don't want to talk?"

"If I do, you'll just get mad at me again."

So something *was* eating at her. "I won't be angry if you tell me the truth, I promise. People who love each other should be able to share their feelings. Sometimes you just have to be careful about how you put things so you don't hurt someone else's feelings," John told her, hoping she wouldn't say anything terrible about the woman he loved. "But keeping secrets doesn't do anyone any good."

"You're sure you want me to be honest?"

He squeezed her shoulders. "Positive." At least he hoped he wouldn't be sorry.

"Well, you're always telling me to be an adult," Kim said, looking up at him through wary eyes. "But you don't think of me as one unless it suits your purpose."

Whatever he'd been expecting, it hadn't been this. "Hmm, want to explain?"

"If you really thought I was grown up, you would have told me about Mom's coming back to town right away instead of waiting like you did."

"I'm sorry about that, Kim. The timing was just bad."

"Mom said it was because you didn't want us to see her."

"Well, she was right about that. At first, I *didn't* want you girls to see your mother, but it was because I thought you'd been hurt enough," he explained. "Then I realized that I was wrong, that I was being overprotective. I figured seeing Kate might be the best thing for both you and Tracy. Something kept coming up and I kept putting off telling you for a better time. It just took longer than I expected."

"You shouldn't have been so mad that we saw Mom, anyway."

"I was angry with *her* because of Tracy, sweetheart. I didn't want to force your sister into anything she didn't want to do. You know she's never gotten over your mother's leaving. Not that it was easy for you," he quickly added, remembering how he'd misjudged Kim's feelings about Kate's return. "I thought given some time, Tracy might come around."

"And you were angry with me because I let Mom buy me some clothes you didn't like," Kim stated.

"Now that's not true. I was angry with you because you lied," John said, keeping his tone gentle. He didn't want her to think he was angry now, not when they were communicating so well. "I don't care if your mother wants to buy you things. I just want you to be honest with me, Kim. No more lies. I hope you can see the difference."

She stared down at her hands. "I guess so."

Though his daughter was silent, she wasn't relaxed. And she was chewing on her lower lip. From experience, John could tell there was more on her mind.

"Since we're on a roll with this honesty stuff, anything else you want to tell me?"

The teenager took a deep breath and gave him a quick glance before staring into the fire again. She shrugged her shoulders, and John gave her another encouraging squeeze.

"Come on. Might as well get it off your chest," he urged.

"Well ... if you thought of me as an adult, you wouldn't have invited Miss Flannery along on this camping trip without asking my opinion. You tell me to stop acting like a kid, then, next time I turn around, you treat me like one."

There it was. Her resentment of Gillian was finally in the open. Since she'd brought up the subject, John felt he, too, needed to be honest.

"Sometimes you don't act very grown up ... like with Gillian." Kim stiffened under his arm as he figured she would, yet she didn't pull away from him. "Don't you like her even a little?" he asked hopefully.

"She's all right ... for a teacher."

"But you still don't approve of my dating her?"

Kim frowned up at him. "I want you to be happy, Dad. If she makes you happy, I guess it's okay with me."

John smiled and kissed the frown away. "Now that's a grown-up thing to say." She didn't sound like the same self-centered teenager who had been driving him crazy for the past month. "Thinking about someone else other than yourself is a step in the right direction, kiddo."

"So, Gil ... Miss Flannery makes you happy, right?"

"Very."

"I knew it all along," she said with a resigned-sounding sigh.

The suspicion Gillian had voiced now crystallized in his mind. "Kim, you haven't been thinking your mother and I might get back together, have you?"

"No!" she said vehemently. "I thought about it for a long time because I wanted us to be a family again. But I guess I wouldn't *really* want you to." When he gave her a startled look, she said, "As much as I've missed Mom, I haven't missed the arguments you always used to have. You weren't happy and neither was she. I don't think you two were ever meant for each other."

"We thought we were a long time ago, but people change." John didn't want Kim to think that everything could always be worked out by logic as Gillian seemed to believe. "And people who love each other *do* argue."

"But they should also want the same things," Kim said in a flash of grown-up insight that amazed John. "You and Mom never did."

John could hardly believe her sensitivity to his and Kate's relationship. Kim had been only twelve when her mother left. Kids were sometimes too sophisticated because they were forced to grow up too fast. And as the elder of his daughters, Kim had always had the most responsibility even if it sometimes appeared that Tracy was the one who could be counted on. For years, Kim had been caught in that awful nebulous state of being half child, half woman. And now it seemed that she was ready to complete the transition.

"You really are growing up, you know that?" he murmured, wrapping both arms around Kim and giving her a fatherly hug.

"Am I?" she asked as she hugged him back. "Is it okay to be scared when you're grown up?"

"It's fine to be scared, Kim. I'm scared sometimes."

"Come on, Dad. You? I don't believe you're afraid of anything."

"That's how much you know. I get scared that I'm not raising you girls right. I'm scared that I'll lose you."

"To Mom?"

He laughed and tweaked her nose. "To some handsome man who'll come along and sweep you off your feet."

"Geez, if I ever get married, you won't lose me. You're always going to be my father, for pete's sake."

"And you're always going to be my daughter."

Her smile faded. "You're thinking about getting married?" she asked in a small voice.

John figured it would be in his best interests to keep the idea general, especially since he hadn't come to any decisions himself. "I've thought about getting married again lots of times in the past five years." That was certainly the truth. "A guy gets lonely, you know, even if he has the two best daughters in the world."

"Besides which, you just never found the right woman before."

He pushed a loose strand of auburn hair from her forehead. "Maybe you're even more grown-up than I realized."

She gave him a look that reminded him of Tracy at her most impish. "Does that mean I don't have any curfew?"

"No, smarty, that means I expect you to have more patience with your old man and to tell him when something is bothering you. It means we can sit down and discuss things together more than we have in the past."

"Like your getting married."

That she was serious but not upset made John smile. "Hey, don't rush me."

"Deal. But if that's what you want, Dad, I guess it's okay with me."

"Thanks, sweetheart. But don't jump the gun, okay? I'll let you know when I'm ready to make that decision," John assured her. He gave her a loud smack on the forehead. "Enough serious talk. This is still supposed to be a fun weekend. How about you and I getting a real big fire going for breakfast? We'll surprise Tracy and Gillian."

"Great."

He and Kim went to work setting up larger logs. They joked and laughed while they worked, and John felt better than he had in weeks. Things were going to work out fine between the girls and Gillian, after all. Now all he had to worry about was getting Tracy to the point where she could accept seeing her mother. Maybe he was expecting too much of her, and himself, by trying to work out the problem on their own. Perhaps he ought to give serious thought to family counseling. Involving a professional couldn't hurt.

The fire was rebuilt and flaming, and they'd started taking food from the trunk of the car before the tent zipper signaled someone else was awake. A sleepy Tracy crawled out of the tent followed by Gillian.

"Morning," Gillian called, her smiling blue eyes finding his immediately.

"Morning," John and Kim returned in chorus.

"Hey," Gillian said, "since you girls made such a great breakfast yesterday, I thought your Dad and I could cook this morning."

"Okay," Kim said.

"Are you sure you know how to cook over an open fire?" Tracy asked, her voice full of concern. "It can be pretty tricky, you know."

"Your Dad can give me pointers. If I burn anything, will you eat it anyway?"

"Sure. I used to burn stuff. It's okay."

John laughed. "We could use some water. How about it, girls?" He held up the collapsible two-gallon plastic jugs, both of which were empty.

Kim and Tracy each took one and raced down the path to the facilities. They were barely out of sight when John pulled Gillian into his arms for an enthusiastic kiss.

"Now that's the way to say good morning," she murmured with a happy smile.

"Sure is. And what a great morning it is."

"I think it's pretty special myself."

"Why's that?"

"I didn't mean to eavesdrop—" she squinched up her face into an endearing expression "—but you and Kim were only sitting a few yards from the tent."

"You heard our conversation?"

"Part of it, anyway. That she's accepted our seeing each other made my morning."

"Mine, too." John kissed her again, more thoroughly. Hands poked at him and a grinning Gillian pushed him away. "Hey, what's the big idea?" he demanded.

"We're supposed to be starting breakfast, remember? The mushy stuff will have to wait."

Grinning, John gave way. They would have lots of time for mushy stuff if he had anything to say about it. And for once, he wouldn't have to worry about Kim's disapproval. The future was looking rosy, indeed.

CHAPTER TWELVE

GILLIAN MET ELAINE PARKER and Wes Meyer in the hallway on her way to the classroom the following Wednesday night.

"You're early, too, hmm?" she observed with a smile, certain she'd interrupted a very personal conversation. Elaine and Wes had been whispering and laughing together as she approached. "You must be anxious to get started."

Wes grinned. "This project has been pretty interesting all right." He exchanged glances with Elaine, who was wearing a bright blue dress that complemented her brunette coloring.

"We've learned a lot," Elaine agreed.

And they'd gotten a lot closer, Gillian silently added, noting Elaine's shy but happy expression. If the couple wasn't dating already, they surely would be soon. Not that they'd be making a public announcement as John had last week.

Wanting to allow the couple their privacy, Gillian headed for the classroom. "See you in a few minutes."

"Right," Wes murmured, turning back to his partner.

Gillian smiled, pleased the evening was starting out on a positive note. But then, she'd been in a good mood since Sunday, having reached a new level of understanding with John . . . as well as Tracy and Kim. On the way back to Indianapolis, they had actually joked with Gillian, and everyone had joined in when Tracy sang along with the soft-rock lyrics on the car radio. The future was looking bright.

The future.

Kim had asked John if he planned on getting married, and he hadn't said no. But he'd also said he didn't want to be rushed, so maybe he only wanted to see a lot of her.

"Only two weeks left, aren't there?" Wes asked, entering the classroom with Elaine and interrupting Gillian's thoughts. "Do you run the project for six weeks in your high school classes, too?"

"The full project is set up for eight weeks. But it can last longer. In one sociology class, we worked on it most of the semester."

"Well, I'm going to miss our couple." Wes waited until Elaine took a seat, then eased down in the desk beside her. "Especially now that we seem to have ironed out the worst of their difficulties."

"We've got Mrs. M's brother-problem solved," Elaine added. "Our grocery bills were so high—we don't have the income that some of the other couples in this project have—and he was eating us out of house and home. We told him he'd have to get a part-time job after school."

"Sounds like a reasonable suggestion." Gillian sorted the evening's envelopes.

"Of course, we don't have anyone playing the part of Mrs. M's brother, so we don't know how things would really turn out," said Wes. "There's a limit to the game, so to speak. You know, I have an idea—have you ever thought about expanding the project logistics, maybe making it into a video game?"

The man was perfectly serious, so Gillian tried not to chuckle. "Do you really think it's that entertaining?" Personally she figured Wes might think differently if he'd had a less diverting partner.

"It was a lot of fun," Wes insisted. "I really learned something…and got to know Elaine. How about giving us the last two weeks' worth of assignments before we split up? There won't be any more group meetings, but there's no reason we can't finish up on our own."

This time, Gillian couldn't help but grin. "You want more assignments? Sure, I guess I can make you some copies." And she couldn't help feeling a little flattered despite Wes's ulterior motives. Usually a perfectionist who was never quite satisfied, she had to give herself credit once in a while.

Her feeling of self-confidence was shaken a few minutes later, however, when the Talbots arrived. Frowning, Derek greeted Gillian quickly and brushed past to take a seat, leaving his wife standing alone beside the teacher's desk.

Arlene Talbot seemed tense. "Don't you think we should discuss our problem with Miss Flannery, darling?"

"I already know there's no answer to the problem," said Derek.

Arlene shook her head and addressed Gillian, carefully lowering her voice. "He's being so stubborn. I've never seen him like this before."

"Let's talk about it in class," Gillian suggested.

"I'd rather talk to you alone." Arlene stepped away and took a seat beside Derek.

Was the Talbots' problem really that serious? Gillian wondered, wishing she could draw them aside immediately. But the other group members were arriving now, including the Bigsbys and John. She smiled warmly in return to John's greeting and then got down to business.

Asking for general feedback as usual, she dealt with a minor question from one couple and went on to announce the reason for the Fosters's two-week absence. On Monday, she'd received a letter from that couple. Serious family problems had forced them to take a trip out of town. She hoped the family problems weren't too awful but was relieved the Fosters hadn't just dropped out.

As soon as the group was finished with the general discussion, Gillian sat down beside John to review the newest slip they'd drawn. He seemed quiet but mellow, examining the addition thoughtfully.

"It's a good thing I didn't use our savings for that newsletter business. This says our apartment building has been sold and we have to move. That could be expensive."

"We'd have gotten by, even if you had invested in newsletter equipment," Gillian assured him, trying to be supportive. She still felt a little guilty for giving him a hard time about his idea.

"Together we can do anything, I'm sure." He leaned closer to whisper, his breath feathering across her cheek. "We'll soon have to find some other excuse to see a lot of each other. In two weeks, the project will be over."

"That's what Wes and Elaine were complaining about."

"Complaining?"

"They asked me for more assignments, so they could continue working with their couple. They think the project's fun."

John laughed. "Cute. Not that I can't come up with some more original excuses for playing house."

His heated gaze made chills crawl up and down Gillian's spine. Still, she knew they had to deal with the problem at hand. "Let's make some notes about the details involved with the Xerxes moving." She opened her spiral.

"If you insist."

Working quietly together after that, they made a few lists before the end of the session. When Gillian led a short, final group discussion, she noted that neither of the Talbots joined in and decided to approach them afterward.

"Do you have anything against going out for coffee tonight?" John asked quietly while everyone gathered up their materials.

"I'd love some coffee." And anything else he had in mind. But first Gillian had to talk to the Talbots. "Can you meet me outside in a few minutes? I need to discuss something with Derek and Arlene."

"Mr. and Mrs. Grouch?" He quirked his brows. "All right, maybe you can straighten them out. I'll wait for you downstairs by the front door."

Trying not to attract attention, Gillian quickly caught up with the other couple just as they were about to leave the room. "Why don't you stay for a few minutes after class?" she suggested. "I'd like to help."

Derek's expression was as remote as it had been when the meeting began. "I don't want to keep rehashing this situation."

"That's just it," Arlene complained. She gazed at Gillian. "He's not doing his part on this project anymore."

Derek crossed his arms over his chest. "It's pretty discouraging trying to break through a brick wall."

"But you're taking this too seriously... it's just a game," Arlene insisted.

"Right." Gillian hoped he'd see reason.

"I know it's a game." Derek adjusted his striped tie. "But I don't play games I can't win, whether it's Trivial Pursuit or the stock market. If you start to lose at most games, you can change your strategy. It's not like this." He tapped a finger on his notebook. "I'm nothing like this Mr. K. What a loser. No one with a half a brain would take a middle management job in a specialized industry these days."

Arlene frowned. "But you're only playing a role, like in a play or a movie."

"Well, I don't like my role. Furthermore, I don't want to argue."

"You're being impossible—"

"And there are only two weeks of the project left," Gillian cut in. "You've been doing great so far." Though she had to admit Derek Talbot had been acting annoyingly peevish since last week. "I don't blame you for hating to argue."

"Really? And do you realize that arguing is a natural outcome of the project you've set up, Miss Flannery?" Derek said accusingly. "This is no way to inspire kids to go out and take on life. You have to offer them more options or they'll get discouraged. They shouldn't have to lower their expectations."

"Now, Derek . . ." Arlene was looking at him disapprovingly.

Feeling defensive, Gillian realized Derek was frustrating her own expectations. How could he say that arguing was a natural outcome of her project?

"I only wish that everyone had the best options to choose from in real life," she told him. "Unfortunately only a small percentage of people make as much money as they'd like. And most people have some kind of problems with their family." But she saw that she'd have to soften her stance—he was in no mood to understand. "If it will help, why don't we just say that Mr. K gets a job. Make one up for him if you can't find it in the paper." That should satisfy the difficult man.

Derek shook his head. "Oh, no, you said that was unfair. I don't cheat."

Wanting to tear out her hair, Gillian managed to keep her voice even. "Then what *do* you want to do?"

Derek checked his watch. "Leave. It's getting late." He glanced at his wife and then at Gillian. "Don't worry about Mr. K, I'll come up with my own solution for him. Maybe he'll take off for another city and look for a job there."

"Without me, darling?" Arlene acted surprised. "Remember, we bought that condo together."

Derek shrugged. "You can have it if you want."

His wife tried to object, "But—"

Derek silenced his wife with a wave of his hand. "You know, sometimes people come to a parting of the ways, communication fails, whatever . . . and I'm tired." Shoving his notebook into his briefcase, he headed for the door. "I have to finish some paperwork before I go to sleep. Thank God, I have a real profession."

"I can't believe it." Arlene turned to Gillian in disgust. "I'm seeing a new side to the man I married—one I don't like!"

Appalled, Gillian wondered if the project was actually interfering with the Talbots' real marriage. Otherwise, why would Derek mention failure and a parting of the ways?

"We have to talk out your problems," she told Arlene, then realized Derek had gone off without his wife. "Is he waiting for you?"

"No, we brought separate cars." Arlene sighed. "Maybe Derek is right about talking serving no purpose. I'm ready to give up. I suppose life has been so perfect for us, we're not used to serious problems. We've always had an ideal marriage. Derek and I both love our careers and our children and have wanted the same things from life. We've rarely had a disagreement, not even in the couples' workshops we've attended. That's why this project thing has been such a shock. We go around and around every time I try to work with him. Crazy, isn't it?"

The Talbots had always had an ideal marriage? Gillian felt even worse. "I can understand why you're upset." The situation upset *her*. And Derek was being illogical, obviously unwilling to try to work things out.

Looking uncharacteristically downcast, Arlene gathered up her purse and notebook. "I need to go home. I have some work to clear up, too."

"Please call me," Gillian urged. "I want to help."

"All right, maybe I will."

"How about tomorrow evening?"

Arlene merely nodded. "I suppose these things just happen sometimes. Maybe Mr. and Mrs. K are incompatible. Maybe nothing can be done." She walked away.

"That's not true. Something can always be done," Gillian called after her, still concerned for the state of the Talbots' real marriage, afraid that the project had caused a terrible rift.

Shoulders slumped, Arlene continued down the hall. Worried and distracted, trying to remember all the projects she'd done with her high school classes, Gillian sorted the envelopes she'd brought that evening and stacked them between the pages of her spiral. She'd had to deal with a compatibility problem between two students only once during the past few years, and in that situation the boy had been emotionally troubled.

But the Talbots weren't troubled. There was no comparison. What if Derek was right? What if her project was seriously flawed? At the moment, Gillian could believe almost anything, the talk of arguments and failure having scared her nearly witless. Arlene had seemed sadly reconciled, but Gillian couldn't accept that "these things just happened sometimes." How nebulous. How illogical. That kind of explanation made no sense.

If it did, then her new relationship with John could be severed as fast as it had been forged. The scary thought made a cold lump settle in the middle of her stomach. She picked up her spiral, accidentally dumping several envelopes out onto the desk. She paused to scoop them up.

Of course, she and John had been at odds a lot lately . . . could that mean they weren't really compatible? So much could happen in a complicated situation.

When she knocked a couple of the envelopes onto the floor, she cursed softly and sat down on the chair to retrieve them, then managed to push them under the desk. Now she'd have to get down on her hands and knees.

She cursed louder, "Damn!"

"Do teachers wait until they're alone to swear?"

Nearly smacking her head on the edge of the desk, she jerked upright and whipped around in the chair. John was standing in the doorway grinning.

"Careful, you almost gave yourself a concussion." He came toward her. "Having problems? I saw the Talbots leave and wondered what was keeping you."

"I've been trying to get these blasted papers together."

"Hmm, the Talbots must have upset you," he said knowingly before stooping to pick up the errant envelopes, then placing them in her hands. He planted an understanding kiss on her forehead. "Don't let them get to you. Those two are neurotic."

"Maybe, but it was this class that drove them over the edge. I'm afraid they're headed for divorce."

"Divorce?" John looked startled.

"They said their couple isn't very compatible."

"Oh, their *couple*," he said with a laugh. "Well, everybody isn't, you know."

"*My* couples are," she insisted, not admitting her fears concerning the Talbots' real marriage. "All twenty-six of them. My students have always been able to work things out. But Derek isn't willing to cooperate. He doesn't like the way I've organized this project."

"Too bad for him. I told you the man was spoiled." Taking both her hands, John pulled her out of the chair to face him. "You were bound to run into someone who disagreed with your ideas sometime. Maybe your high school students have been afraid to admit any dissatisfactions."

"You mean you think there's something wrong with the project, too?" Had John been withholding the truth as well?

"Come on, don't be paranoid. I think the project is great. But you can't please everyone, and nothing's ever perfect. It couldn't be or we'd be assistants to God and helping run the cosmos." Grabbing her jacket, he slid an arm around her shoulders and drew her toward the door. "Let's forget about Derek Talbot and go have some coffee."

But Gillian couldn't forget about the Talbots, at least not yet.

Nothing is ever perfect.

Some people aren't compatible.

The moment she'd heard those phrases, she found herself wondering what else could go wrong. She only prayed that she and John were on solid ground. She was head over heels in love with the man and would be devastated if their relationship didn't work out.

GILLIAN FELT BETTER after she'd relaxed with John over coffee, but she still had doubts about the Talbots and the marriage project that carried over into the next day. As soon as school was out, she went on a nervous shopping binge before she remembered she'd asked Arlene to call her. She hurried home to check the answering machine, disappointed when the little red light wasn't blinking.

Well, maybe Arlene would call later... unfortunately, probably while Gillian was having her planning meeting with John. Surely he wouldn't mind waiting a few minutes while she talked to the woman. He knew how concerned she was over the situation.

Glancing at the clock on the fireplace mantel, Gillian realized he'd be arriving soon. She dropped her packages on the couch and hurried into the bathroom to touch up her makeup and brush her hair. She was placing drops of French perfume behind her ears when she heard the knock at the front door. She ran to answer it.

"Hi," John said softly, drawing her close. "You smell good." He nibbled her lips and ran exploratory hands down her sides and over her hips.

"Hi, yourself." She nestled against him eagerly.

The night before, she'd been disappointed that he hadn't come upstairs when he'd dropped her off. She would have enjoyed an hour or two of feeling safe and secure in his arms. But he'd had to hurry off to help Tracy with some homework assignment.

He kissed her lingeringly, his mustache soft against her upper lip. "Mmm, you taste good, too. Are you sure we have to work on the Xerxes' moving problem tonight?"

"There's not that much to do."

"Good."

Slowly he walked her backward to the couch, easing her down onto the cushions. Paper crinkled beneath her.

"Just a minute." Sitting up, she grabbed her purchases and tossed them onto the carpet. A couple of boxes slid out of one of the paper bags.

"More dollhouse furniture?" John remarked, catching sight of the new miniature dining room table and bedroom set she'd purchased. He sat down beside her and picked up one of the boxes. "Those rooms are going to get a bit crowded, aren't they?"

"I'm going to redo several of them. Besides, varnishing and upholstering relaxes me."

He laughed. "I can see you're the perfect kind of woman for a renovator to have around."

"In more than one way." She slid a seductive hand into the vee of his open shirt and gazed at him meaningfully.

But his expression was lazily sensual rather than heated. He kept his arm around her shoulders and leaned back into the couch. She leaned back as well, figuring they had plenty of time.

"Speaking of furniture, I saw a couple of ads for two-bedroom condos in the newspaper. Isn't that what Mr. and Mrs. Xerxes should be looking for?" He joked, "Maybe you can talk your bank into giving us a loan."

"Maybe. But we'd have to look at those condos first. They should be large enough for an expanding family."

"We only have one baby."

"So far. But there are going to be a couple of little additions. Remember when I told you the Xerxes wouldn't be parents for a year or so down the line? Our final printout specifies that we'll have two children eventually. The baby you added makes three."

"Three?" He looked surprised. "Can't our first baby count as one of the two on the printout?"

"You added the baby. The final count is three."

"Whew, two are enough work, and I'm speaking from personal experience."

Something about the way he said that bothered Gillian, making her think about the children she'd always dreamed of having. Since he claimed he enjoyed fatherhood, she'd just assumed John would be willing to have another baby if they ever got married. And though she was more than willing to play stepmother to Kim and Tracy, she also longed for the experience of raising a child herself. No promises or plans had been made one way or the other, but Gillian couldn't help feeling disappointed. She frowned.

"So what are we supposed to do for this assignment?" John asked. "Do we have to check out the floor space on these condos for real?"

"Hmm?" Still distracted, she mulled over what he'd just said. "Uh, no, of course not. List the Xerxes' requirements in your notes. We have to be aware of it, that's all. Everything is geared to being realistic about life in this project."

"Uh-huh. And what's so realistic about our couple having three kids instead of two? Just because you organized it that way doesn't mean we have to go along with it."

She frowned. "We're not supposed to change the original logistics." As he'd insisted in the first place. And she felt personally involved over the issue of the third child. "You can't change everything to suit yourself in real life."

"Yes, you can," he insisted stubbornly. "At least you can try. It sounds like we're only being *realistic* when the decision is made by you and your printouts."

Not liking his tone, she was annoyed. "As creator and coordinator, I have to exercise some control."

"Playing assistant to God, hmm, like we were talking about last night."

That he sounded as if he was teasing didn't help her mood.

"*You* were talking about cosmic assistants, not me." Were they going to fuss every time they got together now? "I have to set some limitations or my students would go wild and imagine they were rock stars and had millions of dollars and summer homes on the French Riviera. I'm trying to help kids be practical about life.''

"But that doesn't mean they have to aim for the lowest goals.''

"The goals we set aren't too low. No one is starving or homeless. You're beginning to sound like Derek Talbot.''

"Maybe the man has a point. Why don't you let him create a job for himself, if it means so much to him?''

Gillian couldn't believe John was taking the other man's side. "I suggested he do just that, but he refused.''

John chuckled. "The guy's really got a bee in his bonnet, hasn't he?''

"I suppose you could say that.'' Gillian only wished she felt half as amused.

His grin disappeared when he saw she was serious. "And I've gotten under your skin, too, haven't I?'' He gazed at her closely. "The Talbots' problem really has you crazed.''

"I'm not crazed!''

"Just tense then.'' He parted his knees and motioned for her to sit on the floor in front of him. "Come here. I'll rub all that tension out of your back and neck.''

"I'm not that tense.''

"Sure.''

She didn't stop him when he slid her off the couch and down onto the carpet, however. Removing her glasses and setting them on the coffee table, he massaged her temples, moving his fingers in light circular motions. Then he brushed her hair aside and kneaded the muscles of her neck and shoulders.

"You're all knotted up.''

"I've had a hectic day.'' Enjoying the sensations he was creating, she groaned and tilted her head to one side.

"Have you really spent the whole day worrying?''

"Only when I had time to think about the Talbots,'' she admitted. "Arlene said she would call me tonight, but I haven't heard from her.''

"Then maybe she'll call tomorrow. You shouldn't feel so responsible. If the Talbots are unhappy, it's their problem.''

She relaxed into his strong, supportive grip. "But I want to be sure they're okay. I can't help blaming myself if something goes wrong.''

"You really care, don't you?" he said softly. "I've always appreciated that about you. I was aware of it from the first night we met." Leaning forward, he lowered his head to kiss the back of her neck.

Though the soft touch of his lips incited another kind of tension within her, his statement relaxed her fears a little. John appreciated, respected...and loved her, probably just as much as she loved him. She had to remember that.

"Mmm. Feels good."

"And this will feel even better."

Entangling his fingers in her hair, John kissed her throat, her ears, her temples. His breath was warm against her skin. Gillian threw her head back so he could cover her mouth with his own and gripped his knees as he deepened the kiss, his tongue searching. Warm hands slid over her shoulders, along her arms, her sides, then tugged at her sweater, unfastening the bra beneath, gently cradling her breasts. Her nipples swelled to his touch and desire spiraled sweetly within her. She moaned.

He shuddered slightly and broke the kiss. "Surely we can find a more comfortable position for this."

"I'll get up."

"I'll help you."

Hands around her waist, he pulled her up and back, pressing her tightly against him. Feeling his arousal through all the layers of clothing, she rocked her hips in a slow, sensuous dance.

He took a deep, ragged breath and turned her around to face him. "It's been too long."

She agreed, "A whole week."

"I dreamed about getting you off by yourself during the camping trip." He kissed her again hungrily. "But it was impossible."

Not to mention inappropriate, considering his daughters were always around.

"Just imagine," he went on huskily. "All those trees, the fresh grass, the open sky, and you and me alone."

"We don't need trees to get in touch with Mother Nature." Encircling his neck, she bit his lower lip and pulled him toward the bedroom.

"And we definitely don't need clothing," he added, unbuttoning her skirt and sliding it down over her hips, letting it puddle into a soft heap on the floor.

Her slip followed, then her sweater and bra. She quickly peeled herself out of her panty hose, then unbuttoned his shirt and unfastened his belt. Laughing, he lifted her and carried her across the threshold, then laid her on the bed.

When he backed away to take off his shirt, she reached for him and teasingly commanded, ''Come here.''

He laughed and knelt beside her, then levered himself over her until their bodies were parallel. ''A little demanding, aren't we?''

To show his own power, he kissed her fiercely, thrusting his tongue inside her mouth. Welcoming the invasion, she gloried in it, unzipped his pants and pushed them down over his hips so she could caress him intimately.

Making animal sounds in his throat, John rolled over and rid himself of his shoes and pants. Quickly he removed the last shred of covering between them—her lace-trimmed briefs—then drew her solidly against him, skin against skin.

''Is this natural enough for you?'' he whispered, before lowering his head to suckle at her breasts.

She didn't answer. The sensations he was causing rendered her speechless. Kissing and touching and exploring each other hungrily, they might have been apart for a year rather than a week. Emotions building along with her passion, she was more than ready when he slipped inside her.

As they moved together in the age-old rhythm, she'd barely caressed the corded muscles of his back and moved her hands to cup his hips before she was lost. She kissed his arched throat, bit the soft flesh between neck and shoulder. He, too, cried out.

Seconds later, resting on his elbows above her, he let his breathing slow. ''I love you, Gillian.''

''And I love you.''

The affirmation was as satisfying as their lovemaking. She stared into the warm amber depths of his eyes and touched his whisker-roughened cheek. He kissed her before rolling over and cradling her against his chest. His heart beat strong against her ear as she closed her eyes.

They lay together quietly for several minutes before he asked, ''What's this? A nightgown?''

She glanced up to find him fingering the lacy white garment she'd tossed across her pillow after getting dressed that morning.

Ribbon-trimmed and sheer, it had spaghetti straps, a bustier bodice and a long bias-cut skirt.

"Uh-huh."

He let out a low whistle. "Must be made out of silk... and the top's almost transparent. You really have a thing for this fancy stuff."

"I like pretty sleepwear," she admitted.

"And lace bras and underpants and slips."

"Do you think I'm too extravagant?"

He laughed and smoothed back her rumpled hair. "I think that dreamy romantic you keep hidden in your dollhouse is peeking out the windows again." He notice her teasing pout. "Not that you're not totally feminine." He held up the wispy nightgown. "But you have to admit your outer wardrobe is pretty practical compared to this."

"Would you rather I wore low-cut blouses with ruffles? Long skirts with yards of petticoats?"

"Naw, the underwear is fine. I'll have double the fun when I take your clothes off."

"I like the sound of that." And the long-term involvement the statement implied.

He examined the nightgown's lace bodice closely. "Actually I wouldn't mind seeing you in this right now."

"You want me to put it on?" All right, she was game.

Taking the nightgown from John, she slid off the bed. Dropping her eyelashes seductively, she slowly lowered the garment over her head in a reverse striptease. "Like it?" She slowly paced up and down the length of the room, stopping to pirouette before her lover, fully aware the gown revealed far more than it concealed.

"*Like* isn't a strong-enough word for the way I feel."

Could any words describe the way he was looking at her? Snared anew by the sexual tension between them, Gillian quickly came back to bed. With a satisfied murmur, John pulled her down on top of him. He raised the skirt to her waist, then drew the nightgown up over her head.

"But I just put it on," she teased.

"So I could take it off," he told her, silencing any more protests with a heated kiss.

AN HOUR LATER, Gillian fixed them both some coffee and cake and served it in the living room. Wearing pants, no socks or shoes, and his shirt unbuttoned to his waist, John accepted the snack gratefully. He'd only had time for a few bites of dinner. As soon as they finished eating, she cuddled next to him and he drew the afghan back over them.

Still enjoying the afterglow of their lovemaking, he nuzzled her ear, inhaling the fresh scent of her hair. "We're great together, aren't we?"

"Mmm." The noncommittal murmur was followed by, "Do you really think we're compatible?"

Was she joking? "You have doubts?" He drew back to gaze at her questioningly.

"I didn't mean romantically." She lowered her eyes and picked at a loose thread in the afghan. "We do argue an awful lot."

"We express our opinions honestly," he countered. "And having differences is only natural."

"Is it?" she asked seriously. "Sometimes...well, I'm not sure...but I can't help wondering if we want the same things in life. Maybe that's the real cause of our disagreements. And perhaps we need to use a different approach for working out our problems."

She sounded unhappy.

"We might not agree on everything, but we seem to have similar goals and hopes and opinions." At least, he'd thought so up to now. And, to tell the truth, if not, he didn't particularly want to discuss problems at the moment. "We fell in love so quickly. It'll take some time just to adjust to each other."

In the meantime, he wanted to enjoy the heady feeling of falling in love. Perhaps he was being selfish, but Kate's arrival had precipitated enough difficulties in his life. When he was with Gillian, he wanted to luxuriate in their love, to play, to dream, to escape. He'd have to return to his problems only too soon.

Reminded of that, he glanced at his watch.

"Do you have to go?" she asked with a frown.

"In a little while."

The kids would be expecting him. He knew Gillian deserved a man who could stay all night and spend the weekends with her, but for him, that was impossible. Too bad Kate was so difficult and Tracy was so set against seeing her mother. If only that problem were worked out, he could make his ex-wife happy by letting her have the girls for a long weekend while treating himself and Gillian to an uninterrupted couple of days.

"You love me in spite of our differences, don't you?" he asked, only half joking.

"Of course." She took a deep breath. "I'd like to discuss our goals and hopes in more depth some time, though. I think that will ease the tension and stop us from arguing over small, unimportant things."

Tension? Suddenly the room felt thick with the stuff.

"Are you angry with me?" he asked.

"No."

"Then what's wrong?"

She shrugged. "Nothing specific. I just want to make sure we maintain open communication. That's the best approach to keeping a relationship vital."

John didn't care for Gillian's tone. She sounded as if she was lecturing. Obviously something *was* wrong . . . something she was reluctant to talk about.

"Do you want to open up and tell me something?" he probed. "Is that it?"

She drew away slightly, taking part of the afghan with her. "Do you have something *you* want to tell me?"

She was eyeing him in an odd manner. He hated the reminder of the endless occasions when Kate had demanded he "talk" when he hadn't even known something was supposed to be wrong. His ex-wife had more than once knocked on the bathroom door when he was showering to ask him what he was thinking about. Now Gillian was doing the same sort of thing. Maybe he really did have a communication problem.

"I've told you everything that's important to me," John said honestly. "If there's anything else, I'm not aware of it, but I promise I won't hold anything back. A person doesn't assimilate information like a computer."

She looked offended. "I didn't expect that. But surely I deserve to know about some things . . . if we're working toward a more serious relationship."

Uh-oh. She must be talking about marriage. He felt a little uncomfortable, not that he hadn't already considered the idea as an option for the future. For now, he didn't know what to say, but Gillian went on.

"Um, I don't want to push you." She rose from the couch, dropping the afghan and wrapping the kimono she was wearing more closely around her. "I just think we should be straight with each other before things get too complicated." She definitely seemed uncomfortable when she blurted out, "I want children."

"You mean right now?"

"Well...within the next few years. I'd like to have at least one, maybe two." She turned to face him. "Not that I wouldn't make room in my heart for yours as well. Do you want more children?"

Suddenly he realized the argument about whether the Xerxes were going to have two children or three had struck a nerve. She must have taken the issue personally.

"Uh, right off hand, I'm not sure what I want," he finally said. Despite her disclaimer, Gillian *was* pushing him, making John feel cornered. "I'm still raising my two girls. I haven't thought about having any more."

"Well...it isn't exactly fair to ask me to continue getting involved if children aren't an option, is it?"

He frowned. "No one's saying they're not an option, but we need time to get to know each other before we even consider it. We only met a month ago."

Both her voice and eyes seemed sad. "I'm just trying to avoid a broken heart."

"You're projecting. I have no intention of breaking your heart," he insisted.

John rose, meaning to take Gillian in his arms, but she paced away from him.

"Good intentions often go awry. We're taking a big chance."

"Any relationship is chancy."

Though, much as he disliked admitting it, a divorced father of two might not be the best choice for a never-been-married woman with no family of her own—at least not on the face of it. But he believed he was the right man for Gillian and was trying to figure out how to convince her of that fact when the phone rang.

Gillian jumped. "That must be Arlene." She hastened to grab the extension on her workstation. "Hello?" Her eager expression changed subtly and she gazed at John. "It's for you."

He stepped forward and took to the receiver, concerned when he heard Tracy's voice. "What's wrong?"

"She...Mom's coming over. She just called."

Kate was invading his house again? He saw red. "I'll be right home, sweetheart. You don't have to see your mother if you don't want to."

Gillian had gathered his socks, his shoes and his belt before he'd hung up. "Another family crisis?" she asked, handing him the clothing.

"I'm afraid so—my ex-wife again. I'm sorry," he apologized, pulling on his socks, then his shoes. "I want to clear the air, too."

"Maybe we can continue the discussion tomorrow."

He thought fast. "Let's see, I have a meeting with my lawyer after work, then I need to talk to David. I only wish I could be more specific about time."

"That would be nice." Her face was tight as if she were resigned to the inevitable.

"I have so many complications in my life at the moment," he tried to explain. "I know it's not fair to ask you to deal with my problems."

"Uh-huh."

"And this difficulty with Kate keeps escalating." He grabbed his jacket where he'd left it lying on a living room chair. "I never know what's going to happen next."

"Yes, you *do* have pressing responsibilities."

"True, I do."

John didn't appreciate Gillian's tone or her expression. As a matter of fact, he didn't care for the tension she'd created between them, starting with her doubts about their compatibility and ending with her demand about having children. It was as if she were looking for reasons to end their relationship.

"What really is going on here?" he demanded.

"I don't know what you mean." Her lips thinned into a tight line and she crossed her arms over her chest defensively.

"Baloney! Look at you. Where's the soft, loving woman of a few hours ago?"

"Where's the loving man?" she returned. "He disappeared the moment the phone rang!"

"I'm sorry if I'm not like some single man who has all the time in the world to wine you, dine you and romance you. As much as I would love that luxury, I have to take care of other things first...."

He stopped short, suddenly aware he'd told Gillian she wasn't number one in his life.

Her lips curved woodenly and she shrugged. "I guess I'm 'the other woman,' huh?"

"It's not like that. I'm not married, for God's sake. But you're being unreasonable." And he was having difficulty seeing reason himself at the moment. "Why are you trying to start a fight?"

"I'm not."

"You could have fooled me!"

"I hate fighting! I told you that." She brushed by him to stare at her dollhouse. "Two people who can't work things out don't belong together."

"Is that what you're trying to prove?" John felt his temper getting away from him. "That we don't belong together?"

"I'm just trying to be cautious."

He whipped her around to face him. "So cautious you're willing to give up a relationship of a lifetime out of sheer fear?"

"That's ridiculous."

Gillian shrugged free of his grasp and John could see he was getting nowhere with her. She glanced at the clock.

"You'd better go. You told Tracy you'd be home right away."

John could hardly force himself to leave, but he really did have to get home. "Maybe we should back off a little until the Kate thing is cleared up," he suggested. Maybe fixing one problem at a time was the sensible thing to do.

Her expression was at once stricken and accepting. "You mean not see as much of each other?"

"Maybe that would be best until everything is worked out. Then I can devote my undivided energies to our relationship." Would that make her happy? He couldn't tell from the way she was acting. He also couldn't help feeling hurt that she didn't tell him she wanted to see him, no matter the situation. "So we'll put our relationship on the back burner until I have more time?" He willed her to say no.

"That would be the logical solution."

Wonderful. Gillian wanted a real relationship to be as logical as those in the marriage project. John's temper flared anew.

"All right, then! We'll see each other only to work on the project until my situation is more favorable."

He headed for the door, hoping she'd call him back.

She didn't.

Before exiting, John turned toward Gillian. Back stiff, she was busy gathering up the coffee cups. She didn't even glance his way. Jerking the door open, he plunged down the steps and across the porch, then strode across the lawn toward his car.

Damn it all! How could Gillian say she loved him, then let him go like this?

And he'd been stupid enough to give her the suggestion.

CHAPTER THIRTEEN

GILLIAN HAD NO INTEREST in going out on a date with another man. But she feared that dating was exactly what Ty Spencer had in mind as soon as she met him on the Indianapolis health club's tennis court.

"Gillian," he said warmly, engulfing her hand. "It's great to see you again." He glanced admiringly at the length of leg revealed by her tennis skirt. "When Vicky called and asked me if I was interested in going out with you this evening, I jumped at the chance."

"Playing tennis will be fun," she agreed, trying to create the right tone in a tactful way.

Had Vicky implied a double date along with the doubles match? Unwilling to continue feeling bad about John and the way he'd walked out the night before, Gillian had only agreed to some friendly diversion before taking off for her parents' place for the weekend. She drew her hand back, stepped away and looked around.

"Have you seen Vicky and her partner?"

"They're in the locker room."

She glanced toward the locker-room doorway, relieved when her sister appeared there a split second later.

"Hi!" A happy expression on her face, Vicky rushed to give Gillian a quick one-armed hug. "And how are you, Ty?"

He grinned, and they made small talk for a few minutes until Vicky's partner appeared. When Gillian recognized him, her mouth dropped open.

"Tim!"

"Gillian!"

Her brother-in-law swept Gillian up in his arms and whirled her around. She mussed his dark hair, a little longer now than it had been on the Fourth of July, the last time she'd seen Tim.

"I've missed you," he said, setting her down.

She noticed Vicky frowning, and Ty gazing at them curiously, but she didn't care. "I've missed you, too—you and your silly jokes."

One Christmas, Tim had leaped out of a big package wearing a reindeer outfit, and he often pulled similar stunts or teased people mercilessly during family dinners.

"Um, Gillian already knows him," Vicky hastened to explain to the psychologist. "This is Tim Harper, my date."

Date? Gillian started. While the men shook hands, she drew her sister aside.

"Why are you introducing Tim as your date?" she whispered.

"Because we *are* dating," Vicky whispered back. "And it's not the same as getting back together, so don't get any ideas."

Thinking her sister was crazy, Gillian just shook her head.

"Don't tell Ty we're married. It'll destroy the illusion. And dating's a lot more fun, let me tell you," Vicky went on. "I forgot how good Tim kisses."

"Ready to play?" Tim asked the women. He placed a possessive arm around Vicky's shoulders and winked at Gillian.

She smiled and let the others decide who would serve first and which side of the court each couple would get. In spite of Vicky's disclaimers, she felt good about her sister going out with her estranged husband. The more time that Tim had to work on Vicky, the better. Maybe they'd be living together again by Thanksgiving.

On that upbeat note, Gillian ran to her end of the court, determined to play so hard and fast, she'd have no time to think about John. She'd already lain awake half the night tossing and turning and talking to herself, rehashing their last discussion. What kind of man would tell the woman he loved that he was putting her on the "back burner"?

"Your serve!" Tim yelled, tossing the ball onto the other couple's court.

Ty sent the ball spinning, and Gillian flexed her knees, keeping her eye on the others. They played several sets, Gillian concentrating on the game, noting that Ty was as smooth with his backhand as with his compliments. Furthermore, he laughed at Tim's jokes and magnanimously ignored Vicky's mistakes. Gillian had to admit he seemed like a nice guy. By the end of the match, she was sweaty and exhausted, but she'd had so much fun, had released so much tension, she didn't care.

"Gee, it's too bad we can't play another hour," Tim complained. "Are you sure somebody else booked the court at eight?"

"They're already waiting." Vicky jerked her head toward the two men who'd been watching them for the last ten minutes. "Besides, I'm hungry, let's go get something to eat."

They showered and changed, then drove to a nearby restaurant in Tim's car. Stuck in the back seat with Ty, Gillian again felt uncomfortable. Obviously determined to impress her, he asked her endless questions about her background and interests, then made a big show of helping her out of the car and into the restaurant. Luckily all the booths where they'd have to sit too close were full, so the couples were seated at a table.

Ordering quickly from the moderately priced menu, they settled down with drinks. Thirsty after the tennis match, Gillian had a tall Tom Collins. They'd gotten on to the topic of sports before they'd left the car. Ty picked up the subject, asking her about skiing.

"I've only skied once or twice," Gillian admitted. "In Wisconsin."

Ty grinned. "Wisconsin, huh? Not quite the challenge of Aspen or Taos but still a wonderful escape from the doldrums of winter. I belong to a ski club myself."

"Escape from winter? It was pretty darned cold."

"Well, if you really want a different scene, you should try the islands when the north wind blows. Like diving?"

"I don't know how." Though she'd always wanted to learn. She didn't tell Ty that, however, since she was a little tired of the constant upbeat chatter.

He went on, anyway. "Learning to dive is easy. Most community colleges offer lessons. Or you could book yourself into a tropical Club Med and learn right there."

"That sounds like fun," Vicky piped up. "I've never been to a Club Med."

"Want to go this winter?" Tim asked her.

"I only wish. I don't have that kind of money."

"That's okay, I can pay for us both," Tim offered. "I've been working a lot of overtime. It's too lonely sitting around at home alone."

"Aw, poor baby." Vicky reached across the table to squeeze his hand.

Gillian smiled at the romantic gesture.

Her sister stared into Tim's eyes. "That's so sweet of you. And we didn't have a real honey—"

She stopped in midsentence and glanced at Ty as if to see if he'd understood. He didn't seem to have caught on.

"Most Club Meds have great food," Ty continued, trying to recapture Gillian's attention. "You should see the feasts they lay out for the guests at Puerto Vallarta."

"How many of the clubs have you visited?" she asked curiously, thinking Ty must be a very busy person, what with diving and skiing and all the other sports activities he'd mentioned.

"I've been to a half dozen. It's fun to try a new place each time. But Club Meds aren't just a swinging singles hot spot anymore, you know. Some of the clubs even have special facilities for kids. And babies. Personally I would rather avoid the singles scene nowadays. At thirty-three, I'm looking for commitment."

He was only three years younger than John, Gillian thought, but what a difference between the two men. Ty Spencer seemed so much less substantial. But then again, she told herself, she hardly knew him. Ty had different experiences and talking about sports and singles spas didn't let her get to know the real man.

Ty took a sip from his glass of wine. "It's hard to find the right person. I had a steady girlfriend for a couple of years, until we finally realized we weren't compatible enough for marriage."

Compatible. At the moment, Gillian hated the word. "That's too bad."

Ty shrugged. "These things happen."

Great! She really wanted to hear that phrase again, too. Annoyed by the conversation—the very subject she'd been trying to forget—she kept silent. She glanced across the table at Vicky and Tim, who were leaning close and making eyes at each other. The kick she'd felt under the table a minute ago must mean they were playing footsy. She hoped they'd realize *they* were right for each other.

"I think it's very difficult to find a potential mate," Ty went on. "There are so many problems involved in the process."

"Like what?" Gillian asked, wondering what he'd say.

"Oh, everything," he said nebulously, obviously not wanting to get too personal.

Not that she blamed Ty. It was just that she was certain that John would have been quite specific, no matter what she asked him.

Ty paused to take another sip of wine, then glanced toward the rear of the room. "I wish they'd bring our salads." He turned back to Gillian and changed the subject. "Do you like football?"

Sports again. Suddenly wishing she were home alone, Gillian said, "I hate football." Having sometimes enjoyed watching the sport with her family on holidays, she felt a little guilty at the fib.

"How about ice hockey, then?"

"A blood sport? No, thanks. They might as well kill one another in the first hour and be done with it. The Romans would have cheered them on." My goodness, she was being negative, she realized. She really didn't like hockey but she supposed she shouldn't put down Ty's interests.

"Uh, interesting viewpoint." Ty raised his eyebrows. "Well, I know you like tennis. Did you see the last Wimbledon tournament?"

"No, I don't watch television." Another fib. "It's bad for the brain."

She had, indeed, missed Wimbledon, but she had nothing against watching television. Amazed at herself, feeling her face flush, she suddenly realized she was trying to start an argument with Ty.

But he didn't act offended. He continued glibly, "Well, I suppose television could be bad if you did nothing else but watch it. But surely sports are a little different, don't you think? You can't be present for every live performance."

"Uh-huh."

As Ty went on to explain—tentatively, however—the mental and physical healthiness of loving sports, Gillian realized she'd pushed the man to test him. He didn't like confrontation. John, on the other hand, would have immediately challenged her outrageous negative statements, teasing her and dropping innuendos, finding other ways to make the conversation stimulating. Argument-hater that she professed to be, she was surprised to realize she'd actually enjoyed going around and around with John, as long as they hadn't been discussing a truly serious issue.

"I didn't like the way they televised the summer Olympics," stated Ty. He paused as if he expected Gillian to say something. "There was far too much boxing.... Um, I know you probably didn't watch it, but wouldn't you say three hours a day was a little much?" He paused when she didn't answer. "Am I boring you? I've been rambling on and on."

Poor Ty, he'd finally realized she wasn't paying much attention the past few minutes. It wasn't his fault she'd been shunted aside by another man.

"I'm sorry, I'm a little distracted. I'm so hungry, I've been staring at the food on the other tables. Thank goodness, our salads are coming now."

The tossed salads and bread had indeed arrived. As soon as the waitress put the plates down, everyone ate. Between bites, Gillian tried to make Ty feel more at ease. They weren't on a date, but that didn't mean she couldn't be pleasant.

"What kind of work did you say you do? Psychological research?"

He nodded. "For a cereal company. I compile statistics on what American families are buying and offer theories as to why. It's a lot of computer work, but I'm in complete charge of the surveys."

"Do you really find that as interesting as working with people?" she asked.

"You mean as compared to doing therapy? No, I wouldn't claim that statistics are as interesting as patients." Ty leaned back in his chair. "But they're also a lot less depressing. I guess I'm a purist, and human emotion doesn't fit into any kind of logical format. I gave up trying to do that a long time ago."

"You gave up on emotion?"

"I stopped trying to fit it into a format. Emotions are so ephemeral. I decided I could never trust the heart without involving some logic." His smile was boyishly charming as he tapped his forehead. "The old knocker is so much more reliable, don't you think?"

Usually she would agree, but just now Gillian longed for a depth of emotion she wasn't getting from Ty... the kind she'd had with John just the day before, whether they were making love or arguing. Ty's remark about logical formats preyed on her mind. Could she be guilty of running relationships in the same way? Had she started the fight because she'd been afraid her own emotions were getting away with her?

Uneasy, she tried to push the thought aside and concentrate on conversation and dinner. She'd spent hours on heartache-level introspection the night before. John seemed to be dominating her life whether or not he was actually present.

As USUAL, there was no peace and quiet in the Flannery household that weekend.

"What the heck did you do with the TV remote?" Stuart Flannery yelled at the top of his lungs, as if his wife couldn't hear him in the very next room.

"Look between the couch cushions, that's where you usually lose the thing!" Carolyn yelled back, pausing before she placed Saturday night dinner—a roast beef—in a large pan.

"I wasn't on the couch last night, *you* were!" Muffled cursing followed.

"I didn't use the remote! Look between the chair cushions!" Her mother shook her head sadly and gazed at Gillian. "He can't find anything. It's ridiculous—only fifty-five and he's going senile."

"What's he watching?" Gillian asked, noting her father wasn't paying any attention to her after inviting her to visit.

But she'd expected such behavior. He'd been outside routing through the garage that morning while she'd eaten breakfast, had gone back out after lunch and now wanted to watch television. And when it came time for her to go tomorrow, he'd complain that he hadn't seen enough of his middle daughter.

"Oh, he's watching wrestling or the roller derby or something. He likes to see people whomp on each other," her mother said, reminding Gillian of the ice hockey discussion she'd had with Ty. Carolyn glanced at the table where Gillian was cleaning carrots on a chopping board. "Can you cut up the onions when you're done with those?" She frowned. "You don't need to scrape them down to nothing, you know."

"Oops."

Gillian immediately put the skinny carrot aside. She must have gotten carried away at the task in hopes of tuning out her parents' bickering. She picked up another carrot and watched her mother bustle around the kitchen, thinking Carolyn Flannery still looked young despite her harried life. Her mother was trim, and the gray that flecked her light brown hair almost made it look streaked.

"Here's the onions." Her mother handed her a half dozen.

As the older woman prepared the oven, Gillian went to work on the other vegetables, wrinkling her nose at the pungent odor. Feeling blue, having spent another restless night trying to sleep, she wondered if she should call her remote-controlled answering machine and play back the messages again. John hadn't phoned her last night or this morning, but there was the chance he'd done so this afternoon.

She hadn't had time to tell him she would be visiting her parents. But then, she thought resentfully, *he* didn't have time for her at all. She sighed, and her eyes filled with moisture.

"Thinking hard about something?" Her mother peered down through her bifocals, her eyes sharp. Wanting to know all, she was always trying to wheedle secrets out of her children.

Gillian brushed away a stray tear with her forearm. "These onions are getting to me."

"For heaven's sake, don't touch your eyes. Put a piece of bread in your mouth to sop up the fumes."

Gillian took the proffered bread and made short work of the onions. She decided she should definitely phone her answering machine. Arlene Talbot might have called. She'd almost forgotten about the poor woman in light of her own troubles. But after she'd washed her hands and dialed her number on the Flannery's kitchen extension, she was disappointed to hear nothing but the beeps that meant the message tape was empty.

"Who are you calling?" her mother asked.

"Myself."

"Not inviting anyone else to dinner, are you?"

"No, of course not. Did you?" Gillian's parents liked to have their children over whenever possible, not to mention friends.

"I asked Jeff to come by, but he said he has a date."

"Too bad." She didn't see as much of her brothers as she did of her sisters. "Couldn't he bring Anne along?"

"Jeff broke up with Anne. He has a new girlfriend." Her mother looked disapproving as she wiped her hands on a dish towel. "He always said he wanted to be a bachelor, that he'd had enough of marriage and kids growing up in a big family. I guess he's going to do just that. He's thirty-four."

"Maybe he'll change his mind when he meets the right woman."

"I hope so. I'd like some grandchildren one of these days. Donald's divorced," Carolyn Flannery complained mournfully, referring to her oldest son. "And who knows about Vicky."

"Hillary's married to Bob now."

"Finally, after living with him for two years. They really should have made it legal, you know. Young people these days are mixed up...."

"Now, Mom," Gillian cut her mother off, knowing she was going to get a lecture on how "nobody's going to buy the cow if they can get the milk free." She carefully changed the subject. "How's Jeff running the company?" Since Donald had his own real estate agency in the suburbs, Jeff had been approached to take over many of his father's duties at the small trucking company the Flannerys owned. "Is Dad happy with him?"

"Jeff's been a godsend for your father and his blood pressure."

"Good."

"And Stuart is doing so much better with the reduced hours. I only wish he could afford to take early retirement."

Gillian wished he could, too. But her parents hadn't been any more practical about money than marriage or children. They were open-handed with cash, had let themselves fall into the trap of early marriage, and had shelled out seven children before they'd thought twice. Not that Gillian didn't love them fiercely. She remembered the good times and the bad in the old days when they'd had the rambling old house with five bedrooms and a roof she used to daydream on. Her parents hadn't moved to this smaller place until Vicky had graduated from high school.

She helped her mother finish up the dinner preparations, then sat down at the table with her to visit. A couple of times, her mother tried to bring up John, but Gillian carefully skirted the subject. Instead, she got her mother to talk about her garden club and the occasions when Carolyn hired herself out to play the piano for local weddings or funerals.

"At least I make some extra spending money." Her mother rose to set the table.

"And you spend plenty," remarked Stuart Flannery, blustering into the room. His thick white shock of hair made his intense blue eyes look even brighter. He came over and patted Gillian's shoulder. "It's good to have you home, sweetheart."

"I don't spend any more money than you do," her mother objected. "You demand the most expensive cereal in the world." She looked at Gillian. "Can you imagine spending three dollars for a small box?"

Fingering the napkin holder, Gillian tried to interject peace. "Well, that's the price of groceries nowadays."

"And this stuff has nuts and honey in it." Her father's tone was defensive. "It has good fiber. It's healthier for you. I saw it on TV."

"You ought to have a TV glued to your face," growled her mother. "You watch it enough. And earphones, too. The volume is always too loud."

Gillian pulled out a paper napkin and meticulously folded it into a tiny square.

"Yeah? Well, I'm gonna have to watch more TV if I have to keep hanging around this house. I can only bowl so much every week. The doctor is nuts. My blood pressure isn't that bad."

Her mother looked worried. "You listen to the doctor, Stuart! You have to take care of yourself."

"I think you should listen to the doctor, Dad," Gillian added. Opening up the folded napkin, she started tearing it into tiny, even shreds.

But her father paid no attention to either woman's remark. He addressed his wife, "You don't want to lose me, huh? Now that you've gotten the best out of me." He raised his hands and looked heavenward. "Help me please, God. Women use a man and leave him a shell."

Her mother sniffed. "You should have been an actor."

Nerves jangled, Gillian gathered up the shredded napkin and stood up. "Come on, both of you, please settle down." She thought her father was teasing but she wasn't sure.

"Listen to your daughter, Stuart. Dinner is almost ready. Sit down and be quiet."

"Now she wants to put a muzzle on me!" Gillian's father complained.

The unlocked back door suddenly swung open, making everyone turn.

"What's this about a muzzle, Dad?" Smiling, Vicky stepped into the kitchen and approached to hug her father.

"Victoria, what a nice surprise!" Carolyn kissed her youngest daughter. "We didn't see you arrive."

"We parked the car in the alley. Dad has a bunch of stuff piled in the driveway."

"I'm cleaning out the garage." Stuart Flannery opened the door further and looked out eagerly. "Did you bring Rose and Ginny?"

"No, just Tim."

"Tim? How nice!" Carolyn gushed. Their mother had been very upset over the separation.

Seeing the new guests' arrival as a welcome addition, Gillian again greeted Tim enthusiastically when he came in. Sure enough, he set a light tone to the conversation until dinner was ready.

When they sat down to eat, Gillian's parents limited their disagreement to a small argument over the way the potatoes were prepared. Her father wanted them scalloped, not mashed, with plenty of salt. He didn't give Tim a hard time as usual, probably because the older man knew Vicky's marriage was still on shaky ground. The young couple seemed to be in a good mood, almost acting as if there had been no months of living apart. At the end of the meal, the sisters helped stack the dishes. Vicky asked Tim to assist in the cleanup as well.

"Men aren't exempt from housework," she stated.

"Who's arguing?" Tim pinched his wife and made her squeal as he passed by her with a bunch of glasses.

Gillian handed her mother a pile of plates to rinse for the dishwasher. Of course, her brother-in-law would probably do anything to be near his wife at the moment. But maybe he'd learned new and better habits, behavior that would draw them back together and make them happier.

"Well, I'm exempt from this kind of stuff," said Stuart loudly, heading for the combination living and dining room.

"You could stand to do some housework!" Carolyn yelled after him. "It's a good way to exercise."

"They're always impossible, aren't they?" Vicky whispered to her older sister.

Gillian nodded and wiped off the table.

When the dishwasher had been turned on, Tim sidled closer to Vicky. "Want to stick around for a while? What about that movie?"

"Let's go to the seven-thirty."

"Okay, let me know when you're ready." Tim wandered off to join Stuart Flannery in the living room where the television was already blasting away.

"This is the second date you've had with Tim in two days," Gillian remarked to Vicky as their mother rinsed pots and pans.

Her sister nodded. "And I'm having a wonderful time. Tim is so much more romantic. I can hardly believe it."

"Sounds like you're into heavy dating already."

"It could lead to something serious," Vicky admitted. She giggled. "As if we weren't already married. Do you know we're actually talking about some of our problems? Notice how he helped with the dishes?" She wriggled her eyebrows. "Watching a man do housework turns me on. Tonight we might go all the way."

Gillian laughed, happy something was working out for someone. She also appreciated that Vicky hadn't mentioned John—not that she'd expected her sister to do so, since that would be rather insensitive. Vicky hadn't mentioned Ty, either. Gillian had cornered her in the restaurant bathroom the night before to tell her she wasn't interested in getting involved with a new man.

Vicky and Tim left for the movie a half hour later. As soon as the door closed behind them, Carolyn told Gillian she hoped the couple would patch things up.

Gillian agreed. "Another chance for grandchildren." Which, sadly enough, she didn't know if she'd be able to provide for her mother.

"It's not just that. They love each other."

"Unfortunately love doesn't stop them from having problems," she said, thinking about John.

"Any close relationship is bound to have problems. Even good friends fight." Her mother took the cover off the coffee maker. "Want some coffee?" When Gillian nodded, she measured out some grounds and turned the machine on.

"I think fighting is terrible," Gillian stated, wondering if her mother really knew how strongly she objected to her parents' continual arguing.

"There are worse problems in the world. Besides, it's impossible to go through life without disagreeing. I don't know anyone who always compromises and says exactly the right thing when they're supposed to." Her mother looked thoughtful. "I had an uncle who never ever got angry, I guess, but he was a priest." She shrugged. "And who knows, maybe we only saw his best behavior because he was visiting my family."

Not particularly interested in discussing her great-uncle, Gillian pushed on, "Fighting upsets me."

"You mean between your dad and me, don't you, dear?" her mother said matter-of-factly. "I know our arguing was hard on you kids. When we were younger, we were even worse. We really got carried away sometimes."

"I was always afraid you would get a divorce."

"But it never went that far. Stuart and I loved each other deeply, still do. We wanted to stay together."

"But you did separate."

"That was only for a few months. *Because* of that time spent apart, we knew we belonged together."

"That's not what Aunt Dolores said." Gillian could still see her aunt sitting on the porch swing while she explained the awful truth to her niece.

"Do you remember what people said way back then? You were only twelve or thirteen."

Feeling a bit teary-eyed, Gillian sighed. "I remember what Aunt Dolores said very clearly. I was worrying about you and Dad, and she told me you two would never be able to get along, that you had married too young and were complete opposites. She said Dad was never coming back to us."

"Never coming back? Oh, how awful!"

"I couldn't sleep for nights after that."

"What a terrible thing to say to a child. Dolores could never keep her mouth shut, and she was always looking on the dark side." Her mother stepped closer to put her arms around Gillian. "And you always took things far too seriously, love. You were a sensitive and dreamy child."

"I believed Aunt Dolores."

"You were at an impressionable age."

True. Was Aunt Dolores's pronouncement the reason she'd avoided arguing most of her adult life?

"You always brooded a lot. I don't know why you didn't ask me about the situation at the time, though."

"I was afraid to. Maybe I *am* too sensitive."

She stood so they could hug with heartfelt feeling. Her mother patted her on the back, then drew away to meet Gillian eye to eye, a big smile on her face. "Your sensitivity shows your intelligence. Your father and I have always been proud of your accomplishments."

"Thanks, I'm proud of you, too." At least that the Flannerys were honest and hard-working and tried to raise their children with decent values.

Her mother kissed her cheek. "Now, let's sit down and have a cup of coffee and talk you into a better mood." She reached for the coffee maker.

Gillian sat. Now that she thought about it, the incident on the porch swing seemed to have hung over her like a black cloud all her life. Had her aunt's negative outlook traumatized her in some way?

Her mother served the coffee and sat down.

Gillian gazed at the older woman. "You don't think you and Dad were . . . wrong for each other, then? Or that you got married too young?"

"Maybe, maybe not. Who knows the answer to questions like that? I only wish there was a complete book of rules to follow in life."

Rules. Gillian thought about the marriage project. "I try to prepare kids for future relationships and responsibility in my sociology classes."

"I think your marriage project is a wonderful idea. People should be more aware of possible problems. Otherwise, they'll think love should be just like a movie. I'm happy you're trying to improve society. Still, nothing is ever going to be perfect. Despite all our hassles, your father and I have been together for more than thirty years." Her mother took a sip of coffee. "How are your classes going this fall, anyway? How's the adult marriage project you said you were working on?"

The situation in which she'd met John. To keep her mother from bringing him up, Gillian hastened to say, "It's fine except for the Talbots. They seem to be having problems in real life."

"They'll work it out if they care deeply enough about each other."

"There you go again, stipulating that everything's wonderful if two people love each other. Do you really think that makes the difference? Love may not be enough."

"If love is more than attraction, it makes a big difference. You can read books and take psychology classes, but a marriage isn't going to work unless you have the depth of true commitment."

Commitment. Gillian thought about her situation with John. Her mother went on, "People who are really committed will do whatever is necessary to work things out."

Gillian certainly hadn't tried to stop John from walking out.

"When it comes down to it, you'll know what to do if you listen to your heart."

The statement struck a deep chord within Gillian. Listening to her heart instead of her head, she made a promise to herself. As soon as she saw John face to face, she was going to tell him she didn't want to wait until he had his ex-wife problem worked out. She'd felt so heartsick since they'd parted, she was willing to do whatever it took to remain together. And if they decided to get married and he didn't want more children . . . well, she'd just have to deal with that. While she wanted children of her own, she'd mistakenly put more importance on that than on being with the man she loved. She'd been wrong.

"Hey, Carolyn!" Stuart yelled from the other room. "Are you and Gillian going to come in here and watch TV with me or not? I hardly get to see her and you're hogging her all to yourself. And is that coffee I smell?"

"We're coming in a minute, and I'll bring you some coffee!" Her mother shouted in return, then turned to Gillian. "Isn't he impossible? He harps about not seeing you enough, but, of course, *you* have to join *him*."

"He's something else."

"But he'd move mountains if you ever needed help. You know that, don't you?"

Gillian nodded. "He'd move mountains for any of us."

"He's a big mouth but at least he has a heart to match."

Gillian daydreamed about moving mountains for the rest of the evening, imagining every vanquished peak brought her closer to John. She was sorely tempted to give him a call, then decided to give him some space. Hopefully the separation would help them both appreciate how much they needed each other.

CHAPTER FOURTEEN

"HI, THIS IS GILLIAN, I can't pick up the phone..." began the same recorded message John had been hearing for four days.

"Damn it all, where are you?"

Unwilling to speak to her unless in person, he slammed down the receiver before the message could play out. It was five-thirty on a Monday night, for God's sake, and her last class had let out at four. Had Gillian taken off for parts unknown? Or was she sitting around, monitoring her messages, intent on avoiding him?

John was certain she hadn't been hiding when he'd dropped by on Saturday night and then on Sunday afternoon. She just hadn't been home. So where was she? Was he going to have to camp out on her doorstep to get the chance to see her?

Thinking he might do just that if he didn't talk to Gillian soon, John quickly tidied up his office, locked up and headed for home. The girls would be starting dinner soon, and he didn't want them to have to wait for him. He also wanted to talk to them about the family counselor he'd contacted that afternoon. The woman had been very positive about setting up an appointment to discuss their problems. Maybe something could get straightened out.

When he reached his house, John left his truck in the driveway and unlocked the front door. Throwing his hard hat onto the coatrack, he stomped into the kitchen and got a can of soda out of the refrigerator. He stared at the package of defrosting steak in the sink—Tracy's handiwork.

Where was Tracy, anyway? John wondered, used to the twelve-year-old being on hand to greet him. He cocked his head to listen, suddenly aware of the house's unusual silence. No music? No television?

"Tracy!" he called, going out into the hallway to gaze up the stairway. "Kim!"

No answer.

"Kim?" John called again. "Hey, anybody home?"

Silence. The house had an empty, deserted feeling.

Trying to ignore a growing uneasiness, John bounded up the stairs. He quickly searched the girls' bedrooms, finding Tracy's textbooks plunked down on her desk, proving she'd been there right after school. He was surprised to find Kim's room neater than it should be at this time of day, however. As soon as she came home, the teenager liked to change clothes and strew the outfit she'd worn to school about the room. Then she'd lie down on her bed and phone someone. John noticed that the bedspread—he demanded that the girls make their beds each morning—wasn't wrinkled at all.

If both girls left the house, they were supposed to leave a note for him. Had Kate dropped by and whisked them off to the mall again? If so, he'd be furious.

The sudden, piercing sound of the doorbell nearly made him jump out of his skin. He ran downstairs and was surprised to find his neighbor standing outside. "Sarah."

Her expression concerned, Sarah Bigsby started talking before he could say another word. "I came over as soon as I realized you were home. I saw Kate drive off with the girls."

Damn. Exactly what he'd been afraid of. "When?"

"About an hour ago. And something seemed kind of strange. I'm probably sticking my nose into your business, but it looked like Kate was pushing Tracy into the back seat. There are bushes in the way, though. I can't be sure."

"Thanks for telling me." Sarah was a kind woman and a concerned citizen, someone who'd undoubtedly heard gossip about his ex-wife being back in town and who cared about him. His heart beat faster, his bad feeling accelerated. "She's stolen the kids, hasn't she?"

Obviously realizing he was upset, Sarah hastened to try to calm him down. "Surely not. I just thought you should know where they were. I would have called you at work if I'd felt it was an emergency."

But obviously Sarah had been disturbed enough to talk to him now. Still, he willed his pulse to slow down.

"Kim went willingly?"

Sarah nodded. "She got into the front seat of the car. It was a burgundy-colored, two-door compact."

"A Ford Tempo." John had seen Kate drive off in the car after having lunch with her. "Then they must have gone shopping and will be coming back."

John breathed a sigh of relief. Kim *was* a little old for one woman to kidnap. But he was still irritated with the teenager and even angrier at Kate. How dare they force Tracy to go with them? He was going to ground Kim for the rest of her life.

"If there's anything else I can do..." Sarah stepped back as if ready to leave.

"Just keep your eyes open. I appreciate it. And thanks again. Maybe I'll take a ride over to the mall." He paused, indecisive. "Or maybe I should wait for a while."

"You could miss them if you went driving around."

After his neighbor left, however, John found himself pacing the hall restlessly. He couldn't sit down. He didn't feel like being patient. What if Kate *had* stolen the kids? What if she'd bribed Kim into heading for California?

Entering the kitchen, he stared at the clock. Six-thirty. If Kate had taken Kim and Tracy away from their home, he was giving her a head start and might never find the girls. Frustrated, feeling helpless, he slammed a hand against the woodwork. He shouldn't have been so stubborn about arranging visitation rights in the first place. When he realized Tracy was troubled over the idea of seeing her mother, he should have called a family counselor right then. And he shouldn't have had that argument with Kate the other night after Tracy had called him and he'd left Gillian's place.

Not that his stubbornness was any excuse for Kate's actions.

After prowling around the kitchen for a while, John put the steak in the refrigerator. The meat would spoil if left in the sink, and he certainly wasn't going to cook it; he didn't feel in the least bit hungry.

He glanced at his watch. Six-forty-five. He couldn't stand much more of this infernal waiting. But what to do? Call David? His brother and sister-in-law could only offer him sympathy. As could Gillian. No doubt she'd be thrilled to hear that he had another problem with his kids and his ex-wife.

He simply had to take action. Since the mall was open until nine o'clock, he decided to go take a look.

An hour later, he was still driving around the mall's parking lot, still searching for the burgundy Tempo. His stomach was tied in knots. He'd even been inside the place and had given a description of Kim and Tracy to the mall's security guards. He was certain Kate wasn't there, at least not now. Finally he drove down the road, checking the cars in the strip malls along the highway. But the action was futile—he couldn't possibly visit every store in Greenville and its neighboring communities.

If only he could get rid of the awful hunch he had.

If only he didn't feel so alone.

In desperation, he stopped at a pay phone and called his house, hoping against hope that Kim or Tracy would answer. The phone rang twenty times before he gave up. Without even thinking, he put the quarter back in and dialed Gillian's number.

"Hello?"

For once, the soft voice wasn't coming from an answering machine. And he could hear her clearly in spite of the passing traffic.

"Gillian." He gripped the receiver hard.

"John . . . where are you? I can hardly hear you."

"I'm in a phone booth near the main highway. I'm dealing with a bad situation."

She caught her breath sharply. "What's wrong? Did you have an accident?"

"No, nothing like that. I'm okay, though I'm not sure about the kids. I think Kate has stolen them, taken off for California or something."

"Oh, no! If you want, I can go to the police with you."

The caring emotion in her voice made a lump form in his throat. He swallowed, then admitted, "I could use your support." And her love, whether he deserved it or not.

"I want to help. Where exactly are you? What's the nearest street?"

"Meet me at my house. With luck, maybe this will turn out to be a nightmare and Kim and Tracy will already be home."

"I'll be there right away. I love you, John."

"I love you, too, Gillian," he stated emphatically before hanging up.

And he would tell her how much he needed her as well, as soon as he saw her face to face. He'd been stupid to let her put him aside for any reason and had known that the moment he'd mentioned the back burner. He should never have left without setting things straight. He only hoped Gillian would forgive him and stand by him despite his messed-up life.

"I WANT TO GO HOME!" Tracy insisted again tearfully.

Kate stared into the rearview mirror, her heart sinking at the sight of her daughter's puffy little face. Tracy had sobbed openly when they'd first started out and continued to sniffle with every passing mile.

"But we're going some place better," Kate said reassuringly, trying to keep her voice from shaking. She glanced at Kim, who sat oddly silent in the passenger seat. The situation hadn't been what she'd expected. She thought Tracy would have settled down by now. "You'll like Chicago. It's exciting, a real city. It has great shops, especially on Michigan Avenue."

"But we aren't going there just to shop, are we?" Kim stared at Kate with a discerning expression.

"Well, I thought we could stay there a few days and see how you liked it."

"Uh-huh. You're planning on having us live there, aren't you?" Kim pointed out, "I saw your suitcases in the trunk when we stopped at that service station."

Kate had opened the trunk to find her road atlas. She'd noticed Kim looking over her suitcases but had hoped her daughter wouldn't read her true intentions. She'd intended to take the girls to Chicago, ostensibly for a shopping vacation, while at the same time letting them get used to living with her. She'd planned to do her best to sweeten the transition, so they could start all over....

"You're kidnapping us!" Tracy wailed. "That's against the law!" Gathering her knees beneath her, she pounded on the back window like a trapped animal.

"Please, don't get hysterical." Kate slowed the car, her heart pounding. "It's not kidnapping," she insisted. "I'm your mother. You can't steal children who are already yours, and I'm certainly not going to hold you for ransom. I love you."

Tracy settled down, but she let out a choking sob. "You don't love me or you wouldn't have gone off and left me."

Kate couldn't stand it. "I left your father, not *you*."

"Then you should have stayed and tried to work things out," Kim told her mother. "I mean, you could have gotten a divorce and stuck around to see us, instead of running off with some guy."

"Yes, that was the worst thing I've ever done in my entire life." Kate sniffed, trying to hold back her own tears. She felt compelled to tell her side of the story. "I was unhappy with your father and wanted to leave him but thought that I couldn't do so unless I had another man."

After all, life was impossible without a man to take care of her, or so she'd thought then. And she'd been sure that John didn't love her anymore. There had been little romance or excitement left in their marriage. Using their savings without her approval had been the last straw.

"Running away was selfish and irresponsible of me," Kate admitted. "I didn't realize that I would be separated so long from my children." Or that the precious, irreplaceable bond would be broken between them. Could it never be mended?

"If you care so much, take me home," Tracy demanded from the back seat. "You still don't care about what anyone else wants or you wouldn't try and take everything away from us. I want to live with Dad."

"But what about me? Can't you live with him part of the year and spend the rest of the time with me?" Though when she'd set out, Kate had intended to sue for complete custody as soon as she got settled in Chicago. "He won't even let me see you!"

"Dad asked me to see you but I said I didn't want to." Tracy scrunched down in the seat. "And I still don't and I don't want to live with you. I already told you, I don't have a mother."

The utter rejection really pierced Kate's heart. Tracy's continuing hostile behavior was too much. She choked, an errant tear running down her cheek. "How can you hate me so?"

"It's natural to hate someone who goes off and leaves you," Kim broke in, her voice controlled but angry. "Tracy was a little kid when you left. She had nightmares."

Kate dabbed at her face with a tissue, imagining Tracy's pain. "My poor baby."

"She screamed and cried herself to sleep," Kim continued. "And I agree with Tracy, you should take us home. I don't care about the shops in Chicago or how exciting it is. I didn't come along for shopping anyway. I was trying to protect Tracy...and to get a chance to say a few things to you."

"You came to protect Tracy?" Did Kim think she would really harm her own daughter?

"You strong-armed her into the car. I wasn't going to wrestle with you."

"I didn't mean any harm."

"But what you're doing is wrong. If I'd known what you were actually planning, I would have run back in the house, locked the door and called Dad." Kim's expression was as accusatory as her words.

"I can't go through with this." Spotting an exit, Kate pulled off the freeway and stopped by the side of the road. "All right, I'll take you back to Greenville." Chalk up another mistake. Her life seemed to be filled with them. Tears flowed down her cheeks. "I can't do anything right. I've dreamed of seeing you for so many years." Her voice broke. "Can't you try to forgive me? Tell me how I can make up for the pain? I just want to see you once in a while."

"Just once in a while?" Tracy echoed, sounding hesitant.

"Please, I'll settle for anything. However many days or hours you choose." And she would force herself to remain patient. "I'll even leave you alone forever, if that's what you want." Though she wondered if that would kill her.

"Well, I guess I can *think* about seeing you." Tracy sat up straighter. She cleared her throat. "Um, you don't have to cry so much."

Kate's expectations rose. "You'll think about it?" She swallowed and dried her eyes. "Please, you'll really consider it . . . ?"

"Yeah, we could get together once in a while," Kim broke in, sounding embarrassed and also sorry for her mother. "If Tracy wants to, that is. But don't try to buy our favors with presents. It doesn't work."

Kate nodded. "Okay, I understand. I wasn't going to be able to buy many more as it was. I was running out of money." One of her credit cards was already over the limit.

"What kind of salary does a saleswoman get?" Kim asked.

"A low one, unless I make a lot of commissions." In Chicago, she'd planned on trying to get a job at Bloomingdale's, one of the better-paying department stores.

"Gee, I suppose I should take the stuff you bought back to the mall right away," Kim offered.

Kate was touched. "Don't worry about it."

"But taking them was wrong anyhow, and Dad already ordered me to return them. I thought you owed me something. I wouldn't have taken them in the first place, though, if I knew you couldn't afford it. All I really wanted was to have things back the way they were before you ran away."

Kate's eyes filled again. "That's impossible, Kim. I can never go back to your father."

The teenager nodded, looked sad. "I know it's impossible."

Kate would take the girl in her arms if she wasn't afraid it would be pushing things.

"Besides, Dad's got Miss Flannery," Tracy said, though she didn't sound as if she were trying to be mean.

Kate pushed down the jealousy she felt whenever she heard the other woman's name. Not that she was upset over John, just concerned that Gillian Flannery would steal the love and affection she still wanted from her children. She had to admit that her fears about that had probably contributed to her irrational actions.

"I'm glad your father's happy," Kate said, knowing that John's romantic involvement was another situation she'd have to learn to deal with in a patient and adult manner. She started up the car and did a U-turn. "And now I want you to make sure *you're* happy. I'm taking you home."

She'd been crazy to think money or a little attention would make up for an absence of five years. She now knew she was going to have to win back her daughters without bribes. At least John had raised them with enough compassion to make that possible. Now, if only he didn't hold this escapade against her....

"WHO KNOWS where Kate's taken the girls," John complained bitterly when he and Gillian came out of the Greenville police station. "They're minors. I can't believe we have to wait twenty-four hours to file a missing persons report."

Gillian rubbed his arm reassuringly. "I suppose the police want to make sure about the situation. Don't worry, though, Kim and Tracy can't disappear."

Gathering her close, John gazed down at her. "Can't they? Haven't you heard the horror stories about parents who kidnap their kids? Some of the children have never been found."

She knew he couldn't help feeling discouraged. They'd already driven by Kate's apartment building, talked the janitor into letting them in, only to find that Kate had cleared out all of her personal items. A bad sign. And, since it was long past closing hours, there was no use checking the store where she worked.

"Kim's not exactly a child, and neither is Tracy. They'll get to a phone."

"True. Kim is especially good with phones." He smiled grimly.

Considering the circumstances, Gillian was a little surprised that his sense of humor was still functioning.

"We might as well go back to your house," she said.

He opened the door of the truck and helped Gillian step up and get in. When he got himself settled, she scooted close.

"I'm shocked that Kate was this desperate."

"I guess she'll do anything to get her own way," said John. He started the vehicle and pulled the truck out into the street. "You're probably wondering how I ever got hooked up with such a woman. Kate's impulsive, and she was always spoiled and selfish, but when she wants, she can be warm and can focus her attention on you and make you feel like you're the most important human being on earth. I was looking for that when I was nineteen."

"That's understandable."

"Kate's less-attractive aspects came out as I got to know her. And I have to admit I probably exacerbated them with my own impulsiveness and difficulty communicating."

"You're not impulsive, just decisive."

"Thanks. Hopefully I've mellowed. I married Kate three weeks after we started dating. I'd say that's pretty impulsive. And remember when I came up with that newsletter idea and didn't consult you first? I was thinking about me—er, Mr. Xerxes."

"But your idea wasn't so off base."

"Maybe not, but I skipped the whole communication process that you're so hot on."

"Well, it wasn't as if you weren't taking your wife into consideration," Gillian said reassuringly. "You didn't actually spend the savings that belonged to both of the Xerxes. You talked it over before you got that far. Your communication skills have obviously improved over the years."

"I talked over my business venture idea with Kate, too, but she wouldn't have any part of it. And I felt I had more of a right to say what happened to our money than she did, since I was the one who'd made it and saved it by working at a job I hated."

"I can understand your viewpoint . . . but I can also see why she was so upset."

John slowed the truck and turned right onto the street that led to his house. "If David and I hadn't acted when we did, we would have lost the deal."

"You could have waited for another opportunity," Gillian pointed out.

"True, though I doubt Kate would ever have agreed, not even if we already had the new house she wanted so badly. Her priority was financial security, and my quitting a 'real' job to open a business was too much for her to handle. That first year was pretty rough financially. Now that I think about it, communication wasn't the real issue. The problem was that Kate didn't believe in me . . . and we didn't want the same things."

"If she'd really loved you, she would have tried to see your point of view," Gillian said with certainty. "Well, all that's in the past. Everyone has problems, me included."

He grinned crookedly. "A few small ones. For example, you could be home more often, so I could reach you," he said, though she'd already explained about visiting her parents for three nights—she'd stayed over on Sunday to please her father.

"You should have left a message," she told him. "I called my answering machine repeatedly."

"Okay, then that's *my* fault."

"But I'm not perfect," she said, wanting to clear the air.

"Well, you try to be. That's why you get so carried away with logic and organization. Sometimes you're too idealistic. You can't plan a relationship the way you do your dollhouse. All the planning in the world can't make two people perfect."

"Guilty as charged," Gillian said with a sigh. "But the past month has taught me better, I hope. I've always hated arguing and stressful situations, but I've come to realize a little bickering between two people who care is a natural outlet."

John placed his arm across the back of the seat and cradled her shoulders. "And real arguments can always be resolved if two people love each other enough. The best we can do is be our true selves and to work on what ails our relationship. I can't promise that you'll never be hurt, but I'll try my damnedest to bandage up your emotional cuts and bruises."

Leaning against him, she said softly, "I couldn't ask for anything more."

After all, she couldn't cower in fear her whole life. She had to take a chance on love sometime. There were no hard and fast rules. Every marriage was an entity unto its own . . . even her parents'. A willingness to work out any problems as John had just promised was enough for her.

John startled Gillian out of her thoughts as they approached his driveway. "Oh, my God! That's Kate's car parked next to yours!"

Stepping on the gas, he sped toward the drive and brought the truck to a squealing halt behind the Tempo. He threw open the door and jumped down. Gillian did the same.

"Come on," he urged.

"Are you sure you want me to go in?" she asked, not exactly comfortable. "I can wait out here."

John caught her firmly by the waist and held her tightly against him. "No, please, I'd like you to come with me. I want us to face this together, with you on the front burner where you belong."

John's words made Gillian throw caution to the wind. She would stand by him, no matter how unpleasant the scene. The door was unlocked, the living room empty, as was the kitchen. He drew her toward the family room. Seated on the couch beside Kim, Kate glanced up when they entered. Guilt immediately flickered over the other woman's features.

Tracy rose from the chair she'd been perched on. "Dad!" When the twelve-year-old ran forward to hug her father, Gillian stepped back.

John held onto Tracy fiercely. "Where the hell have you been?" he asked Kate.

His ex-wife shrank against the couch cushions. "I don't blame you for being angry, John. I did a very bad thing. I was going to take the girls to Chicago. I—I meant to apply for custody."

"What stopped you?"

She glanced over his shoulder at Gillian, then back at John. "I know you expect the worst of me, but I really have changed. I was feeling desperate at the time, but our daughters gave me what for. They demanded I bring them home."

Letting go of Tracy, John looked at Kim.

"She said she was taking us shopping, Dad," explained the teenager, "but that's not why I went along. I wanted to talk to Mom."

"And she wanted to protect her sister," Kate stated. "I...I sort of forced Tracy into my car."

Before John could respond, Tracy said, "Aw, I could have gotten away if I really wanted to. I'm not a little baby. Kim didn't have to protect me. I just didn't want to punch anyone, especially not my...my mother."

"Your mother?" Kate smiled tremulously. "Oh, sweetheart..." She swiped at her eyes with a tissue, then crumpled it in her hand. "The girls talked some sense into me before I got too far. That's why I turned the car around. You've done a good job of raising them. On the way back to Greenville, we talked about the past five years. It might take me a long time to catch up, but I intend to be around permanently."

Calmer now, John motioned for Gillian to join him on the loveseat opposite the couch. Heart pounding rapidly, telling herself she would survive a possible confrontation, she slid in beside him.

"This is Gillian Flannery," he told Kate. He gripped her hand reassuringly. "We've been seeing a lot of each other."

"So I've heard." Kate nodded stiffly and her voice was tense. "I only wish we could have met under better circumstances."

"The circumstances are fine if things are getting straightened out between you and your daughters," Gillian told her, certain that Kate was uptight about her own involvement with John. No doubt Kate would be more relaxed if she were on better terms with her daughters.

"At least we're working toward solutions," Kate agreed, then turned to John. "I won't contest your custody, so you don't have to worry about that. I'll be happy if I can see the girls. I'll leave when up to them."

Perhaps Kate *had* changed, Gillian thought. She sensed the last of John's anger fading. His ex-wife's expression was so vulnerable that Gillian felt sorry for her.

"I'm sure we can work out some visitation rights," he said. "I have one stipulation, however."

"What's that?"

"I want you to attend family counseling with us for a while."

"Agreed. I certainly don't want my daughters to be scarred because of my problems."

Her respect for Kate growing, Gillian only hoped the other woman wouldn't disappoint her daughters again.

"Is that okay with you girls?" John asked.

"Sure." Kim looked a little shaky. "I want to feel better about the divorce and everything." When Kate reached out to take her hand, the teenager responded by grasping her mother's tightly in return. "I hated you when you left, Mom. But I loved you underneath. That's why I was so mad."

"Oh, darling." Kate enclosed Kim in a tearful hug. "I love both my babies. I thought of you every single day and night that we were separated." She released the teenager and looked toward Tracy. The younger girl sobbed and ran into her mother's arms.

Watching the emotional display, Gillian couldn't help but be touched. Her own eyes grew moist, and John cleared his throat. In a minute, they'd all be crying. Tracy broke the tension. After hugging her mother, she backed away, dragged a tissue from the pocket of her corduroys and blew loudly.

"I suppose it's okay to see a psychiatrist if that will help us get along better," the younger girl said. "But does that mean we're all nuts?"

John laughed. "No, pumpkinhead, it just means we'll have someone helpful to talk to. But she's a social worker, not a psychiatrist. Everyone can use outside help at times."

Kate wiped her eyes and checked her watch. "I suppose I'd better be going. It's a school night and it's rather late." She started gathering up her stylish-looking purse and coat. "Will you call me tomorrow?" she asked John.

"Are you still going to have the same work and home numbers? We stopped by your apartment building tonight and the janitor thinks you sneaked out on the lease."

"Oh, my, I'll have to talk to him." Kate widened her eyes and fluttered her hands in a nervous gesture. "I've paid my rent, and I didn't quit my job, so I assume those won't change. I left this evening rather impulsively."

"Well, don't get that impulsive again," John told her. "Tracy and Kim are going to be depending on you."

A hurt look crossed Kate's lovely face. For the woman was classically beautiful and naturally feminine, Gillian thought. No wonder John had fallen in love with her when they were young.

"I won't betray my daughters' trust again," Kate promised. "When I left Indiana, I thought I had to depend on a man. It took me years to gain self-confidence and the knowledge of how to get along on my own."

"I can understand that," Gillian said. Not all women were raised to be self-sufficient and independent.

Kate smiled at her for the first time, one woman to another, and Gillian felt things really were going to work out for everyone. John rose and walked his ex-wife to the door. Tracy followed.

Kim smiled at Gillian, her expression shy but friendly. "What a night! Have you been driving around looking for us?"

Gillian smiled, too, warmed by the girl's seeming acceptance. "For a couple of hours. You dad was so worried about you. We *both* were," she amended.

Their eyes met in true understanding for the first time. "You're good for Dad," Kim said softly.

It was the closest thing to an apology she would get, Gillian figured, but it was enough. "He's good for me, too."

As only a teenager could do, Kim changed the subject without blinking an eye. "Say, did you have a big dinner? I'm starved."

John was just coming back into the room, Tracy on his heels. "Did I hear someone mention food?"

"There's steak in the refrigerator," Tracy told him. "But we'd have to cook it. I'm starved too. Mom bought us hamburgers, but I was too upset to eat."

"So what do you want to do?" John asked. "Go out to the all-night coffee shop or order in? I don't care if you're up late. You can even miss school tomorrow, if you want to." He glanced slyly at Gillian. "Don't tell, okay?"

"Deal."

Kim scooted forward on the couch. "How about pizza?"

"Yeah, pizza!" Tracy agreed. "I'll call Ricardo's and have them deliver. Mushrooms and sausage? Is that okay, Dad?"

John nodded.

Then Tracy looked at Kim. "Or plain hamburger will be all right, too."

"No, order it with everything," the teenager told her sister. "I'll pick off what I don't want."

"But you don't like mushrooms."

"But *you* do," Kim insisted.

"Stop already!" John said. "Order two pizzas. Just get on that phone and tell them to hurry. I'm hungry."

At the sight of both girls rushing neck and neck out into the hallway, Gillian laughed.

John plopped down beside her and took her in his arms. "Don't be too amused. This loving sensitivity toward one's siblings is only going to last a few hours."

"Then we should enjoy it while we can."

"And we should enjoy this—" he kissed her soundly, his lips moving firmly over hers "—while we can, too."

"Mmm." Gillian wound her arms around his neck and kissed him back fiercely. "I'll take the good with the bad, as long as I'm important in your life."

"Like I said, you're on the front burner. And that's where I want you to stay."

Gillian couldn't argue with that.

EPILOGUE

"So we're declaring the marriage project a big success," announced Principal Fowler when Gillian had finished her report and the participating PTA members had given their feedback at the November meeting. He scanned the auditorium. "And do you all agree that Miss Flannery should resume the assignment in her sociology class?"

"We do," Sarah Bigsby said. "It'll be an excellent learning experience for our kids." Other people around her also murmured their assent or nodded their heads.

Wes Meyer rose to his feet. "I think Gillian Flannery deserves a hand for a job well done."

Gillian adjusted her glasses and smiled, a little embarrassed when everyone applauded, even the Talbots. She'd been very concerned about that couple, especially when they'd gotten a "divorce" for Mr. and Mrs. K. Luckily, though, they'd then made up and "remarried." Both Talbots claimed their real, flesh-and-blood marriage was stronger as well, because they'd had to deal with the unusual challenge.

Her face warm, Gillian stood up on the small podium. "I think you should also give yourselves credit for doing a good job. I've really enjoyed working with all of you." She grinned, making eye contact with the project participants in the audience, stopping with John. He quirked his brows in a teasing manner. "I'm going to miss you." Though, hopefully, she'd be seeing plenty of *him*.

"Well, we don't have to remain strangers, you know," Sarah Bigsby said. "There's nothing to stop us from getting together once in a while." She and Calvin had come through the project with flying colors. Nearly opposite in personality, they were already used to bickering and compromise.

"How about having a class reunion once in a while?" Arlene Talbot suggested. "You're all invited to our place for a New Year's party in January. My husband already suggested it." Smiling at Derek, she reached for his hand.

"Sounds great," added Wes Meyer, who was seated next to Elaine. They had finally admitted they'd been dating and seemed very happy.

Sarah went on, "In celebration of our 'graduation,' several of us have brought refreshments tonight." She waved toward the hallway. "Help yourselves as soon as the meeting's over."

"Food?" Principal Fowler looked very interested. "All right, this meeting is over right now."

Everyone laughed and drifted toward the hall.

More than pleased with the project's outcome, as well as happy for more personal reasons—Vicky had called over the weekend to say she'd moved back with Tim—Gillian mingled with the crowd exiting the auditorium and helped herself to a piece of pie from the tables that had been set up outside. She was about to pour John and herself some coffee when he caught up with her.

"Coffee, pie or me?" he said softly, draping an arm around her waist.

"I'll take all three," she stated, ebullient.

He pretended to scowl. "Food is as important to you as love? How unromantic."

"I'll show you romance later on, Mister," she whispered in joking threat.

"Promise? We'll have the whole night—the girls are staying over at Kate's."

"Again? The family counseling must be going well."

And Kim had been quite friendly with Gillian the past couple of weeks. The teenager had even bragged to her friends that she now had a personal tutor.

"Actually I suggested that Kim and Tracy stay over there tonight, it being a special occasion."

"The end of the project?"

Most of the PTA members were still helping themselves to the refreshments, so he pulled her off to the side for some privacy. "And the beginning of a new one."

She raised her brows in question.

"I'd like to remain partners." He pulled an envelope out of his jacket's inner pocket. "I made up plenty of options for us to work with. Want to draw a slip?"

"Is this a joke?"

He just smiled. Curious, Gillian put down her coffee and immediately reached into the envelope to draw out a small slip of paper. When she unfolded it, her eyes widened at what it said:

Will you marry me and love me for the next sixty-three years?
One or two children (new) very likely.

"Oh!" She didn't know whether to scream or cry or blush.

"Just 'oh'? What happened to 'yes'?"

She felt overwhelmed. "You *are* asking to marry me, aren't you?" she asked, willing her heartbeat to slow down. His method was so unusual, she wasn't sure. "What's on the other slips in the envelope?"

"Interested in options? You're not getting many." He took her in his arms. "The other slips say the same thing, except that they state a different number of years from sixty to a hundred."

"A hundred? We'd be a hundred-thirty-something."

"Don't worry about our old age. You still didn't give me an answer." His expression showed he was a bit nervous, possibly insecure, certainly not as confident as he was trying to act.

"Yes, I want to remain your partner," she stated, meeting him eye to eye. Of course, he just had to be creative with his proposal. "Yes, I'll marry you, John."

"Thank God." He kissed her.

"Yeah!"

The celebratory cry came from Wes Meyer, who had happened to overhear. Wes tapped his spoon on his cup. "There's a wedding announcement over here." He waved his arm and pointed to John and Gillian. "The teach is getting married."

"Kim and Tracy have both given their approval," John told her as a huge round of applause began.

Gillian grew warm as she met all the smiling familiar faces.

"Uh-oh, I didn't mean to make a public announcement," John muttered.

Then he shouldn't have proposed to her in public. But, for once, Gillian didn't care. "They might as well know up front. Otherwise, they'll make up their own gossip about it." She kissed him.

When they broke apart, Sarah, Arlene, Derek, Calvin, Elaine and the others gathered around to give their congratulations to the happy couple.

"You're all invited to the wedding." John scrunched Gillian to him in a bear hug. "After which we'll be playing house for real!"

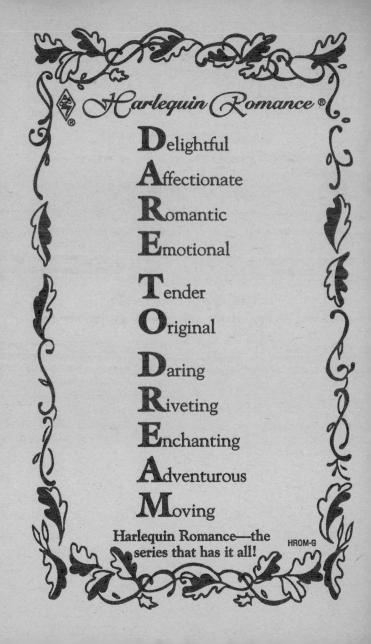

Harlequin Romance ®

Delightful
Affectionate
Romantic
Emotional

Tender
Original

Daring
Riveting
Enchanting
Adventurous
Moving

Harlequin Romance—the
series that has it all!

HROM-G

HARLEQUIN  PRESENTS®

HARLEQUIN PRESENTS
men you won't be able to resist falling in love with...

HARLEQUIN PRESENTS
women who have feelings just like your own...

HARLEQUIN PRESENTS
powerful passion in exotic international settings...

HARLEQUIN PRESENTS
intense, dramatic stories that will keep you turning
to the very last page...

HARLEQUIN PRESENTS
The world's bestselling romance series!

**Harlequin®
Historical**

If you're a serious fan of historical romance,
then you're in luck!

Harlequin Historicals brings you
stories by bestselling authors, rising new stars
and talented first-timers.

Ruth Langan & Theresa Michaels
Mary McBride & Cheryl St. John
Margaret Moore & Merline Lovelace
Julie Tetel & Nina Beaumont
Susan Amarillas & Ana Seymour
Deborah Simmons & Linda Castle
Cassandra Austin & Emily French
Miranda Jarrett & Suzanne Barclay
DeLoras Scott & Laurie Grant...

You'll never run out of favorites.

Harlequin Historicals...they're too good to miss!

HH-GEN

HARLEQUIN®

I N T R I G U E®

THAT'S INTRIGUE—DYNAMIC ROMANCE AT ITS BEST!

Harlequin Intrigue is now bringing you more—more men and mystery, more desire and danger. If you've been looking for thrilling tales of contemporary passion and sensuous love stories with taut, edge-of-the-seat suspense—then you'll *love* Harlequin Intrigue!

Every month, you'll meet four new heroes who are guaranteed to make your spine tingle and your pulse pound. With them you'll enter into the exciting world of Harlequin Intrigue—where your life is on the line and so is your heart!

Harlequin Intrigue—we'll leave you breathless!

INT-GEN

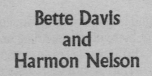

Bette Davis
and
Harmon Nelson

Legendary film star Bette Davis met Harmon Nelson, her first of four husbands, when they were students at Cushingham Academy in Ashburnham, Massachusetts. They married August 18, 1932, but divorced six years later. The pressures of Bette's stardom were too great for the couple to overcome.

In her autobiography, *This 'n That,* Bette listed four factors that contributed to a failed marriage: money, a shared bedroom, an inability to communicate, and sex.

B-DAVIS